Pride Publishing books by Bellora Quinn and Sadie Rose Bermingham

Elemental Evidence
Breathing Betrayal
Burning Boundaries
Surfacing Secrets
Digging Deeper

Wanted
Demon Familiar

Elemental Evidence

DIGGING DEEPER

Bellora Quinn &
Sadie Rose Bermingham

Digging Deeper
ISBN # 978-1-78686-371-3
©Copyright Bellora Quinn & Sadie Rose Bermingham 2018
Cover Art by Cherith Vaughn ©Copyright August 2018
Interior text design by Claire Siemaszkiewicz
Pride Publishing

DIGGING DEEPER

Dedication

Over the last few years, there have been many people to thank for their help and support in the writing of this series. We are overwhelmed with gratitude toward our families, our friends and our lovely readers, who have given boundless encouragement and advice and cheered us along the way.

Elemental Evidence is now at volume four, and while we once naively imagined that this book would mark the end of the series, we now know there are still more adventures to write for Jake and Mari. Their stories are not yet complete.

So, as we continue to document their journey, there remains one person we must yet thank for her amazing work. Our wonderful editor, Rebecca Scott, has been a teacher and motivator, who has supported Elemental Evidence from the start. Thank you, Rebecca, for your keen eye, great sense of humor and unfailing enthusiasm for our boys. You're the best.

Prologue

Tamara opened her eyes to total darkness. A black so profound that, even after blinking several times, she could still see nothing. There was no sound beyond the dull thump of her heartbeat and, most alarming of all, she couldn't do more than wiggle her fingers and toes. Her breath seemed to bounce right back in her face. There had to be something solid mere inches in front of her but it was like she was in a straitjacket. She couldn't lift her arms to feel it. Her head was throbbing and she began to panic.

Another, harder effort to move her arms got them to shift against the pressure holding her down. Crumbs of something warm and soft fell between her fingers. The weight on her arms and lower body was more than just her own groggy inertia — there was real, physical pressure. She whimpered and struggled in earnest, getting her arms and legs to move incrementally, and more soft, damp crumbs tumbled around her in the stifling, pitch blackness.

I'm underground! My god, I'm underground!

The thought was enough to spike panic in her chest and her heart drummed louder. She kept wiggling and shifting, forcing her fingers into claws and scrabbling them upward. The dirt was loose and gave way, but that didn't make the absolute terror coursing through her abate. Lifting her head, she hit something, about three inches above her nose. It was curved and solid, extending down toward her chest, and she could feel the roughness brushing her nipples when she tried to push herself upward again. Was she naked? How had that happened? Had the house collapsed on her in her sleep?

Disturbingly, she could not remember anything leading up to this moment. Her last clear recall was of leaving work, heading off to meet with a few mates for a drink before going home. Nothing special, not the kind of bender that would have wiped out her memories of going home afterward.

How long had she been like this? She tried to force the panic down, some shred of logic asserting that she would use up what little oxygen she had if she continued panting. She couldn't help it, though. Her mind kept screaming that she couldn't move, couldn't see, couldn't breathe!

In addition to clawing at the damp earth, she moved her legs, pushing up and trying to bend her knees, even shifting her hips up and down, all in an attempt to make the dirt sifting around her pack down under her body and give her increased space. It was working, inch by inch. She was getting room to move, even as more and more soil shifted over her like a dry cascade. She just needed to keep on wiggling. By doing that, she might get free. If she was buried shallow enough.

If she was several feet under, though… No, she would not think of that. She had to keep the panic at bay.

Shift, shift, wiggle, wiggle.

She had almost made enough room for her hands to dig.

How could this have happened? How had she gotten here?

Tamara struggled to recall her last memory again. Calling in at the pub for a pint of cider after work, a quick laugh with friends, then…nothing. She didn't remember talking to anyone or going home.

Shift, wiggle, shift, wiggle.

She had enough room to bend her elbows and knees. All she could do was keep at it, keep going, keep swallowing the panic every time it threatened to engulf her. Tears stung her eyes. What if she was buried so deep it was all useless? It didn't matter. She couldn't just lie there and accept her fate. She would keep going until she was either free or she ran out of air.

Shift, wiggle, dig, shift, wiggle, dig.

She was getting handfuls of dirt. It was easier to move. Tamara kept going, clawing faster. Without warning, her fingers met no resistance. Her hand was free. Cooler air swirled over her exposed skin and she thrust upward, forcing her arm higher, tearing at the ground until her other hand joined it. Breathing was harder. The air that fanned her face didn't ease the burning in her lungs. With both hands, she raked at the ground and at last her fingers touched the rough wooden arch covering her face and part of her torso. She shoved at it as she sat up and sweet air rushed into her starved lungs.

Tamara sobbed with relief and spit dirt that had fallen from her hair out of her mouth.

"What the fuck?" a man's voice demanded. "Oh my lord. Oh my god. Are you all right?"

She had no idea if she was all right or ever would be again. Someone bent over her, trying to help her up, and she panicked, conscious of the cold air on her skin. Tamara screamed.

"Don't touch me! Get away from me!"

A flashlight beam cut through the misty gray of early morning and a small dog yapped like a mad thing as it ran around in circles.

"Stop! What are you doing there?" That was a different voice. She recognized the dark navy uniform and the high-viz vest of a police officer beyond the bobbing torchlight.

"Help me! Help me, please!" Tamara screamed. The man who had his hands on her backed off at once and Tamara had never been so glad to see a police officer in her life. The uniformed figure hurried up to them and pointed a finger at the man.

"Keep your hands where I can see them!"

"I wasn't doing anything!" the man protested at once, sounding like he might burst into tears. "I was trying to help her."

Tamara sobbed and crossed her arms over her body, trying to cover herself. The dog was still yapping away like it was demented. She wished it would shut up. It was making her headache worse.

"I don't know how I got here. I was buried under the ground."

"It's all right, love. I'll call for an ambulance." The copper radiated calm. He knelt and put his waterproof jacket around her shoulders, looking up. "You!" He pointed at the man again. "Put your hands on your head and turn around."

Chapter One

"Mama, you've not forgotten what happened in Paris, have you?"

Dr. Annabel Gale was busy making scrambled eggs, while her sole offspring perched on a stool at the edge of the island unit in their open-plan kitchen and perused the documents from her oncologist she had given him to read. The twenty-four-hour news channel burbled away in the background. On the TV screen, police tape surrounded an incident somewhere in Highgate, but there were many incidents in London, so many that they failed to raise an eyebrow most of the time. She did not look up at him but a smile tugged at her lips. Her son, Ilmarinen—named in honor of her Finnish ancestors, for an ancient Suomi wind deity, and resentful of that fact since childhood—loved to find fault with the many and various consultants she selected in the battle to fix her allegedly incurable ailment. It did not stop her reaching out to anyone she believed might have a cure.

Anni was not a fantasist. A competent medic and a specialist in tropical medicine, she knew that the cancer in her blood stood a high chance of beating her. Until it did, though, she was going to find new and interesting ways of fighting it. The experiments all made for good research papers, if nothing else.

"You know as well as I do, when you have seen as many specialists as I have, there is an outside chance that one of them at least will be..." She paused to consider her words.

"Bogus," Mari filled in, without looking up from the glossy brochure in his hands.

"Don't be childish," she admonished.

"I'm not being childish. Monsieur Colbert was a fraud, plain and simple. He'd have milked you dry, if you'd been more gullible. And you'd still be sick." Mari raised his head, staring at her with open defiance over the résumé in his hands. He had her sharp blue eyes, the family genes inherited from her father and his mother before them.

"I thank you for acknowledging that I'm not in my dotage yet." She exhaled. "Do you want breakfast or should I just give it to Tonka?"

Her elderly Staffordshire terrier pricked his ragged ears and lifted his brindle nose off his neat, white forepaws at the mention of his name. His whipcord tail wagged once or twice in momentary enthusiasm.

Mari set the booklet aside and beamed at her across the island that separated their cooking and living spaces in the rear of the house. French windows in the lounge area looked out over a rare square of green space behind their neat, white-painted Georgian terrace, filling the room with light and what passed for fresh air in the capital. Tonka settled down in his dog bed by the windows, having satisfied himself that neither food nor walkies were seriously on offer, while Anni spooned eggs onto a plate. She pushed it across the counter toward her son, watching him with maternal tenderness as he helped himself to crisp wholemeal toast and devoured it with the appetite of a man twice his size. He was tall, like her estranged husband Troy, and her father, but she worried that he was too thin for a man approaching thirty, even if he did burn off excess calories with his daily runs in the park. At least he had a boyfriend now. His solitary status had been another of her concerns since his return to London.

"No Jake this morning?" she asked, keeping her tone casual as she ground a scattering of fresh black pepper over her eggs.

He glanced at her with narrowed eyes and a warning frown. "Clearly not."

"There's no need for snark. It was just a question. You're still being nice to him, aren't you?"

"Mama, he doesn't belong to me. Jake has his own life, you know."

"I do know." She turned away to hide a tiny grin, all the same. If there was a problem, she would be able to see it. Mari was hopeless at hiding his emotions around her. At the moment he was frustrated but not despondent, and she was content. A little teasing was good for him. It prevented him getting too serious and self-absorbed.

Mari put another forkful of food in his mouth likely so he didn't have to talk. For a few minutes they continued to eat in companionable silence, but as her son put his utensils down on the empty plate in front of him, his expression was solemn again.

"What?" she asked, aware that there was a question coming.

"You trust this one?" He nodded toward the brochure.

"She seems reliable. I looked into the testimonies of her previous clients and they all check out. She's an Elemental, Ilmari. I thought that would appeal to you." Annabel took a last mouthful of breakfast and tapped the side of her coffee glass with her fork as she chewed and swallowed. She knew Mari was still watching her as she took her tablets with the last few gulps of strong, dark Italian coffee. He could be possessive and sometimes a tad controlling — a trait he got from Troy — but she didn't love him any less for it.

"She's a bloody faith healer," Mari said with a huff of dismissal, which also uncomfortably reminded her of her ex.

"No one understands what you do either. Does it make your gift less genuine?" Annabel shook her head. "I realize you feel the need to protect me, though, for all my days, I have no idea from what, but let me try this. If she can do what she professes she can, it might well be the key to our wildest dreams. What's the worst that could happen?"

"She turns out to be another charlatan and we're a quarter of a million pounds in the red for nothing," Mari replied succinctly.

"That's my decision to make," Annabel told him. "You promised to support me when you came home from Barcelona. If you don't want to do that anymore, you could always move in with Jake."

She saw him open his mouth and waited for him to remind her that, technically, the house was his, transferred to him by her mother during the springtime, when they'd both been worried about her health, and on the condition that he didn't abandon her. Annabel Gale was still annoyed about that.

To her surprise, he made a thin line of his lips again without saying a word. That was so uncharacteristic that she wanted to find reasons for it.

"Everything is okay with you and Jake, isn't it?"

He uttered a breathless laugh. "Mama, we spent one night apart in the last fifteen. I haven't offended him. He's not left me for a newer model. We're good. He had an early start yesterday and I had work to do last night. That's all."

"I'm glad to hear it." She sighed, collecting up the breakfast plates.

"I'll do those," he said in a curt tone, rising and taking them from her. "You seriously believe this healer can help you?"

"If I don't try, we will never find out, will we?" she said, ever practical. Her gaze found his and, to her relief, he at least returned her smile. He looked tired, though, and she worried that he had been working too hard since he'd started his new job. Whenever she asked him about it, all he said was that he wasn't able to discuss his work but she wasn't to worry.

"I can ask your father for help, Ilmari. You don't have to work yourself to death to raise money for me."

"I'm not going to do that, Mama," he said in that patient way of his, sliding plates into the kitchen sink and running the water so that he didn't have to look at her while he lied. She saw the defensive twitch of his shoulder blades through his shirt but played along.

"I'm glad to hear it. I don't want to have to have words with your boss about this."

"Mama, I'm not at school. I work for MI5. You do not have the right to tell my manager off like she's one of your patients." Anni couldn't see his face but she could hear the note of amusement in his voice all the same.

"Ohh…you're no fun," Anni teased.

"I'm going to come with you tomorrow," he warned. "I want to meet this Solana woman before you give her everything we have."

"Of course," she demurred, folding her hands in her lap as he rinsed the plates and slipped them into the drying rack, focusing all his frustration into the simple task of putting the correct items into the proper slots and holders.

"No arguments?" He looked over one shoulder at her, a wisp of ice-blond hair tumbling over one eye. After drying his hands on the dishcloth, he tucked the renegade strands behind one ear as he turned to lean against the counter.

She wondered when her baby boy had grown so tall and handsome. He had been a child in her eyes for so many years, even after he'd gone off to work in Barcelona. Since then he had gone through so many changes, not all of them good ones. In the past few months, she had seen a new maturity in his bearing. He seemed to have found his purpose in life and pride warmed her heart. Jake Chivis was a lucky man. He and Mari made such a striking couple and she loved the light that Jake had put back in her precious Ilmari's eyes.

"No. I want you to meet her. I think you may find that you have things in common," she said. "I hope very much that you'll like her, Ilmari. I do."

"Then I hope I do, too, Mama." Mari unfolded himself and came to her, kissing her hair. "I'm going for a run. I might pop round and see if Jake's awake before I go in to work. I'll get changed there. Don't wait around for me."

"Don't be late," she reminded him.

He just laughed at that and left her to watch the news.

Chapter Two

A ripple of pops went down Jake's back as he stretched his arms over his head. He yawned and, with a little grunt, pulled on his sweats in preparation for his morning run. A knock on his door interrupted his plans.

The street-level door had a buzzer, but half the time it was broken. Even when it worked, his new neighbors across the landing kept sticking a brick in the jamb to prop it open so their friends could breeze in and out. Still, he could count on one hand the number of times someone had come up and knocked directly on his apartment door, barring visits from Mari, who now had his own key.

"Detective Cordiline, you look like hell," Jake greeted the man as he opened the door for him. He said it casually, but alarm bells were going off in his head. The last time the detective inspector had shown up unannounced on his doorstep, he'd been investigating the possible homicide of his previous neighbor.

"Thanks for that, Chivis," the gruff London copper told him with a shake of his head. There were dark shadows around his storm-cloud blue eyes. If he'd gotten any sleep the night before, it didn't show. "Have you got time for a quick word before you slope off to the comfy desk job?"

"Envy doesn't suit you," Jake told him. "Besides, it's Sunday. You want coffee?" he asked, stepping back to let him in.

"You read my mind." Cordiline cracked a smile that mellowed the stark lines of his face. He rubbed a hand across his unshaven chin and pushed his fingers through his short, dark brown hair. Jake thought he was sporting a few more silver strands than he had the last time they'd spoken. "I forget what a normal week feels like. Sometimes I'd kill for a quiet life. Then I wonder if the boredom wouldn't finish me off."

Jake poured two mugs, added cream and sugar to one and handed it to Cordiline, who accepted it with a nod.

"I'm sure every cop feels the same at some point, Inspector. But philosophy isn't what brought you over this morning. What's going on?"

Cordiline settled on the edge of the sofa and took a sip of coffee before he set his mug on the chrome-and-glass table. He laced his fingers between his knees and Jake could practically see him composing his thoughts.

"I'm here to ask for a consult, Chivis," he said.

A heavily laden pause followed that statement. Jake remembered their last conversation, which had been fraught with tension over his unofficial involvement in a murder case. If John was here asking for favors, it was something serious.

"I'm all ears."

"I don't need to tell you that this is hush-hush," Cordiline warned. "You are not to repeat any of this." He paused again and took a gulp of his coffee.

"I know how to handle confidential information, John." Jake frowned. Cordiline's reluctance was obvious—which meant he'd either hit a wall in his investigation and had no choice but to ask for help or had received orders from on high to bring him in on a case. He wasn't sure which would create more animosity.

"Good. I'd have thought so, but I have to give you the official line." Cordiline set the mug down on the table again. "We've had three very nasty rapes on our patch in the last few weeks. The perp uses the same MO every time. The victims are doped. SOCO says metabolites of flunitrazepam and ketamine were found in the blood of the previous pair, and they suspect they will find the same from this morning's victim. After he assaults them, the perp buries the girls in a shallow scrape that allows them to dig their way out. In all three cases, he's put a sheet of balsa wood over the girl's head and shoulders before covering her body, presumably so that she can breathe as she's coming round from the roofies. So far, he's not killed anyone, but in my experience, it's only a matter of time."

"Jesus, he fucking buries them alive?" Jake suppressed a shudder. There were few things he could think of more horrible than waking up trapped underground.

Cordiline leaned back, sighed and pressed his knuckles into his eyelids for a moment. "This guy is a sick bastard, Jake. There's no apparent rhyme or reason to this one. The girls don't know each other. They don't work together. They don't live in the same areas.

There's no shared boyfriend history. As far as we can work out, nothing links them. He's just picking random young women."

"And you're at a dead end. I'm assuming you want me to see if I can pick up any memories? Do you have anything from the victims I could handle? Clothing, jewelry, anything they had on them at the time of the assault?"

Cordiline shook his head.

"He leaves nothing on the victims—no clothing, no accessories. All jewelry, including piercings, he removes and...maybe he keeps them as trophies." Cordiline shrugged. "What we do have is a suspect in custody. I understand it's a big ask, given the situation, but if we knew we had the right guy, it would save us time. He's been questioned and maintains he's innocent. So far, there's no evidence linking him to any of the crimes other than his presence when the last victim was found, and she can't remember ever seeing him before."

"I'd be happy to see if I can give you confirmation, sure. Just as long as you realize it's not a guarantee I'll pick anything up off him. Even if I do, it's not admissible in court." Jake tried to keep from sounding bitter, but he could hear a hint of it in his own voice. He couldn't help it. Part of why he'd agreed to take his current job at UCL was the opportunity to advance Elemental studies to the point where they were taken seriously in the mainstream.

"Anything you can give us that will help," Cordiline said. "If he's our man, we can focus on building the case. If not, we know we still have a serial rapist out there somewhere, and he's escalating."

"All right, let me get changed and I'll go with you to the lock-up," Jake told him and headed off toward the bedroom.

* * * *

Mari kept to a steady run as he dodged the early-morning tourists around the top end of Baker Street. He hadn't spotted Jake anywhere on their regular route so he headed through Marylebone to Jake's flat. When he got there, the street door was off the catch and he let himself in and made his way to the landing, prey to a sudden wave of anxiety. He contemplated knocking, then steeled himself and slipped his key into the lock instead, letting himself in.

"Oh, there you…" The words died in his mouth as the figure on the sofa turned to face him and he realized it wasn't Jake. His heart jumped hard. "What in the world are you doing here? Where's Jake?"

The moment Mari uttered his name, Jake appeared in the short hall from the bedroom, pulling a shirt on. As soon as he saw him, a big smile flitted across Jake's face—for all of a moment. It died as he took in Mari's expression.

"What is it? What's wrong?" Jake asked, coming to him at once.

Mari glanced briefly from Jake's open, ingenuous face to Cordiline, who was trying very hard not to smirk. He looked at his lover again, smoothed all evidence of jealousy from his features and slid his arms around Jake's neck to plant a kiss on his mouth.

"I was worried about you," he soothed. "You didn't run?"

Jake gave him a searching look but put an arm around him and returned the kiss. "I was about to, but the inspector here dropped in and asked me to do a bit of consulting. Are you sure you're all right?"

"I'm fine...totally fine." Mari beamed at him. He pointed upward, toward his deliberate grin. "See? Is he staying for breakfast, or does he want you to go with him right away?"

Cordiline rose to his feet, drained his mug and set it down on the coffee table with a clunk.

"It can wait until later, if you have to be somewhere. We can hold him until tomorrow morning," he said with a nod to Mari, who just eyeballed him in silence.

Jake glanced back and forth between the two of them, so Mari offered him a placid smile, while his eyes shot furtive daggers at Cordiline. Jake said, "Yeah, that might work better. I'll call you when I'm on my way."

"You know where you're going, yeah?" Cordiline said in a mild tone. "They're moving us all up to Kentish Town, so I'm working from there this week."

"I've been there."

Mari noted that Jake didn't add that it had been while he was being questioned about their unofficial involvement in their first case together. That was a sore point with the DI at the moment.

"I saw the scaffolding. Have you got the builders in?" Mari asked.

"No. Albany Street's been decommissioned. They're gonna pull it down and build some expensive flats, I imagine." Cordiline raised an eyebrow. "That'll suit you, I'd have thought."

"So I won't have the benefit of your charming company for much longer? I'm gutted," Mari told him, not even trying to disguise the fact that this was far from unhappy news. Kentish Town was at least a mile away. If it meant that Jake accidentally ran into John Cordiline less often, it was a good thing, in his opinion.

"I'm sure you'll feel the same when your neighborhood crime figures go up," Cordiline said, with a smirk that told him his sincerity was doubted. He headed for the door. "I'll be seeing you, Jake."

As soon as Cordiline was gone, Jake pulled Mari close and locked both arms around him.

"You are not seriously still jealous, are you?"

"What? I turn up at my boyfriend's flat and find an old guy — one who I know is already perving on him — sitting on his sofa, while he's half-naked in the bedroom… Tell me again how you think I should feel, Chivis?" Mari kissed his cheek to show that he wasn't truly angry, but he wished it was easier to make Jake see how the cozy relationship he had with Cordiline affected him. "I know he's a cop. I understand that there is cop stuff going on between the two of you that's just business." He sighed. "But I can't help it. He fancies you. And I totally want to kill him for it, every time I catch him leching over you."

Jake's chuckle was a warm, husky sound in Mari's ear that went a long way toward chasing his jealousy away.

"He was sitting on my couch, drinking coffee. I'd hardly call that leching. Did you have a good run?"

"Mhh-hmm," Mari conceded. "It was okay. I missed you. Mama was grilling me about why you didn't stay last night." He paused. "So, Inspector Gadget wants your help again? I thought he told you not to get involved after that business with the euthanizers?"

He snuggled up to Jake, in spite of his promise not to make himself late for work. It wasn't entirely his fault, after all.

"I don't know if it was his idea. He seemed hesitant to even ask," Jake said. He wrapped his arms around him more tightly. "It might be his higher-ups suggested it, and he was just delivering the message. I can't give you the details, but they have a suspect in custody for a series of rapes but no real evidence. If I can tie him to the victims, they'll still have to build their case the old-fashioned way, but at least they'll know they have their man."

"Oh my!" Mari sighed and pulled him into a full-body embrace. "I can't even object without sounding like a total bastard, can I?"

He didn't let go, though. It might only have been one night without his precious Jake, but that didn't mean he hadn't missed him.

It was strange for him to be so relaxed with another man. After the disaster of Barcelona, Mari had believed that he would never again be completely at ease in a physical relationship. The nightmare with Tomas Arregui had left him doubting who and what he was. It had made his love life a no-go zone for nearly three whole years. Jake had cut right through all that anxiety in mere months. He made Mari feel human again, deserving of love and desire like a normal person — something he had almost stopped hoping was possible.

"What if he is their rapist, though?"

"Well, that's sort of the point, babe," Jake told him.

It hurt him to think that Jake might be forced to see that sort of darkness. Even when he knew his lover was strong enough to cope with the evils of modern society, Mari still wanted to protect him from anything that might make him feel bad. It was ridiculous. Jake had been a cop in Detroit, one of the toughest cities in the world. It was far too late to shelter him from the harsh cruelties of life.

"Is it fair, asking you to go into his head like this?"

"You know what they say about fairness. It doesn't exist. I'll be fine, Mari. I'm not looking forward to it, but if he harmed those women and I can see what he did, it ends there. If he didn't do it, they still need to be looking, before anyone else gets hurt."

Mari pressed his forehead to Jake's, running his fingers through Jake's hair, then kissing his lips.

"You are wonderful," he whispered. "Never forget that."

"Mm, you're pretty fantastic yourself," Jake murmured. "I missed you last night." He stroked his hands up and down Mari's back, over the curve of his ass, and Mari pushed back into that touch with a mischievous glance.

"I imagine you did." Mari wriggled encouragingly. "And you are going to miss me again." He glanced at his watch. "I have seven minutes then I have to get ready and go. I could kill your tame copper sometimes."

"Are you sure you have to run off so soon?"

"Uh-huh." Mari nodded with an unhappy pout. "I promised. There's a gold alert in place. I'm looking into some suspicious emails Ghislaine intercepted last night. It shouldn't take too long, but I need to talk to her about it."

Jake sighed and kissed him. "I hope they're paying you OT for going in on a Sunday. I suppose I'll go see Cordiline's suspect while you're gone. Are you coming back here when you're done?"

"If you want me to." Mari winked at him and planted a kiss on his nose. "Did I leave any grown-up clothes here last time? I can take a shower here with you if I did."

Jake snorted. "You've got at least half the wardrobe taken over. I'm sure there's something in there you could wear."

"Come on then. You can scrub my back," Mari said with a wicked smirk.

As tempting as it was to do more than just soap each other up in the shower, they stuck to a quick but sensual wash. Jake had not exaggerated about the wardrobe, either. There were plenty of clothes for Mari to choose from and he was dried and dressed in an ice-blue, single-breasted Paul Smith two-piece and ready to go in short order.

Chapter Three

It was about even odds which was the worse option for crowds, the park and the busy market streets or cramming into the Underground. Since it was only about a half-hour's brisk walk, and likely to take just as long on the Tube, Jake opted for the open air and set out through Regent's Park. He left its leafy haven of peace behind as he crossed the Parkway toward Camden High Street.

Mari had taken him to the Lock Market on a number of occasions, so he was at least familiar with the area, although he didn't share Mari's love for shopping. He was quietly amazed how Mari could wander from store to store, in and out of this booth and that stall, cooing over prospective purchases and seemingly oblivious to the sardine-can press of people all around.

If Jake wasn't preoccupied enough with trying not to touch anyone or anything that might hold a big jolt of memory, he was forever eyeing strangers, measuring up potential trouble. It got exhausting fast. Today, he avoided the high street, traversed Parkway and skirted the panhandlers at the tube station before heading down the quieter Kentish Town Road. He crossed over the canal and under the railway bridge into the urban environs of Kentish Town itself.

The shopfronts here were less garish and shabbier. A mishmash of clashing cultures called this part of London home, but it was still not as combative as the pulsing heart of Camden. It reminded him in a way of certain parts of Detroit. In the space of a couple of blocks, he saw prettily painted houses on nice, residential side streets give way to stores with foreclosure signs and grills fastened over their windows and doors. Then, on the next corner, an immaculate Greek Orthodox church looked out over a row of cheap takeaway restaurants and a beat-up laundromat. A heavily armored van in Metropolitan Police colors passed him and turned into the next side street, although its blue lights were not engaged. When it disgorged its passengers — a group of young cops in their black assault vests and helmets — he was reminded of what Mari had said about the city being on alert. There was always a sense of potential trouble. It stalked the streets of any big city, but these days there seemed to be a frisson of anxiety everywhere.

The sense was lessened when the troupe of youthful PCs filed into one of the takeaways and began to load up with sandwiches and kebabs. He figured they were on their way to a soccer game somewhere. They would be glad of the chance to eat by the end of the afternoon.

The station house was off the high street, appropriately enough on Holmes Road, which Jake found amusing. His flat was just around the corner from the famous residence on Baker Street, which had been assigned to Conan Doyle's fictional detective, and the coincidence did not escape him. It was a neat, square Regency block with an incongruous palm tree in the front yard, very different from the long, concrete fortress on Albany Street that had been Cordiline's previous HQ. It was a much nicer building but considerably less convenient to walk to, even if the lack of proximity between John and Mari made his life easier in some respects.

Jake sighed at the thought. Juggling his professional relationship with the London cops and Mari's very open hostility toward John Cordiline could get wearing. At least he didn't have to worry about that this morning.

It was not Jake's first visit to Holmes Road, as he had been taken there during his one brief period in custody. He and Mari had been arrested a few months previously, while investigating the disappearance of the brother of one of their university colleagues. Jake passed under the stone arch with its chiseled POLICE motif, through the double doors into the lobby, and rang a bell for the desk clerk. A harassed-looking middle-aged man in an ill-fitting uniform shambled through and took his name before calling up to let Cordiline know he was there. Jake wandered around, scanning the public information posters, semi-interested, until another door opened at the far end of the hall and a younger cop, in a navy sweater and matching trousers with her hair up in a long blonde ponytail, called his name.

She gave him the once-over and a curious smile before taking him up to the second floor, where Cordiline had established control over one corner of a crowded office. From the piles of archive boxes around his desk — like a small defensive wall — he was still very much at the settling-in stage.

"Jake, welcome to the madhouse," Cordiline hailed him over the top of his PC monitor and beckoned him in. "Excuse the tip. It's kind of a dumping ground in here. Thanks for coming."

"No problem. And don't worry, I've seen worse. How long do they expect it to be before you're in your own digs?"

Cordiline's shoulders rose and fell. "How long is a piece of string? I worked at Albany for five years and I didn't even get my own office. Hot desking is a fact of life. Welcome to the modern Force." He flashed a humorless grin. "You want a brew or something?"

"No thanks, I'm fully caffeinated."

"I'll have our suspect moved to an interview room."

"Let's get the preliminary stuff out of the way first," Jake suggested. "If I could get a look at anything he was wearing or had on him when he was brought in, that would be a good start. I might not even have to talk to him if I get a hit on his watch or his belt buckle."

The young woman who had come up with him was still in the office, thumbing through a box of files in search of something. She looked up as Jake spoke.

"Would it be okay if I sat in while you do your thing? Sorry…" she added quickly. "I kind of overheard the DI talking to DS Woodmansey and…I've never met anyone able to do psychic stuff. Not for real. Not outside of films and whatnot. That's…kind of amazing."

Cordiline shrugged and looked at Jake. "Up to you, Chivis. PCSO Ladley is with us as a victim liaison officer. She's a hard worker and she won't get in the way. Will you, Jen?"

"No, sir, I promise," Ladley volunteered right away.

"I'm afraid there isn't much to see," Jake said. "To you, it will look like I'm just picking up random things. But you're welcome to watch if you want to."

"Thanks," she said with genuine enthusiasm. "That would be cool."

"You want to go fetch the suspect's effects for Mr. Chivis, Jen?" Cordiline asked.

"Will do, sir." The woman bounced to her feet and hurried off down the stairs, her ponytail swinging.

"The enthusiasm of youth!" Cordiline exhaled and rolled his eyes. "She makes me tired just listening to her sometimes."

"Don't let the boss hear you say that. They'll put you out to pasture," Jake warned him with a smirk, before bringing the conversation around to the task in hand once more. "So, he's denying any involvement. What do you think, though? You like him for it?"

"The PC who brought him in said that he was standing over the grave when he found them. The girl was freaking out, trying to make him let go of her. He read the guy his rights and brought them both in. The Sapphire team have got the girl, down at St. Mary's in Paddington. They'll check her out and go through her story with her when she's ready to talk. Until then, we've just got Mr. Public-Spirited's account to go off. He says he was walking his dog, in the fucking cemetery, in the middle of the night, and it ran off and started scratching at the ground under the trees. Then up she came, like *Night of the Living Dead*." Cordiline pulled a skeptical face.

"If his story checks out, it's a wonder he didn't shit his pants," Jake said. "He buried her in a cemetery? Jesus."

"I know. Fucking ghoul or what?" Cordiline laughed without a trace of humor. "And they wonder why coppers drink!"

Ladley returned in short order with a bin that held a few bagged items — shoes, wallet, watch and a dog leash. She set the bin down on the desk.

"We can use an interview room, if you want," Cordiline offered. People were coming and going from the office almost constantly, but they paid little-or-no attention to what was going on around Cordiline's workspace.

"Makes no difference to me," Jake said. He pulled out the bag containing the watch. Metal held memories best, and if he were going to get anything, that was the most promising target. He opened the top of the plastic bag and tipped it, sliding the watch out onto the desk. Jen was standing off to one side, hardly breathing, her eyes glued to his every movement. It was unnerving to be scrutinized with such intent but Jake understood the curiosity. Even Cordiline was observing him closely, although he was being cooler about it.

At one time, it might have bothered him, the way they watched, almost like they were expecting him to pull a rabbit out of a hat or perhaps trying to see through some 'trick' he might be playing. Months of being a lab rat at the college had taken the edge off, though. At the same time, he knew that if his talent were ever going to be legitimized in the mainstream, he couldn't act like it was weird, mystical or something to be hidden. He wanted the police to see his ability as just another tool in helping them find the bad guys and get them off the street.

He took a breath and opened his senses, allowing the flow of energy — or power, or whatever you wanted to call it — to fill him. Even that sounded way too metaphysical to explain out loud, so he kept it to himself. He was still getting used to the idea of being able to control his ability to be receptive to any memories an object held, or not.

For damn near his whole life, he had been at the mercy of his talent. He might pick up a memory from a random object any time or anywhere. It had colored how he approached everything. Even something as mundane as going out to eat or riding the bus could be a trial. One minute he was talking with a friend and the next minute a casual brush of fingers against a spoon, or a clothes hanger, or a handrail sent him reeling into a memory of a heated argument between lovers, a frantic mother looking for a lost child, a robbery turned shooting.

And now...now it appeared that the EQ10, the experimental drug he'd been forcibly injected with, had given him something he'd never thought possible — the ability to turn his talent on or off at will. Of course, it could also just as well have killed him, like the other Fire Elementals Roy Corrie had experimented on. He still had the uncomfortable side effect of a rising body temperature when he got angry, too, and that was worrisome.

Even with the bonus ability to keep himself from picking up stray memories randomly, his psychometry still wasn't a gradual thing. When he was on, if there was a memory attached to an object, he didn't fade from the present to the past. It was more like being in one place then being in another, in less than the blink of an eye. It could be disorientating to say the least, and he had to focus one-hundred percent of his attention because he wouldn't get another chance to see the memory. Once it was released to him, it was gone from the object. Jake touched a finger to the metal band of the watch.

He was running down a gravel-strewn lane, mostly in darkness, except for the swinging, bobbing light in his hand that picked out glimpses of the way ahead. There were high, leafy bushes to either side, hemming him in.

"Isolde! Isolde, get back here!" The voice that came out of his throat was male and irritated.

In the jerking, swaying light, he saw the dog at last, in a clearing off the path, digging at the ground. Suddenly the light steadied and he saw something straight out of a horror movie. There was an arm sticking out of the ground, tearing at the soil with dirt-caked fingers and broken nails.

"What the fuck?" he said, as a woman emerged from the soil. "Oh my lord. Oh my god. Are you all right?"

Jake blinked, back in Cordiline's office without any warning.

"You saw something?" Cordiline asked, carefully neutral.

Jake nodded. "I got a memory of him in the cemetery."

Ladley's eyes were as big as two-pound coins. Cordiline appeared less fazed but he said, "Did you see the victim? Were you any... Was he anywhere near her?"

"You were in his head?" Ladley asked in a breathless whisper. "For real? Just from touching his watch?"

Cordiline looked at her with a frown but it was as if he had vanished. She only had eyes for Jake.

Jake glanced from one to the other and answered Cordiline first, "It was dark and his flashlight was bouncing all over the place, but yes, I saw her arm sticking out of the ground and clawing at it. The memory ended so fast that I barely got a look at her. He was standing maybe ten yards away when she sat up. He said, 'What the fuck' and asked if she was all right."

"Did you see him go into the cemetery?" Cordiline asked. "Did you get any sense of how long he was in there?"

Jake shook his head. "He was already running when the memory started, calling the dog. Isolde? I think that's what he said."

"Funny name for a dog," Ladley said. She was still staring at him like he'd turned into one-fifth of a boyband. Jake ignored it. "Will the other things show you different stuff?"

"Possibly," Jake answered, picking up another bag and opening it. "I'll go through the rest of his things but the watch was the best shot. Metal tends to hold on to memories best." He went through every item but, as it turned out, he'd been right, and the watch had been the best, and the only item he got an impression from.

Cordiline drummed his fingers on his desk, a scowl settled between his brows. "You heard him ask if she was okay? Did you get any sense he was playing with her, maybe? Trying to hide guilt?"

Jake shrugged. "I don't know. It's possible he was acting, faking his shock at finding a woman popping out of the ground."

"Why would he act surprised? I'd be surprised if there was anyone else around to see at that time of night, yeah?" Ladley asked.

"No, there wasn't," Jake confirmed. "But maybe he wanted to play hero. If he'd put her in the ground himself, maybe he was banking on her not remembering him. He could have hung around and waited, maybe, so he could watch – or maybe to see if she made it out of the grave or not."

Cordiline gave him a long, cool stare. "Do you think that's what happened?"

Jake blew out a small puff of breath. "No, not really. It's all possible, but..." He shrugged again. "Look. I don't read their thoughts or feelings through the memories. I only see and hear what they saw and heard. There just wasn't anything definitive to this memory. He could just as well have been doing exactly what he said he was doing, walking the dog when he happened on the scene."

"Do you get memories if you touch people?" the PCSO asked him.

"Jen, don't hassle Mr. Chivis," Cordiline said in a mild tone.

"It's all right," Jake reassured them. "Yes, sometimes I do pick up on memories from touching people."

"Could you touch the victim and see what happened to her?" Jen asked, fascinated.

"It's a possibility," Jake answered carefully. "Although I'd hesitate to ask a rape victim to let a stranger come in and touch her in hopes of seeing what happened to her. I could try your suspect, though...if he agrees to it."

Jen shot a hopeful grin at DI Cordiline, clearly hoping that he would jump for joy. He folded his arms and nodded toward the door. "Aren't you supposed to be on the beat in ten minutes, Jenny?"

"He could though?" she argued.

"Mr. Chivis has already pointed out that what he does isn't admissible in court." Cordiline waved her off. "Go and report for duty. I'll let you know if anything interesting crops up."

"Yes, sir," she said. She took a couple of steps but stopped and turned toward Jake. "What about me? Could you do a reading on me?"

Jake sat back in the chair. "I'm not psychic, Officer Ladley. I can't control what I see. I might see nothing at all. I could pick up on what you had for breakfast this morning…or see who you went out with on your last date."

She blushed strawberry-red at the implications of that. It didn't deter her, though.

"Would you see it like a fly on the wall? Or like I saw it? Or my… The person I was with?"

"Jenny." Cordiline didn't snap at her but there was a warning in his tone.

"I'm sorry. I was just interested," she demurred.

"That's enough," Cordiline said quietly but firmly.

She nodded and headed off again. The heavy door closed behind her with a muffled thump.

"Sorry about that."

"Don't worry about it. I've gotten kinda used to living in a fishbowl."

"It's a bit of a floorshow here at the moment." Cordiline exhaled. "We've got a lot of new faces coexisting in the same small space. I could hide you at Albany Street. They all want to know about Elementals here, at the moment."

Jake shrugged. "Well, let's hope I make a good impression. Do you want me to wait while you find out if your suspect will allow the human lie detector to check him out, or will you call me later?"

"Hang around if you like. I doubt anyone will mind. Unless you were expecting another visit from your boy toy?" Cordiline cracked a smirk.

"Watch it." He mellowed, though, and even managed an answering smile. "He's working this morning."

"Working on a Sunday?" The detective chuckled, clearly enjoying the chance to tease. "Didn't think he needed the overtime."

"He's..." Jake deliberated. He wasn't supposed to discuss what Mari did for a living. "His department has a rush job on. He volunteered."

"Very public-spirited of him." Cordiline picked up the phone and made a call down to the holding cells.

It took a while for the guards on duty to arrange for Jake to speak to their suspect but Cordiline ushered things along. It was wasted effort, in any case. Jake was unable to pick up anything from him except the sour smell of nervous perspiration and a sense of indignation that he didn't need any Elemental or psychic ability to see.

He stopped with Cordiline in the hall outside the interview room.

"No luck?" Cordiline asked.

"Sorry. Nothing." Jake was about to leave it at that but he hesitated and Cordiline shot him a knowing frown. "I didn't get anything definitive for you one way or the other, and this is pure speculation, but I think you've got the wrong guy, John. I wouldn't stop looking."

Chapter Four

It was strange to be on the campus at UCL, after a couple of months working for Trafalgar House. Mari was pleased and quite touched to note how many of the Malet Place regulars remembered him and greeted him with smiles and friendly inquiries. It helped that Jake still worked here, and everyone in their respective departments was aware that he and Jake Chivis were an item. He had to sign in, but as he was on official business with an appointment to see his old handler, Professor Karden, and to chat with Anthony Weston — whose SEWN UP project had been instrumental in bringing him and Jake together — gaining access was a formality.

Toby Wainwright in the post room kept him chatting as usual, after his blissfully short meeting with Karden. His old boss had been polite and professional throughout their update session and, in truth, Mari didn't resent him for enforcing the move to Trafalgar House, but he'd been dreading the meeting all the same. It was a relief to escape his stuffy office on the eighth floor and come down to catch up on the gossip with Toby.

"Did Jake tell you what happened to Nolan?" the post boy asked, lowering his voice to a conspiratorial whisper after some vocal appreciation of Mari's new suit. It was a gorgeous McQueen two piece, in cerulean mohair silk, and he adored it.

"No." Mari looked puzzled. Jake had no love for his former workplace tormentor and he was sure that his lover would have mentioned it, had some misfortune befallen Damien Nolan. He hadn't seen or heard about the creep since he had punched Nolan's lights out during an altercation just before his departure from UCL. Mari did not consider himself a violent man, but after three years of ignoring Nolan's barely disguised homophobia, he had been able to take no more. He had not been sure who was more surprised by the knockout blow, himself or Nolan. "C'mon. Tell all."

Toby looked delighted to be the conveyor of virgin news. He leaned forward across the desk, keeping his voice low.

"They are saying—they being the canteen staff, mostly, and you know how none of them can keep their mouths shut—the rumor is that he got caught in the gents at the Carpenter and Carrot during office hours with his dick in some guy's mouth."

Toby's grin grew broader at this last snippet of information and Mari widened his eyes. He cracked up laughing and drummed his hands on the counter in delight.

"I knew it! The lying toad! I always guessed he was a closet case."

"He's denying it, of course," Toby said in an arch tone, "but everyone thinks he's lying. Apparently, Professor Michaelson who runs the CAD team gave him a written warning for skiving and bringing his department into disrepute."

"I love you, Tobias," Mari declared, clapping his hands to either side of the post boy's beaming face and planting a kiss on his forehead. "I owe you big time for this. Thank you. That's the best news I've had in ages."

He was still amused by Toby's story as he made his way over to Jake's office on the fifth floor, planning to share the joy before he returned to work. But as he stepped out of the elevator, the smirk left his face. Two men in well-cut suits passed him on the way out, their heads together in deep conversation. They were both older and one was unknown to him. That was no surprise. The campus was enormous and in three years of working here, he still hadn't met half its employees. As the other looked up from the document they were discussing and his steel-gray eyes passed across Mari dismissively, his heart stopped dead in his chest.

He actually managed to take another couple of strides before his body came to a halt and he turned his head, imagining for a moment that this must be how it felt to take a fatal bullet. Just before the elevator doors closed, his gaze met those of Tomas Garcés Arregui — and his world came crashing down around him.

The shock of seeing his ex, here, in London of all places, drove all other thoughts out of his head. His initial instinct was to find Jake, to tell him and share his outrage. As logic reasserted its control over his brain, he whirled around and hit the elevator button with enough violence that it hurt his hand. When the lift car didn't come up quickly enough, he took to the stairs, racing down to the next level and the next, putting his head out to search for that jarringly familiar figure, rehearsing in his head the words he would have with the bastard for daring to follow him here and disrupt the life he was trying to rebuild in the wake of their ugly breakup.

He reached the ground floor with a flush rising in his cheeks and still no sign of Tomas. Barely acknowledging the departing call of the security guy, he pushed through the barriers and the glass doors that led out onto Malet Place, looking left and right. Still there was no evidence that the man even existed outside his nightmares.

Mari strode as far as the main road, where he stood in the gateway, pushing his hands into his trouser pockets as he scanned Torrington Place in vain. His shoulders slumped, some of the fight going out of him as he wondered if he'd been hallucinating. He deliberated whether to go in and talk to Jake, to see if he could find out more, or just head straight back to work.

As he was making up his mind, a hand clapped on his shoulder and he jumped like he'd been electrocuted.

"I thought it was you," Tomas said coolly in Catalan, his lips twitching around something that wasn't quite a smile. "I couldn't be sure. You've…changed. Have you lost something, Dr. Gale?"

All the erudite words that Mari had composed in his head crumbed to sand in seconds and he was left to stare in dazed incomprehension at the man beside him.

Tomas hadn't altered much at all in the three-and-a-half years since they'd last worked together. His choice of suit was still enviable. Today he wore an Armani two-piece with a double-breasted jacket and slimline pants, in buttermilk with bronze buttons. Coupled with his cream shirt and red and gold striped tie, it set off his Mediterranean tan to perfection.

There was more white in his short dark hair and a few extra lines around those gunmetal-gray eyes, but other than that, he was weathering well.

Mari noted, with some satisfaction, that he was not as tall or as well built as Jake. Something that he'd never previously considered was that there was none of the warmth in his eyes that he saw when Jake looked at him.

All this flitted bat-like through his mind as he stood there staring stupidly at the only man who had ever left him lost for words on a regular basis. So much, in fact, that Tomas had to repeat his name, prompting him with a sly quirk of the lips.

"Marijne?"

He hadn't heard that name in so long. The way Tomas uttered it was like a summoning. It twisted its barbs deep in Mari's gut and left him breathless for a moment, unable to rationalize the rush of adrenaline that single word triggered.

"*Señor* Arregui," he managed to respond. "I…I didn't recognize you."

That was a lie and Tomas must have guessed, but it was the best he could manage until his mouth reconnected with his brain. Why? Why the blazes did Tomas always manage to have this damned effect on him?

He hesitated a moment before holding out his hand and he thought Tomas looked surprised, too, for a heartbeat, before taking it in his own and shaking it warmly. His grip was still strong and he did not let go immediately, but Mari pulled his fingers free as soon as he was able to.

"You look well, Marijne. I was surprised to see you here. Professor Karden told me that you no longer worked for the college," Tomas said with a half smirk. "He hinted at MI5. Of course, he thought he was being subtle, but that has never been his strong suit."

Mari blinked at him. "You've seen Emmanuel Karden?"

"Naturally," his former employer confirmed, though it seemed far from natural to Mari. "Karden has links to some of the finest academic minds in Europe – and connections in your government, too. His business and political connections segue neatly with my own. It was inevitable that he and I would meet at some point. I had hoped that I would see you, but when he told me of your promotion, I feared it was not to be."

Mari was wrong footed by that. He could not think of any reason Tomas Arregui might want to see him that didn't involve a physical fight. When he had left Barcelona, following Tomas' very public attempt to humiliate him, Mari had used his phone and his special talent for interfacing to break into this man's personal IT system and send pictures of the pair of them, naked, in bed, to Tomas' wife. He had no doubt that Tomas had neither forgotten nor forgiven him for this final act of defiance.

"Are you recruiting?" he asked, in order to steer the conversation clear of anything personal and because Tomas didn't seem in a hurry to be anywhere else.

"Why? Are you looking for a job?" The man gave him that not-quite-smile again and Mari was quick to shake his head.

"I don't think that would be a good idea, even if I was," he said as his brain began to recover from the shock. "And speaking of work…" He waved a hand vaguely in the direction of his department by the Thames.

"Does that mean you don't have time for a drink?" Tomas looked a shade disappointed. "Just a quick coffee?"

"I…uh…I have to go," Mari lied. "Stuff to do."

"Maybe later… I'm in London for a few days. Let me give you my number. Call me when you're free."

Mari wanted to refuse but if he did, it would look like he was intimidated. He relented just to get rid of him, tapping the digits into his phone and sending the man a brief missive to confirm that he'd done it right.

Tomas had always been like this, he remembered bitterly — skeptical of his abilities, always questioning him. He could block the number later. He had absolutely no desire to talk to Tomas Arregui. They had nothing whatsoever to talk about. Tomas had never wanted to talk when they were together. Why should today be any different?

He turned this conundrum over in his head all the way back to Trafalgar House.

What do you want from me, you bastard?

The question nagged at him for the rest of the day. By noon, he had a headache, and by the time he went home, his stomach was churning and he texted Jake with an excuse and told him he would see him the next day.

Chapter Five

It was a lovely crisp fall morning and Jake appreciated the beauty of the leafy park turning all colors and the snap in the air as he ran. Yesterday had been stressful, even by Monday's standards, and on top of the regular work-related distractions, he'd been preoccupied with Cordiline's case. He'd wanted to discuss it with Mari and get his thoughts but Mari had texted him just as he'd gotten off work. Anni was feeling anxious ahead of her first session with her 'new witchdoctor', as Mari put it, and he wanted to pamper her.

Jake was worried about her, too, but he could relate. The last thing he'd ever wanted when he'd been feeling low was visitors. So he'd stayed home the previous night and gone over the case files Cordiline had sent him.

He was just coming up to the bench that was his and Mari's favorite meeting place when he spotted Mari heading his way. Jake came to a stop first, taking a moment to admire his boyfriend's long-legged gait. He'd never told Mari but he thought there was something very ethereal about him when he ran. The effortless way each foot landed and sprang back up made it seem as if he hardly touched the ground at all. Of course, Mari would probably just roll his eyes if Jake expressed that thought aloud, so he kept it to himself.

"Mornin', pard'ner," Jake greeted him, in a hokey John Wayne accent.

Mari raised one immaculate eyebrow and good humor twitched at the corners of his mouth. Pampering Anni must have included a trip to the salon because he was sporting a fresh cut, short around his ears, which made the longer top layers cascade around his face.

"What gives, cowboy?" he inquired in a silky tone, making no attempt to play along in the foolish voices game. "Someone steal your horse?"

Jake chuckled and gave him a kiss. "Nice hair. It looks good."

"Thanks." Mari preened.

Jake turned and they matched strides around the Outer Circle. Mari quizzed him about his meeting with Cordiline and Jake could tell he was trying hard not to sound like the jealous boyfriend, but he fell short by avoiding all mention of the inspector's name. Jake still thought his jealousy was misplaced but a small part of him took secret delight in how possessive he was and the pains he went through not to let it show.

"Their perp didn't do it, then?" Mari concluded, when Jake had regaled him with the tale of his trip to Kentish Town. "What happens next, Kemosabe?"

"Correction. I don't think the man they arrested did it. That doesn't mean I'm right," Jake said. "I was hoping you could lend your help on that score actually.

Do you think you could do some digging on him and see if there's anything that raises a red flag — or if he's as squeaky clean as he seems?"

"I can do that," Mari said.

They ran for a few minutes in silence before Jake added, "Kemosabe is actually a derivative of a Potawatomi word. You got the right nation and everything this time." He could see Mari's grin from the corner of his eye and suspected he did, in fact, already know this tidbit, given his penchant for research. "Although it might make more sense for you to be Kemosabe, and me to play Tonto."

"Do I get to wear a mask?" Mari asked, pretending to think about this for a moment.

"How about a blindfold instead?" Jake suggested, just to see the effect it would have.

Mari's eyes glittered wickedly and Jake didn't need to ask if that suggestion pushed his buttons.

"You are very naughty," Mari said with a delighted smirk. "How on earth am I supposed to run when you make me think about things like that?"

"Ah, you are on to my plan to keep you constantly distracted with sex," Jake teased him. "Maybe I'll finally be able to keep up with those damn long legs."

Mari gave him a sharp poke with one finger, trying to get him off balance so he could open up a lead and make Jake chase him. "Mama said to ask if you'll come for lunch on Saturday. She seems to think you need feeding," he relayed, looking back over one shoulder until Jake caught up. "She starts this ridiculous therapy today. I have to go with her to meet her new quack. That should be fun."

"Tell Anni I would be delighted to have lunch with her on Saturday," Jake said and poked him back. "You should keep an open mind, Mari. For her sake, anyway."

"That's what she says," his lover sighed. "I can't help it that the world is full of charlatans, though. Someone has to look out for her."

"I understand, babe. She knows you would do anything for her. But, she's a grown-up and if you treat her like a child, she won't be happy with you."

"I will be on my best behavior. I promise," Mari lied blatantly. "What's going to happen with the girl that got attacked? Does your tame policeman have any other links? Or anything he wants us to look at for him?"

"Just the one guy I asked you to look into," Jake said. "I went over the case files last night but didn't see anything that stood out. If you come up with nothing as well, I may go speak with some of the victims. But I want to avoid that if possible."

Mari wrinkled his nose in agreement. They continued their run in silence for a while, making almost a complete circuit of the huge park, and it was beginning to get busier as they reached St. Andrews Gate.

He had been so quiet that Jake already figured Mari had things on his mind, but he'd presumed it was his mother who occupied his thoughts. It wrong-footed him when, out of the blue, Mari said, "I saw my old boss yesterday."

"Yeah, you came in with me, remember?" Jake teased, thinking he meant Karden for a moment.

"No...not Doctor Death!" Mari elaborated with a scowl. "I meant Tomas, the guy I worked for in Barça. He's here in London. He came to meet with Karden as well, but I didn't see him until I was leaving."

They came to a halt together, just as Mari finished speaking, and Jake took a moment to breathe. "The guy you worked for… You mean your ex? The one that was married and treated you like shit? Did you talk to him?"

"That one, yeah." Mari managed not to look too mortified at the reminder of what Tomas had already put him through. "Not exactly."

"Not exactly? Does that mean you just glared at him, or was he an asshole to you?"

Mari shook his head and looked down at his running shoes, suddenly preoccupied with them. "No, he was polite. I was polite. He asked if I'd come for a coffee with him and I said I had to be somewhere."

Jake reached out and took Mari gently by the shoulders, stepping into his line of sight and forcing him to look up. "If you're worried I'm going to flip out because you talked to your ex, you can relax. I'm not going to pull some jealous macho bullshit. Do you want to meet with him?"

Mari's eyes held his for a couple of heartbeats, unblinking. Then he lowered his head. "No. I don't want to meet him. We don't have anything to say to one another, Jake. That particular ship has sailed," he said in clipped and careful tones. "He… It took me by surprise to see him. That's all."

Jake slid his hand up, curling his fingers around the nape of Mari's neck and using his thumbs to caress his jaw. "Then, if he calls, you tell him that. If he says he wants to apologize, you tell him the best apology he can make is to leave you alone. And if he says he misses you and wants to fuck you, laugh and block his number."

Mari managed a humorless snort at that.

"Tomas Arregui doesn't do apologies," he said in a darker voice. "That's what worries me. He knew I'd be here. He wants something."

"He can go home to where he came from still wanting it then."

Jake saw the way that response curved Mari's lips, ever so briefly. The warmth and humor was still there in his words as he leaned in to kiss Jake.

"I love the way you think," he said, a twinkle in his eyes. "Maybe I should have given him your number."

"I would be more than happy to talk to him for you," Jake said, not even trying to hide his evil grin.

"While I would love nothing better than the chance to eavesdrop on that conversation, I do think it would be unspeakably cowardly of me to delegate responsibility." Mari sighed. He was still wearing a half-smile, though, and his fingers brushed Jake's cheek tenderly. "He can't touch me here, Jake. I'm well protected. Whatever he wants, he'll just have to whistle for it, won't he?"

Jake pulled him in for a kiss and while they normally kissed each other goodbye after a run, before they both had to head off to work, this time he lingered, tasting his lips thoroughly and teasing Mari's mouth open with his tongue. Instead of fending him off with a wink and going on his way, Mari slipped his arms around Jake and rubbed up on him, inviting a longer, slower kiss, uninhibited by the very public setting. He brushed his nose against Jake's as they broke the hungry merging of lips.

"Very tasty," he observed. "Could this be the same shy boy that could hardly meet my eyes the first time we ran past each other in the park? Much as I'd love to fuck you right here, I have an important appointment this morning. Can I come over later?"

"I was just about to ask if you wanted to have dinner after work." He leaned in closer to Mari's ear and whispered, "I'll make you something yummy, then fuck you until you beg for mercy. Sound good?"

"My stars, Chivis! I swear you have the best ideas. I have to go or I will do something that might well get us arrested again. And I promise I won't be sorry, either."

His grin would have put the Cheshire Cat to shame.

Jake kissed him once more because he couldn't resist that delighted expression. "Have a good day, babe. I'll see you tonight."

Chapter Six

Mama's new consultant was called Solana Stellara, and as if that was not enough to make Mari hate her at first sight, her 'practice' was based in a community residential block near Camden Lock Market that had been designed to resemble a basket full of flowers. He thought it was more like a cage and muttered darkly about council planning departments with more money than sense until Mama told him to be quiet or go home.

When he pressed the buzzer on her intercom, a surprisingly deep and musical voice invited them up to a spacious apartment on the third floor, far enough above the bustling high street that the sounds of people going about their daily lives was muted and somehow distant. There he got his second surprise of the day.

Solana greeted them at the door—which had a rainbow plaque with the words 'Enter Your Happy Space' written on it in sparkly letters. He'd been geared up—rather uncharitably, he had to admit—for a tiny, middle-aged lady, shaped like a dumpling, perhaps, with purple hair and lots of cats. Solana, however, was almost as tall as he was, and probably not much older. She was dressed in faded-denim-effect leggings under a long, dark-green shift dress with flowing skirts that split at the sides. A tumble of thick, dark, copper-colored hair fell almost to her waist and was pulled back in a tail with a bright aquamarine scarf. The facial features it framed were strong-boned and — well — rather handsome, even tempered with a shimmer of silvery eyeshadow and a slick of light pink gloss. Eyes that were the color of brushed pewter twinkled back at him with something that was almost recognition. A firm, warm hand suddenly enfolded his in a brief and professional shake. Turning, Solana took his mother's smaller hand in both of her own.

"Dr. Gale," that rich, melodious voice intoned, and a broad smile pulled at the healer's lips. "Welcome to my Retreat. I hope that you will feel comfortable here, and together we can banish the darkness that troubles you."

Mama glanced at him and Mari was conscious of the fact that he'd not uttered a word since the door opened. He opened his mouth. Then he closed it again.

She looked annoyingly pleased.

Solana chimed softly as she walked. There were tiny bells on the bracelets she wore and on the loose ties at the neckline of her dress. Her feet were bare, the toenails painted, like her fingers, in alternating purple, green and white. He took all of this in as they followed her down a short hallway festooned with colorful modern-art prints and posters advertising painting workshops and jewelry-making courses, toward the spacious living and working area that she invited them into.

A large sliding window took up most of one wall, with a long, shallow balcony beyond it, packed with plants. There was greenery, or books, on most of the shelves in the apartment, too. Another wall was floor-to-ceiling shelving with a small stepladder beside it, indicating that nothing here went unused. Colored glass spheres hung in the window, catching the light as they turned lazily in the soft drafts of the air conditioning. In one corner stood a carved desk in some dark, polished wood, with a stylish high-backed, leather office chair in front of it. That and the long chaise, draped in silver lamé, with two round-topped side tables positioned at either end, were the only conspicuous furnishings.

It was a beautiful space. Mari just wished he could make his heart stop racing and appreciate it.

"Please, take a seat," Solana said, gesturing to the chaise. "Would either of you like a drink before we begin? Coffee? Or tea, perhaps? I have a selection of fruit teas if you would prefer."

Mari mutely shook his head. Annabel thanked her and negotiated a raspberry and rosehip infusion and Solana disappeared into an adjoining room to prepare her drink. When she had been gone for around ten seconds, he leaned toward his mother and whispered, "Mama, she's a —"

"Hush, Ilmari," she whispered before he could finish.

"But —" He stared at the doorway through which their host had just disappeared, unable to get a handle on the fear that was making him tremble with the urge to flee. "I think we should go."

"Ilmarinen, you are welcome to leave if you wish," his mama said rather more sternly. "I want to hear what she has to say."

He stared at her. "Mama, this is not going to work. I mean, look at her. She's a faith healer. You don't have a cold or a sprained ankle that she can sprinkle herbs on and it will go away on its own. You have cancer!"

"I am aware of that, Ilmarinen," she retorted testily. "I have seen some of the best and the most expensive oncologists that money can buy. They have failed to heal me. So, *I'm* prepared to look outside the box. She is an Elemental, Ilmari."

"I don't care. There are cheaper faith healers out there," he said, furrowing his brow. "This is just extortion."

"You said you would support me," she reminded him, her voice quiet and controlled.

"I will. I do. But this… I have a bad feeling about…" Mari closed his mouth at the look on his mother's face.

"I expected better, Ilmarinen. From *you*, of all people," she said in a low, warning tone.

For a moment, he was silent, aware that she was backing him into a metaphorical corner. Frustratingly, he could not even argue without making himself look hypocritical. After the shock and discomfort of facing Tomas, this was almost the last straw. At last he uttered a huff of exasperation. "Okay…have it your way. We will listen to whatever this person has to say but, Mama…please don't give her money."

He looked up at the suggestion of movement in the kitchen doorway.

Solana emerged, carrying a delicate teacup and saucer, which she placed on the table beside Anni. If she had overheard what Mari said, she was choosing to ignore it, as she neither defended herself nor chastised him for his opinion of her abilities.

What she said to him instead was, "You are an Air Elemental, are you not?"

Mari blinked at the statuesque healer. For a moment, he was blindsided by the question.

"Who told you that?" he asked at last, keeping his tone polite in deference to his mother, but a sudden chill in his blood raised every hair on his body. He eyed Mama inquiringly but she just shook her head.

"No one told me," Solana said in her soothing, lilting voice. "I can see the shimmer of Elemental energy in your aura. The yellow and gold is what tells me the element is air. Quite pretty."

Mari struggled hard not to roll his eyes. He wondered how difficult it would be to put two and two together and link him to his mother in order to research them both. Being a logical thinker, he found this explanation easier to accept than aura reading. Her comment reminded him of the last police case that he and Jake had assisted on, though. One of the murderers had professed to be able to see his aura. The memory made him shiver.

"What do you know about Elementals?" he asked, skimming over the 'pretty' comment for the time being. It was not the first time someone had told him he was pretty. Once, in another lifetime, he might have been flattered. Now, he found it irritating but had no desire to let Solana discover that. Not on a first meeting anyway.

"I've been one my whole life, so…quite a bit," Solana said. "A Water Elemental, to be precise. I understand your skepticism, Dr. Gale, but I assure you my gifts are as valid as your own. How far are you able to project?"

"Excuse me?"

"Oh, I'm sorry. I shouldn't have presumed. The yellow and gold parts of your aura are so vibrant I thought you would have one of the stronger gifts of Air. Astral projection — being able to leave the body for a short distance — is the most common manifestation."

He was impressed in spite of his determination not to be. Of course, anyone could have found out he was an Air Elemental with a bit of research. It didn't prove Solana wasn't a fake. However, if this healer *was* a genuine Water Elemental, it raised the bar on her potential abilities. One of Mama's not-too-distant ancestors had been one. Though he'd still never met a Water Elemental that could cure cancer.

"That's not exactly what I do, no," he said, conscious of Mama's eyes on him. He would be polite, for her sake, but he wasn't giving this stranger his life story. "My gift is more...technical than that. How long have you been" — *dressing like a teenage girl on a hippy trip?* his mind supplied, as he was searching for the right words. He bit down on that because he thought Mama would probably kill him, and settled for — "practicing?"

Solana looked thoughtful. "I have been reading auras for as long as I can remember. My other abilities developed later."

The answer seemed frank enough, but Mari didn't miss the fact that actually she hadn't told him much.

"So you have a number of skills? That must be useful."

"Do you possess more than one gift, Dr. Gale? It's quite rare, I'm told. In fact, I've never met another Elemental who did." She beamed at him and Mari frowned irritably. He answered a question with another question often enough that he recognized the evasion when he saw it.

He had no desire to get sucked into a conversation with Solana — if that was even her real name, which he doubted — but he'd met precious few people in his life that even understood what he was and what he could potentially do. The chance to talk properly about his gift was a rare one. Even so, he kept his answer curt.

"Just the one, I'm afraid, though it is quite specialized. Aren't you supposed to be talking to my mother? Remember? The one who's sick?" he reminded her helpfully.

Mama nudged him with her foot and gave him one of her sharp, narrow-eyed 'looks'. He feigned an innocent expression and beamed at her the way Solana did.

"Annabel is not the one who's anxious. She has already told me of your natural skepticism. I only wanted to put your mind at ease. Nothing I do will hurt her. The way I work is completely non-invasive. It will, however, take time."

And time is money, of course. Mari thought it but he didn't say it aloud.

"I'm not anxious. I'm just concerned about her" — *mental state* — "well-being," Mari said levelly, instead.

"Perfectly understandable. I am concerned for her well-being, too. I intend to make sure that her sessions here are comfortable and stress-free. Stress can create setbacks and delays in the healing process. Perhaps you would like a session yourself, as a demonstration?"

That was definitely a dig.

"I'm not the one who is sick. I would settle for an explanation of how you intend to banish my mother's incurable cancer, though." He leaned against the raised back of the chaise and folded his arms.

"I suppose you won't take 'magic' for an answer," Solana said, with a hint of teasing. She must have read the look on his face well enough because she held up her hands to placate him. "It's not an easy process to explain, Dr. Gale. I don't perform surgery or prescribe medicine. I don't sacrifice animals to appease deities or pray for their mercy. I don't manipulate the body or provide herbal remedies. All of these forms of healing can help or hinder what I do, but I won't know which until I start. I work directly with the energy centers of the body. Sometimes energy flows too strongly and sometimes it's mired and stagnant. I gradually adjust these flows until they are in balance. Once balance is achieved, healing is the result."

"I can see how that might take a while," Mari said, glancing at Mama for her take on this. She was watching Solana intently, though, and did not spare him a glance this time. He heaved a sigh. "Is this a kind of reiki that you do, then? Is there any...physical contact involved?"

Solana nodded once. "Indeed. Reiki is a form of energy work. Although it can't be proven, I believe Usui Sensei was probably a Water Elemental. Although what I do is not exactly the same. Touch may be involved to some extent, depending on what is needed, but mostly I will work without physical contact. I assure you, however, that I am very professional, and a licensed massage therapist." She softened her expression. "You know, massage might help relieve some of the tension you hold in your spine and shoulders."

That suggestive mirth was tugging at the corners of Solana's glossy lips again. Mama hid a smirk behind her hand as his gaze darted from hers to the supposed Healer's. She was absolutely making fun of him. Sudden anger welled up in Mari's breast and he sat down on it hard because it was unproductive. He had no desire to provoke an argument.

"I am not your patient, Miz Stellara," he said in a very pointed tone. "I have absolutely no intention of allowing you to touch me."

Solana gave him a curious look but only said, "Interesting. Well, if you change your mind, I'd be happy to schedule an appointment for you or recommend someone else if you would prefer it. Tension is never good to carry around, Dr. Gale." She turned to his mother before he could even open his mouth to argue. "Before we begin your treatment, Annabel, do you have any further questions?"

"How many sessions do you think I will need before the cancer responds?" Mama asked her. "I have no problems with repeated sessions, but I'd like some kind of timetable so that I have an idea of what to look out for as the healing progresses."

"It's difficult to say how long. A lot depends on how easily your energies can be balanced. I've never treated anyone with multiple myeloma before. I don't know if it will be more or less difficult than someone with leukemia or ovarian cancer. If you respond well and the disease reacts similarly to leukemia, it might take six months, perhaps a year. As the cancer can lie dormant naturally for a time, we may also need to make follow-up appointments to be sure."

Mama looked disappointed but managed a nod. Mari was less contained.

"A year? At your rates?" he huffed. "You do realize that will bankrupt us!"

"And a specialist in oncology would cost you less and be more successful, naturally," Solana said, and this time she was definitely sarcastic. "Dr. Gale, you have come to me because the other options did not work. Don't think that I do not see this pattern regularly. The treatment will take as long as it takes. I will not lie to you. What you are paying me for is an experiment. It may or may not work. But if we don't try at all, it certainly won't."

"That was my thinking, too." Mama sighed and nodded.

Mari opened his mouth then closed it again because basically he couldn't disagree with what she said, much as he might want to. That irked him more than anything right at that moment. Addressing Mama, he said, "You want to do this. I can tell."

"You know that we have to try," she responded with her infuriating logic. "I'm running out of options, Ilmari. Another cycle of chemo could wipe me out."

He nodded, recognizing when he was beaten. Mama's last session of chemotherapy had been over a year and a half ago but she was still weaker than she ought to be. Every session seemed to diminish her brightness a bit more, and he could not stand to watch it happen again.

"Okay, you have my blessing. We will do this." He chewed on his lips, frustrated but unable to deny Mama anything that her heart was set on, especially not where her health was concerned. He pointed one finger at Solana in warning, though. "If this makes her worse, I will make you sorry."

Mama did not speak to him again for the rest of the morning.

Chapter Seven

"And then, she says this whole sham could take up to a year! I'm telling you, this Solana person has no shame."

"Mm-hm."

"I mean, it's one thing to fleece desperate people out of a few hundred, or even a few thousand, but this person basically wants us to pay her Camden rent for twelve months while she waves her hands around and fondles crystals."

"Mm-hm."

"Did I tell you she had the nerve to say I looked tense? Of course I'm tense! My mother is buying snake oil from a charlatan that brazenly admits she's going to bilk us for the better part of a year."

Jake switched off the flame under the wok he'd been stir-frying their dinner in and transferred the contents to plates. He set one in front of Mari and the other across from him on the tiny folding kitchen table before sitting down.

Mari picked up his chopsticks, using them to stab viciously at a peapod. "Are you even listening to me at all, Chivis?"

"Of course I am. She's supposedly either a crossdressing, or transgender, Water Elemental, who claims to be able to cure cancer in a about a year by waving crystals around and probably playing annoying New Age music. I've heard every word, sweetheart. Eat."

"I can't eat. This whole thing is making me sick," Mari railed and scowled down at the plate Jake had fixed for him.

"Eat, Mari. Starving yourself isn't going to help."

Mari picked random pieces of chicken out of the tangle of noodles and greens and shoved them into his mouth like they'd done him a personal injustice.

"I wouldn't mind," he said, with his mouth still half-full, "but this Solana person behaves like she's doing us both a personal favor. Mama can't talk about anything else, though. She's besotted. It's ridiculous."

Jake swallowed what was in his mouth before saying, "What did you find? Anything? I'm assuming you didn't or you wouldn't be this pissed off."

Mari looked up at him. "What are you —?"

"You spent the whole afternoon digging into her business, didn't you? You were probably on your phone, looking, as soon as you walked out of the door, if I know you. And I do. So? Nothing? No arrests for fraud? Not even a parking ticket you could use to convince Anni she's bad news?"

Mari's chopsticks twitched, then he put them down and dropped his face into both hands, shaking his head. "There's nothing. She's got good recommendations from former patients. About five years ago, she was running a drag club in Bristol Temple Meads then—she claims—a head injury caused her Elemental gifts to flourish. She was helping to restrain a man who was hit by a car and she cured his broken leg. Her mother owns a dress agency in Weston-super-Mare. She was baptized Andrew Calvin but changed her name by deed poll about seven years back. She's thirty-five years old and there is absolutely nothing dodgy whatsoever in her profile." He sucked in a long breath and let it go, looking up at Jake with dejected eyes. "Why does she make my skin itch?"

Jake reached over and put his hand over the top of Mari's, brushing his thumb across the top soothingly. "Because you're scared she'll get your mother's hopes up. Because you're scared she might get *your* hopes up. Babe, this changes nothing. If she's a sham, you'll know it long before we get close to a year being up. And if she isn't…" Jake shrugged. "It can't hurt for Anni to see her."

Mari lifted Jake's knuckles to his lips and kissed them.

"You always say the right things," he said, though he sounded less than happy about it.

Jake offered a fond grin. "Don't be so disappointed. Pick up your sticks and eat. Don't make me force-feed you."

Mari's lips quirked and he picked up one chopstick and tapped it against the plate.

"You want to make me eat, huh? Is that right?" There was a seductive purr to his words that made Jake's abs clench in anticipation of something more than food.

He didn't give away any indication of how that tone sent a surge of heat through him. Instead, he took another bite before answering. "I like to watch you eat. And you need to keep your strength up for later."

"Promises, promises," Mari teased, but he did retrieve his chopsticks and plucked out another piece of chicken, popping it into his mouth and chewing slowly. He swallowed and reached straight away for more. "This is delicious, by the way. Where did you learn to cook?"

Jake ignored the awkward stab the compliment gave him. Cooking was 'women's work', as far as his father had been concerned, but if Jake hadn't learned, dinner would have come from a carry-out carton, or the microwave, every night.

"It's just something I picked up when I was a kid."

Mari gave him a curious look, like something he'd said had touched a chord.

"You've had plenty of practice then," he said, licking his lips and taking his time about it. He put another sliver of chicken in his mouth, chewing slowly, swallowing it with a low, throaty murmur of approval. "No wonder it's good. Are you going to make me eat my greens, Chivis?"

Jake's lips twitched and he suppressed a grin. "Every bit. I want to see a clean plate, mister."

Mari pouted and pretended to think about this while stirring the food with his chopsticks. He nibbled on a bean sprout but put it down again with a manipulative twinkle in his eye. "Do I get a reward?"

Jake lifted his eyes, letting his gaze roam down Mari's body purposefully. "I think Solana is right. You do look tense. I've got something much better than a massage to help with that, if you eat your dinner."

The twinkle became a gleam and Mari tucked away another mouthful. He didn't take his eyes off Jake as he chewed and swallowed with more purpose. After a couple of minutes, though, he put down his chopsticks.

"I'm all full up."

Jake looked at Mari's still not quite empty plate and back at his face. He knew for a fact that Mari was still hungry because he usually hoovered up every last beansprout, but tonight he was likely either distracted or just wanted to see what would happen if he pushed his luck. Jake kind of wanted to see what would happen, too, but he carried on eating his own meal. When Mari just stared at him like a puppy begging for scraps, he said, "Pick your sticks up and eat the rest of your dinner."

Mari whined in sheer desperation. "Jake...damn it! Don't torment me like this."

"Eat!" Jake told him, pushing himself to his feet and pointing to the chopsticks he had just put down. "Did I slave over a hot stove for nothing? Eat your dinner."

Mari's eyes widened but, when Jake just stared him down, he did as he was told, reaching for his discarded chopsticks. There was still a tiny flare of heat in his eyes as he pulled the plate toward him.

Jake stepped behind him and smoothed his fingers through Mari's silky hair. Mostly he moved there so Mari couldn't see how hard he was fighting not to laugh. Mari got off on this stuff, and that—more than anything—was what got Jake hot. Sometimes, though, he was surprised by how it turned Mari on when Jake got bossy or manhandled him. He'd experimented with the whole BDSM thing with a couple of other lovers, but more often than not it had just been playing around. Mari was into it more seriously. Jake couldn't help thinking that, if the shoe were on the other foot tonight, he would have told Mari to fuck right off.

Mari diligently chewed and swallowed until his plate was clean. Jake rested his hands on Mari's shoulders, kneading lightly and bending to kiss the top of his head. Tilting in his seat to look up at him, Mari put the utensils down so he could reach above his head to run his fingers through Jake's hair in response.

"This is really doing it for me. I want you so much it hurts," he breathed.

Jake paused for a second, considering his next move. In all honesty, he could have thrown Mari across the table and taken him at that very moment, but this was part of the game, he knew. Escalation, Jake's research had called it. Of course, he wasn't going to let Mari realize he was onto him.

"All right, sweetheart. Strip."

Those vivid blue eyes went huge and Mari quivered as his fingers worked on the buttons of his shirt and he shrugged it off his shoulders. His skin dimpled with the chill and the rush of excitement that was mirrored in his gaze. He ran his hands down his stomach to his waistband and popped the button of his fly.

"Can I stand up?" he asked huskily.

"Did I say you could?" Jake tried to keep his expression serious.

Mari pouted at him and somehow managed to wriggle his way out of his jeans without actually leaving his seat. He pushed them to his ankles and kicked his feet free of them, looking up at Jake again, reduced to his skimpy blue briefs and the twinkle in his summer-sky eyes.

"You are angling for that whipping, aren't you? I said, strip. All the way, then sit tight and put your hands on the table where I can see them."

Mari licked his lips and Jake knew he hadn't just been imagining it. His pretty mate had a passion for punishment. Their games in the bedroom were not always rough, but when they got that way, Mari was practically insatiable until he'd been spanked good and hard.

"We haven't played a scene in a long time," Mari chided him, letting him know that his thoughts were running on the same lines.

Jake pushed his fingers into Mari's hair and pulled his head back, bending to kiss him, short and hard. "Are you feeling neglected, baby?"

Mari nodded and looked up at him with a soulful stare. "I love how you take care of me. But I love how you keep me in line as well. It really turns me on, Chivis."

"I know it does, babe," Jake murmured against his lips. "And I understand. I'm gonna give you what you need."

Mari shivered again. He was gloriously hard, practically straining right out of those tiny mesh briefs that Jake loved to see him in. He wriggled the skimpy garment off under the table then slapped his hands down on the top, obedient to the last, but a little bit defiant, too.

"Good boy. I think you earned your reward."

Jake picked him up and Mari wrapped his arms around his neck. He carried him into the bedroom and set him down on the bed, kneeling down on the floor between Mari's thighs and kissing him. "I love you. You'll use your word if you need to tonight?"

It wasn't exactly a question but Jake expected an answer. The blue of Mari's eyes darkened at the mention of their safeword and his pupils grew larger, making his gaze seem more intense than ever. Jake had instigated its use once he knew that their initial forays into light bondage and playful hand spankings were never going to be quite enough to satisfy Mari's needs. They hadn't ever discussed how these needs had arisen in the first place. Mari tended to become reticent when Jake steered the conversation in that direction. But he had been persuaded, after much arguing, to accept a means of bringing his punishment to a halt if things grew too unbearable.

That thought, in turn, made Jake angry—the idea of Mari playing these games with a mate who didn't care if he hurt him. Someone had taught Mari to accept that the passive acceptance of pain was his due, something he had no control over. Jake kept the anger under wraps when he had a paddle or a belt in his hand, though.

"I promise," Mari said with a curt nod.

"Say it for me." Jake rested his hands on Mari's knees, looking up at him seriously.

"Kotka," Mari said. It was his happy place, the holiday home of his childhood. When he spoke its name, Jake saw the light that shone for a moment in his summer-blue eyes.

Jake ran gentle fingers down his long legs then reached under the bed frame and pulled out the footlocker where they kept their growing collection of bondage gear and toys. He opened the box and selected a pair of leather cuffs and some thick, leather straps.

"Lie down and bend your knees up. Put your wrists down by your ankles."

Mari made a purring noise and wriggled into the required position at once, with a naughty curl of his lips. He loved to be cuffed or tied up, and his excitement was all too clear.

Jake put the cuffs around his wrists and buckled them, using the trailing straps to fasten his ankles to each wrist so he couldn't unbend his knees or raise his arms. Once he had him strapped down, he spent a moment or two stroking him all over, up his legs and arms and down his chest, everywhere but his straining cock. Mari was already getting that faraway look in his eyes that he got whenever they played like this.

Jake reached down into the toy box and pulled out a slim length of rough rope. This was something that Mari had already hinted he was interested in, but Jake had wanted to be sure he knew what he was doing before he tied up his balls. The last thing he wanted was to do permanent damage to such sensitive parts of his lover and best friend.

He used the end of the rope to tickle just below Mari's balls and fondled them briefly, pulling them down between his thighs before he started to wind the rope around the stretched skin of his sac in a figure of eight.

"Mmmhhh... Fuck!" Mari exhaled, his body curling up off the bed in response to the friction of the cord against the sensitive skin of his scrotum. He kept his squirming minimal, though, until Jake was done binding him.

"Not too tight?" Jake asked.

"No. It's...okay." Mari swallowed, his voice thickening.

"Good." Jake circled his thumb and forefinger over where the rope was wound and lifted Mari's balls. The skin of his sac was stretched tight around them. Jake summoned his courage. What he was about to do went counter to his every masculine instinct. Swallowing his doubts, he flicked a light finger against one of Mari's bound testes.

Jake felt him flinch but the reaction was not as extreme as he had feared. Mari was biting down on his lips but, beyond sucking in a hard breath through his nostrils, he did not make a single sound. He was still fully erect, his cock arching over his sleek belly toward his navel as he squirmed in the cuffs. The leather creaked a soft complaint but held him fast.

Jake stroked a hand up and down one of his lean, hard-muscled thighs. The soft whorls of fine, light-golden hair on Mari's upper leg tickled against his palm and he whispered, "Good boy. You're so beautiful."

Mari's teeth released his lips at last and he gulped in another breath, exhaling, "I love you more than you could ever know, Chivis."

Jake bent his head to lick the spot he'd just flicked, drawing his tongue up the length of Mari's cock and lapping around the glans before closing his mouth around the crown. Mari lurched almost as much as he had when Jake had flicked him. He lifted his hips to get deeper but Jake didn't let him. He swirled his tongue around one more time then knelt up, letting Mari slip free. Jake pushed on Mari's shins until his knees almost touched his shoulders and ran his tongue over the smooth stretch of skin beneath his balls and between his cheeks, swiping the tip over his flexing hole.

"Uhhhhh...oh fuck! Fuck!" Mari yelped and tugged on the cuffs around his wrists. His body jumped and jolted violently at every touch but he didn't ask Jake to stop.

Jake did stop, though, after a few moments of tonguing him. He held him in position, knees up and ass exposed, the wetness of saliva glistening around his hole. Reaching down into the box again, he chose a short-handled flogger with small, hard knots tied in the tails. It took more precision to whip Mari this way, but that was why he picked the shorter instrument. He used it to strike Mari across one buttock, without any warning.

"Mmmmuuuhhhh!" Mari whined, gnawing harder on his lips as his body vibrated from the impact. He twisted and bucked but didn't protest or ask for release. When his eyes met Jake's, they were almost midnight blue, dark with longing.

Jake trailed the tails across Mari's skin then lifted the flail and struck him again. Mari sucked in a sharp breath and Jake smacked his other cheek with the flogger before returning to the first, back and forth. He didn't swing as hard as he could but they weren't light swats, either. Jake started out slow but built up a steady rhythm, gradually increasing both the pace and the force behind the swing.

He'd never thought this would be something he'd get off on, and he certainly wouldn't have if Mari weren't into it. But he was — very, very much. The way he gasped and moaned and whimpered and the way his cock flushed a darker color with the rush of his arousal were all Jake needed to get into the scene himself.

When Mari's ass was well and truly striped, Jake stopped and ran a hand over the red marks. The skin was hot to the touch but Mari didn't flinch away. He pulled on the cuffs, keeping his legs and backside raised and on offer.

"Mari…" His own voice almost startled him, it sounded so deep and husky. "Say something, baby. Show me you're still with me."

"Mmmhhhh, Chivis," his beloved crooned, wriggling under his touch. His normally light tone was also deeper and much gruffer than usual. "I love being your bad boy. You make me feel like I'm flying." Jake eased

Mari's legs down until his heels were touching his ass again and, parting his knees, bent over to kiss him. He combed his fingers through Mari's hair until he broke off the kiss. That was the only tenderness he got before Jake snared the lube. Mari was so keyed up from the beating that, when Jake oiled him and eased two fingers into him, he lurched and tossed his head. Jake pulled them out and slicked lube over his cock, nudging it between Mari's glowing cheeks.

"Ahhh…ohhhh…mhhhh…" Mari murmured something in Suomi which, as far as Jake had been able to establish from asking him in the past, translated as something like 'your father was a devil with a dick like a reindeer'. It sounded much more impressive in the Finnish national tongue—and fifty times hotter, the way Mari growled it as he was riding Jake's fingers or his dick.

Jake pressed into him, pushing Mari's thighs apart and settling between with an ease that had not been possible when they'd first started seeing each other. Sometimes he still needed to coax Mari into a more relaxed frame of mind and body before he could attempt to get inside him, but it was never an issue when the bondage gear and whips came out. The way Mari handed over the reins, completely trusting, scared Jake sometimes. But at least Mari was with him and not someone who would hurt him without mercy. Curling over him, he kissed Mari hard as he picked up almost the same pounding rhythm he'd flogged him with. As his hands slid under Mari's sweat-slick back, he crushed him to his chest, fucking him hard and kissing him with fierce heat.

Mari arched his torso as Jake thrust into him, heels on Jake's shoulders, pushing his hips down to meet each stroke and using the cuffs that locked his wrists against his ankles for added leverage. Though he was naturally lean and almost fey-looking, his physique was deceptive. Jake knew from experience that Mari was physically stronger than many people gave him credit for.

He certainly had stamina and tolerance for pain, in abundance.

"Oh my stars… Jake… That feels good!" he groaned, twisting and thrashing urgently under him. "So big! I love you, Jake!"

"I love you, too." Jake panted, sucking and nipping at Mari's neck. When the moment came, he didn't hold anything in reserve. He pushed deep and held there until the shudders started to taper off, before rocking into him more slowly.

Mari was still hard, purring at the gentler surging between his long legs and the brush of Jake's warm mouth over his throat.

"Mmhm… I am such a lucky boy," he sighed almost drowsily. "I love the way that feels. Love making you come like this."

"Mm," Jake agreed. He pulled out very slowly and came up on hands and knees, looking down at him with a tender smile. "Time to turn over, babe."

He knelt up and helped Mari roll over. With his wrists still bound to his ankles, he was on his knees and shoulders, his ass in the air. Jake leaned over the edge of the bed and grabbed his jeans to pull his belt out of the loops. "Spread your legs wider."

Mari obliged him instantly, wriggling until Jake had space to kneel between his thighs if he wanted to. Mari turned his head and watched Jake retrieving his belt with a yearning sigh.

The first time they had played this kind of scene, Jake had been reluctant to take his belt to Mari, but it had been the beginning of his lover's road toward complete relaxation in the bedroom. Mari could not — or would not — explain it, but he was just more at ease after a spanking. It was not down to childhood abuse. Mari had been adamant that his parents had never laid a hand on him in anger. But someone must have taught him to love punishment, because it had come as no surprise to Mari when the feel of Jake's belt across his cheeks turned him on enough to take things further in their relationship.

Jake put his hand on the center of Mari's back, more to steady him than to hold him still. The flogger was nice and stingy but it was just a warm-up for Mari. Jake doubled the belt over and brought it down hard right at the top of his thighs. Mari jerked but didn't make a sound and Jake swiped him with the belt again, the smack of leather against his skin loud in the small room.

Mari caught his breath, sucking in air hard, as the short, pliant strap seared his skin. Jake guessed that sitting down was not going to be a barrel of laughs for him tomorrow.

"You want to use that word?" he prompted, caressing Mari's heated skin again.

His lover shook his head. "Nuhhh... I can take it."

The low growl in his voice told Jake that Mari was close, though.

Jake belted him once more, in a different spot, higher on his buttocks, purposely avoiding the stripes where the flogger had landed on his skin. He reached under him and wrapped his hand around Mari's jutting cock, giving that a few strokes as well.

Mari moaned, a low, quiet sound that seemed to begin down deep below his ribs and quiver up through him like breaking ice. He had jerked on the cuffs as the belt had fallen across his skin but he didn't struggle. His responses were quiet and controlled, like he was rationing his reactions.

Jake realized that he'd stopped, mesmerized by Mari's pinioned body.

"You are so beautiful. You're always beautiful, but especially like this," Jake murmured, running his hands over Mari's abused backside. "You ready to come yet?"

"Oh yes...always." Mari managed a short bark of laughter but it was laced with an emotion that was not quite humor. His face was turned to the left, eyes closed and features relaxed, but his voice sounded breathless, almost drunk. "Make me come."

Jake reached under him to rub his cock, letting go only long enough to pull the knot in the rope around his balls free. He hadn't tied it very tight but enough that he knew the blood rushing back was going to be exquisitely excruciating. Jake only had to stroke the loose skin of his sac with the back of one finger to make him jolt and whimper.

"Fu-uh-uck!" Mari sang, shaking his head, though he didn't cry 'enough' as Jake tenderly fondled between his thighs. His body shuddered like a jet caught in turbulence. As he whimpered, a desperate two-note sound, Jake gripped his cock and jacked Mari hard. It was fairly unusual for Mari to take so long to reach his release, especially when he was this horny. Jake let go of his balls and slid two fingers back into him, twisting them around inside and fucking him with them as his other hand worked Mari's cock.

A rapid, shuddering sigh slid out of Mari and, just like that, he was there. He came hard, blasting jets of thick warm cum over Jake's hand.

"That's it, such a good boy," Jake whispered, milking him more slowly, bumping his fingers up over the sensitive head and feeling him twitch and shiver. He kept going, though he knew it must be both a pleasure and a torture for Mari to be touched like this, right after he had come. When Mari elicited a last shudder and started to squirm, Jake let him go and pulled the buckle free on one cuff. He gently rolled him over and released the other before towing Mari into his arms and kissing him.

Mari's body tensed briefly under him as Jake unbound him. But when Jake embraced him, his limbs flowed around him like a strong river, dragging him into Mari's undertow. Mari returned the kiss like a starving man, devouring Jake's mouth. His body arched and he undulated against Jake, stretching out their sweet moment of intimacy. When their lips finally parted and they both lay panting in each other's arms, he whispered, "I love you more than life, Chivis. You know that, right?"

The words warmed Jake's heart. He kissed Mari's temple and caressed his shoulder. "I do. I love you, too, Ilmari."

Chapter Eight

"Jake!"

He heard Manny call him as he passed the front of the bar, so he stopped and reversed course, going inside. It was a Wednesday night and not all that crowded.

"Hey, Manny, how's things?" Jake said as he walked up to the bar.

"There's an easier way to say that, you know. 'Awright?' That works for everything."

Jake flashed a grin at him. "Yeah, I've gotten used to hearing it but not saying it. What gives, then?"

"I've got a favor to ask you."

"What? You planning to break your arm again and need me to haul more cases downstairs?" Jake had only recently stopped helping out as Manny's temporary cellarman, since the barkeep had gotten his arm out of plaster after falling down the steps to the basement.

Manny chuckled wryly. "No thanks, pleasant as it was to watch you do that." He set a pocket watch on the bar, an old-fashioned-looking thing with a chain. "I got this and I was wondering if you could, you know…tell me about it."

Jake looked up at him and lifted his eyebrows. He didn't talk much about what he could do and Manny hadn't ever bothered him about it like some people did, so this was certainly unusual.

"You want me to tell you if it's hot?" Jake asked.

"Well…maybe…but more I wanted to be sure that it's not haunted."

Jake snickered. "I can tell you it's not haunted without doing anything. There's no such thing. Even if there was, I've never come across any object that could hold on to a spirit. Just memories. Where'd it come from?"

"One of my punters couldn't pay his bar bill. He brought it in out of the blue and asked if I'd take it as part-payment. Reckoned it was his great-granddad's or something," Manny told him. "He said the old boy was in the war. Was a bit vague about which war. I guess that should have got the old alarm bells ringing straight off, huh?"

Jake shrugged. "Well, if he killed someone and ripped it off, that memory is probably stuck to it. Trauma tends to stick around."

Manny stared at him as if he wasn't sure if he should laugh or if he was serious, and when Jake didn't say he was joking, he quickly swiped the bar with a clean cloth.

"That's fucking spooky, man."

Jake chuckled again then focused. Another watch, this one considerably older than the one he'd read for Cordiline. Hopefully if it held any memories, they were just of innocuous occasions, like a wedding. He took a few moments to open himself up, to be receptive to any memories that might be clinging to the watch, then took a deep breath and let it out slowly. He reached over and touched it.

He watched his breath plume from between his lips as he shivered in the cold. Looking down, he checked the time. Five minutes to eight. He tucked the watch into his pocket as he walked along the cobbled street and straightened his waistcoat. Whistling a merry tune to himself, he turned down an even narrower, darker passage. The sign on the side of the building read Dorset Street. *He heard the clip-clop sound of iron-shod hooves and the rattle of what he imagined was a carriage behind him.*

A slim, dark-haired girl wearing far too little clothing for the chill weather stood in a doorway under a dim light – a gaslight, Jake noted. The way she was dressed and the way he was dressed, coupled with the sound of the horse and carriage and the look of the buildings and streets around him, told Jake this memory was very old, not this century…maybe not even last century.

"Don't you look like a lonely lamb. Why don't you come in and warm your bones?" she called out to him flirtatiously.

He turned toward her. "Now what kind of gentleman would I be to refuse such an offer."

He stepped up onto the narrow flagstone stairs next to her. They went inside and she giggled softly and lifted her hair from her neck.

"Give me a hand with my dress, lovey."

He closed the distance between them and slid one hand up her slim back. He reached the other into his pocket and curled his fingers tightly around something. He took it out, and when he flicked it deftly open and put it to the prostitute's neck, Jake saw it was a pearl-handled razor.

She gasped and he yanked her head up by the hair.

"Don't you make a sound, you filthy whore," he snarled as he pressed the blade harder into the tender skin of her throat. *"What's your name?"*

"M-Mary..."

He cut her, slicing deep and watching the blood spray out in a gory scarlet fountain. "Hello, Mary. I'm the butcher, but you can call me Mr. Kraft – Harold, to my friends." He let her go and laughed at the way she clutched at her throat. He slashed at her again and –

Jake sucked in a hard breath as he came out of the memory, shaken and wide-eyed.

"What, mate? Is it haunted?" Manny asked worriedly.

Jake shook his head and carefully turned the watch over to look at the reverse side of the casing. It was engraved with the initials HBK. *Could it be...?* No. That was too much to believe. And yet if it proved to be true... He heard the sound of those clip-clopping hooves again and recalled the rattle of the wooden cartwheels on the cobbles and how everything had been so dark in the faint glow of the gaslights. Jake swallowed hard. Even if it was true, who would believe him? No, maybe it was safer to leave the past alone in this case. Some mysteries were perhaps better left unsolved.

"No, no, it was nothing. I just got a vague impression of a foxhole and gunfire. Most likely he was right. It did belong to someone's grandfather." Jake set the watch on the bar. He took a rain check on the beer Manny offered him and continued on his way to the gym.

Jake didn't like treadmills, preferring to do his running in the park, even in miserable weather, but he used the weights and the heavy bag. As he'd once told Cordiline, boxing wasn't his thing, but he did know about stance and technique, and pummeling a big bag of sand was actually a good way to work out his frustration. He ran when he wanted to clear his head and think. He hit the bag when he just wanted to release some anger.

He wasn't exactly angry now, but he had spent most of the day brooding. He warmed up with some stretches and basic calisthenics, afterward moving to the weights for a while. When he was done with his reps, he went to the heavy bag hanging from the ceiling in the corner of the gym. He proceeded to treat it like it was the reason for that distressed look on Mari's face all the time he was trying to pretend he wasn't bothered by his ex being in town.

"That one pissed you off big time," a familiar voice remarked, as if summoned by his thoughts. Cordiline slid onto the bench of the weight machine close by and racked up another fifteen pounds, slipping into a slow, smooth pattern of reps that allowed him to talk. "Haven't seen you down here for a while. How's it going?"

Jake threw a right into the bag, using his arm, shoulder and back for maximum power, and landing it where the midsection would be if the bag were a person. The force of the blow made the bag swing and he followed with a left that would have probably broken some ribs. He hated violence, but that didn't mean he had no idea how to fight or couldn't make someone regret deciding they wanted to test him.

"Fine," he answered, shortly.

"It looks it." The detective raised one dark, wing-like eyebrow. After twelve reps he eased off, flexing pectoral muscles that weren't always evident under the smart cut of his shirt and jacket during his day job, and added another couple of five-pound weights. "Looks to me like you need to take your mind off something. A desk job is fine but it's a bitch for not getting shot of frustration. Speaking of… What does your pretty boy get up to when you're down here? He doesn't do the whole gym scene, I've noticed. I'd have thought he'd enjoy the talent spotting, if nothing else."

"He's working late tonight." Jake jabbed a few more punches into the bag. He ignored the rest of what Cordiline had said about Mari.

"He puts the hours in. I'll give him that. This new job must be pushing his buttons. You know, if you're at a loose end while he's working, I might be able to nudge some work your way, Jake. If you'd be interested, that is." Cordiline eased the weights back into their rests and sat up smoothly.

Jake smirked as he pounded the bag. "Trying to pawn off your cold cases, huh?"

"Never let it be said that I'm afraid to try new methods," Cordiline said. "I'm a modern, forward-thinking type of copper, Chivis, and I hate an unsolved case. From what I've seen so far, the same applies to you, I'd say."

Jake rolled his eyes at the attempted flattery and Cordiline continued.

"But, cold cases are for if and when you have time. I'm talking about consulting on current cases."

Jake hit that bag hard. It swung and he caught it when it came back at him, stopping his flow for a moment. He looked at Cordiline expectantly and the DI nodded approval.

"You were right about that idiot with the dog not being the right perp. We let him go. There's no DNA, nothing connecting him to any of the victims."

"That leaves you with no suspects."

"Correct again."

"You want my help with your serial rapist?"

Cordiline acceded. "For starters, yes. And if anything else comes up. The department frowns on using consultants, generally speaking, but seeing as how you are a trained detective on top of your other ability, I think you'd make a good asset."

Jake snorted. "All right, stop with the buttering up already. You want my help with the case, you got it. I can't make any promises on other cases. I do have a job. Remember?"

Cordiline shrugged. "So, quit. You get your PI license and you can start charging clients. In between, you can help us out."

Jake heaved a sigh. "It takes time to build a practice like that."

"I'm sure your boyfriend wouldn't mind helping out with your upkeep while you're getting on your feet."

"He probably would, but I'm not going to ask him." Jake let the bag go and took a swing, following it with a few left-handed jabs.

"You think he'd take issue with it?" Cordiline narrowed his eyes. "I reckoned things were more serious between the two of you, given the death-threat looks he gives me whenever I've had the pleasure of his invariably charming company."

"You want me to lie and say he likes you? Not gonna happen," Jake said with a humorless huff.

"I wouldn't believe it anyway." Cordiline nodded acknowledgment. "Tell him he'd be an asset, too, if he could take instruction and do as he was told, will you?"

"Tell him yourself."

"I'm serious, Chivis. I've talked to the higher-ups about this and they're on board. If, and I mean that, if it gets results, they would be interested in testing you guys out on a case-by-case consultancy basis." Cordiline leaned forward with his elbows on his knees, looking up at Jake earnestly. "Tell me you'll think about it, at least."

Cordiline was just telling him what he wanted to hear. He knew it and still he couldn't help being seduced by it. He didn't hate his job, but he'd worked hard to build a career as a detective before chucking it on the trash heap. He couldn't say he didn't miss it, and what Cordiline was offering was more than just throwing him a bone. He'd be doing what he'd been trained to do. He'd be doing what he truly loved. He hit the bag one more time and set it swinging on its chain.

"I'll think about it."

Cordiline looked satisfied with that and settled into his workout again. For about twenty minutes, they carried on in silence, working up a satisfying sweat. Before Jake hit the showers, though, Cordiline told him, "We're back to square one on the rape case. No new suspect. No new leads, which is annoying. And worrying, given the game he likes to play with his victims. How long do you reckon it will take before he decides to bury one a bit deeper and she doesn't make it?"

Jake grimaced. It was probably not long at all. It was every detective's worst nightmare—a dead end on a serial case where the perp was escalating.

"I'll start interviewing the victims tomorrow."

Chapter Nine

Mari chewed thoughtfully on the end of his phone stylus as he surveyed the list he had just completed. It was quiet after six-thirty at Trafalgar House. Most of the administration staff had gone home by this time of the evening and those of his colleagues that remained were busy in their own cubicles, working on their own projects. Mari had been involved in two investigations for his employers during the afternoon and his reports for those jobs were neatly typed up and sitting in Ashcroft's inbox. The two personal traces he had been working on between his official duties were what presently occupied his mind.

Natalie Craig was the second known victim of the Highgate Cemetery rapist. She had been attacked after a night out with friends and, according to her statement, she never saw her attacker's face. The last thing she remembered before coming to her senses in a shallow scrape, covered in earth, was waiting at the stop for the night bus home. She said that she thought she heard a hissing noise, but it could have been the sound of tires on the wet road.

He made a shortlist of potential ways that people could have made contact with her, based on the material he'd pulled out of the police files on her case. The Met were still trying to improve their online security but as yet they'd not developed a system that could keep an interface out. He liked to tease DI Cordiline about that whenever their paths crossed. They had no way of proving that he'd sleepwalked his way through their files but his opponent for Jake's attention would be aware that whatever he knew, Mari knew, too.

He certainly didn't need telling that their suspect for the Highgate rapes had walked already. That was fine, as he'd already checked out and dismissed the man, William Sefton Smith, from his list of concerns. The fellow was unexceptional in every respect. Besides which, his wife and his neighbor — who was irritated by the practice — had already vouched for the fact that opera-loving Sefton Smith walked his dog, then returned and played Wagner, at the same ridiculous hours, every night.

Mari reopened the backdoor access to Holmes 2, the Home Office Large Major Enquiry System, a shared casebook of ongoing national police investigations. They'd changed the passwords again but it didn't take him long to crack those. Mari didn't even need to interface with the system for that. He'd set up a netbook specially to access Holmes. If the worst-case scenario became reality and he was caught, he could easily get rid of the physical evidence, but Mari was not desperately worried about that eventuality.

Jake admonished him regularly about his hacking habit but it was just because Jake liked to worry. Three attempts on the final password saw him into the system and he navigated his way through the case files until he found what he was after, Natalie's file.

The investigating officer had already checked out her social media profile, which was reassuring. Sapphire, the unit responsible for victim support where there had been a sexual assault, was in full possession of her contact details so he was able to find out her mobile provider and her home ISP by tracking the numbers backward from calls they had made to her.

He closed his eyes and touched the screen, letting his Elemental senses loose to roam the network of her mobile phone company. The sensation was liberating. Mari could never deny it. He loved to slip out of the constraints of his all-too-mortal body and run free in the ether, surging like electricity from one system to another, using the points of contact between service users as his nexus points. He hopped in and out of people's private communications as easily as commuters hopped in and out of tube trains. If he had access to a person's phone line, he could use it as an access point for anyone that had been in telephone or Internet contact with his source number. The communication potential was infinite.

Mari's health was not, though. His main restriction when interfacing like this was the body he left behind. He wasn't invulnerable to the stresses it put on his less-than-substantial frame and the questionably brilliant mind it housed. During the previous quarter, his beloved Jake had even gone so far as to ban him from interfacing completely for weeks at a time.

The thought of not being able to do this still haunted him and left him sick and empty inside. He could not deny it. He was an interface junkie. But it was a gift that was rarely given. He needed to use it wisely.

Hunting for a rapist and potential killer was wise, wasn't it?

He had to have picked Natalie out from somewhere. The most likely sources were to be found in the circles of her work and social life. Her attacker didn't necessarily hang around with her, but there was a school of thought that suggested the majority of victims knew, or were known to, their attackers in some way.

What he needed to do was to analyze the circles that the three victims moved in and see if there were any overlaps. Jake would doubtless tell him that the police were already doing this, but the police weren't able to access the levels of communication technology that he could. Mari swam deeper, trusting his memory to take notes.

He had to do this here. It was more private in some ways than interfacing at home. Mama could intrude on him at the house and Jake might call him and disrupt his concentration. Here, everyone knew what he was and why MI5 employed him. He would not be interrupted unless it was clear that he was not working.

It was his interfacing safe haven.

By the time he logged his tech out and shut down for the night, it was nearly eight-thirty and he was nursing a slight headache. Even so, he messaged Jake as he was leaving to see if he wanted to grab something to eat. Jake responded and they arranged to meet at a delicious Thai place close to his apartment that they both loved.

He knew that Jake had been to the gym as soon as he stepped through the door and the maître d' showed him to the table where his love was waiting already. There was a glow to Jake when he'd been working out. His dark curls were damp and sexily tousled and he exuded a delicious, healthy vibe that never failed to get Mari hot for him.

He bent to kiss Jake softly on the mouth before taking his seat. "Good evening, hot stuff. I hope you've worked up an appetite."

Jake nodded with enthusiasm. "A bit, yeah. I ordered some spring rolls as a starter for us. How was your day?"

"This is why I love you." Mari snared a bite-sized roll of crispy pastry and vegetables, wolfing it whole as he settled into his seat. "I've been busy. But I did get time to look at the records on the girls that your stalker's psychopath has been inhuming, he'll be pleased to hear. Tell him that their security patches still aren't up to scratch, by the way. A ten-year-old could have hacked them easily."

Jake sighed and ate a spring roll. "He's not my stalker, and you can tell him yourself. Did you find anything interesting in your search?"

Mari reached over and stole another roll. "The girls are all of an age, early twenties. They live within three miles of one another. No work in common, though. They don't seem to hang out in the same areas, so our psycho has his work cut out selecting them, or he likes to change his locale regularly. One had just left work and blacked out before she got home. One was waiting for the bus and doesn't remember getting on it. The first one had been out with friends at a club and left alone. I can't find any friends in common and I spent a long time on their Internet histories. He's random, this one."

Jake didn't bother to feign surprise. "That's pretty much what was in the files from Cordiline that I've already seen." He paused for a moment and added, "Speaking of, I ran into him at the gym. He'd already told me they cut their perp loose and don't have any new leads."

Mari nodded again, still chewing. He swallowed and poured some water into the glass by his place setting.

"He walked this morning. Case notes hint that the psych evaluation found him a shade on the eccentric side, but there wasn't any physical evidence to suggest he'd even picked up a trowel, let alone dug a grave recently. The girl he stumbled across did some volunteer work locally and she'd been to a funeral at Highgate in the past three weeks, which was kind of spooky." He took a sip of his drink and made a cursory scan of the menu, even though they both knew what he would select. "Not stalking you, huh?"

Jake rolled his eyes. "We go to the same gym. It's not like I see him there every time I go."

The conversation was put on hold for a moment while the server came and took their orders.

"Even though we haven't found anything yet, John asked me to stick with the case. I'm going to interview some of the victims," Jake said when their waiter returned to the pass.

"Uh-huh, John now, is it?" Mari winked as Jake narrowed his eyes. "Oh, calm down. I don't mind. I think it's funny, if you must know. And a bit sad." He helped himself to the last spring roll and gestured with it as he added, "You should start with the first girl, Emily Redbridge. She seemed to remember more than the other two. Funny thing that she works at the Bun Shop, the café near Waterstones on Torrington Place. I must have seen her before but I can't visualize her."

"Would you like to go with me?" Jake asked.

"Will there be free almond croissants?" Mari asked, popping the roll into his mouth and managing a dignified grin with his lips pressed shut as he consumed it.

Jake gave him a raised eyebrow. "She's a rape victim, Mari. We're not going to talk to her where she works. Besides, I don't think we'll find out much that she didn't already tell the cops just from talking to her. Since they weren't left with any of their possessions, my best hope is to pick up a memory with a handshake. It doesn't happen all the time, but it's worth a shot."

"Then I'm surplus to your requirements," Mari said, and wiped his hands on his napkin. "I'm not good with emotional women. Unless she lets me play with her phone, I can't do anything more by being there than I could remotely."

Jake turned those big brown eyes on him like a puppy-dog. "C'mon, please? I can't just knock on her door, ask to shake her hand and leave. If you could just talk to her for a minute?"

Mari fired him a skeptical look. "Jake, the last time you asked me to come to a potential murder victim's final stop and keep people talking, we got arrested. Is that wise?"

"That was your plan, if you remember," Jake told him. "This is a totally different situation. We're not talking to suspects for one thing, and we're not doing anything even remotely pushing the boundaries of legality. I don't get why you always say you don't do well talking to people. I've never seen you have any trouble. You have a talent for it."

"Flattery will get you nowhere, Chivis." Mari rolled his eyes. "I talk to people because it's the only way to get them to do what I want. I don't do it because I get a kick out of it."

Jake sighed dramatically. "Well, I guess I can always ask Cordiline to go with me instead."

"You know, he'd love that." Mari exhaled, laughing under his breath at Jake's bald-faced cheek. Honestly, if he didn't love this man so much, there would be no putting up with him. "If you're that desperate not to go alone, I suppose I will have to come and hold your hand."

Jake leaned closer to kiss him. Their meals came shortly after and they spent the rest of the evening talking of more pleasant subjects. Mari drank more wine than he'd intended, but Jake kept ordering another glass for him every time it looked low. When they left the restaurant, Jake put his arm around him as they walked toward the apartment.

"There was something else I kinda wanted to talk to you about," Jake said. "Cordiline suggested he would like me, possibly us, to take on more consulting work for the police."

The space between Mari's eyebrows contracted and he made a conscious effort not to frown.

"That 'possibly' hints at conditions he knows I'm not going to like. What does he mean, exactly?"

"Well, mainly that you'd have to play by their rules. And, uh, 'do what you're told'. Although I'd take that with a grain of salt because consultants are usually given a lot of leeway, as long as they're working within the law. Anyway, I told him I already had a job but he asked that I at least think about it."

Mari considered this for a moment, enjoying the warmth of Jake's arm around his waist as they walked. Less than a year ago, he'd have laughed at the idea of such a silly thing meaning so much to him, but Jake had changed so many of his old opinions in that short space of time.

"Have you? Thought about it, I mean?" he asked, curious about what his partner in love and crime was thinking.

Jake shrugged. "It would be doing the work I was trained to do. And it's why I agreed to join the university program to begin with, so that we are treated legitimately by the legal system on a global level. Having our work be recognized this way would be a big step in the right direction."

Mari turned his head to one side, taking in Jake's handsome, earnest features as he listened to his words. He experienced a small glow of heat and pride in his man as Jake gave voice to his deliberations. They had argued before about how best to use the gifts they had been born with, and though they had differences of opinion on that matter, he knew in his heart that Jake shared his belief that Elemental resources should not be wasted.

"It would be," he agreed, slipping one arm around Jake and letting his hand rest on the man's hip as they walked. "I have a job, too, and I have to be careful how the other things I do impact on that work. Let me talk to Ashcroft. If he agrees, I will help."

Jake offered him a tender smile. "Your boss seems determined to keep you happy. I'm sure they won't mind you moonlighting occasionally with the local cops. I'm not sure it would be as easy for me, though."

"The university are pretty flexible, on the whole. As long as you don't do anything to bring them into disrepute, I think they would let you take on consulting work. And if you get Weston to okay it and start feeding the results into the Program, the world's your oyster, frankly." Mari stopped and pulled Jake around to face him as they reached the front door to his apartment building. Impulsively, he touched his mouth to Jake's lips in the softest kiss.

When their lips parted, Jake didn't pull away, hovering his mouth close before he returned a tender kiss of his own, whispering into Mari's mouth, "As much as I'm sure Weston would love the prestige of one of his guinea pigs working for the police, I can't do both, Mari. Even just two or three cases at a time is a full-time job."

As Jake turned to unlock the door and Mari followed him into the hallway and up the stairs, he was mulling over this admission. When they were snug in the warmth of his lover's tiny flat, he rested his hands on Jake's hips and drew him in closer again, touching his nose to Jake's as he gave voice to his thoughts.

"You want to take this on as a career? To quit the university completely? That's a big step. Your permission to stay hinges on the job you already have, and this would be freelance, right? You'd need some extra support to live in London, unless they were paying you top dollar, which I can't imagine."

"It wasn't a serious job offer, babe. The police are always dealing with cutbacks. They can't afford to pay most of their consultants much, if anything. That's what they have 'real' detectives for." He paused again before saying, "It's private work that actually pays. If I wanted to take on more work from the police, that's what I'd have to do, unless I suddenly become independently wealthy."

Mari touched his cheek tenderly. "You'd need somewhere to live. I can't see the university letting you stay here if you bailed on them. London is expensive, Chivis."

"It is. Which is pretty much what I told Cordiline. At the moment, it's not feasible, to think of trying to build a PI practice here."

"But you could do it, if you didn't have to worry about that," Mari breathed, leaning in to touch his forehead to Jake's. "If it was somehow feasible, would you take that chance?"

"I don't know. It's a big risk."

The hesitancy in his voice, and the sudden vulnerability of his expression, tugged at something in Mari's chest. He was abruptly short of breath. ·

"Do you want to take the chance?" he asked. "Would you want to stay here, under your own steam, I mean? If there was a way of doing it?"

"Mari…what is going on in that head of yours?"

He cupped Jake's face in both hands. "Just answer the question, then I'll tell you."

Jake pulled Mari closer. "I went to school for law enforcement and worked my ass off to make detective. It's what I've always wanted to do. The thought of being able to do it again is a big carrot dangling in front of my face. So yes… If I can't have my old career, this would be the next best thing."

"Then tell him 'yes'," Mari said, kissing the tip of his nose and letting him go. "Tell him you'll do it."

Jake laughed. "It's not that easy. Were you not listening to the 'why it's not possible' part?"

Mari nodded, taking a deep breath. His heart was racing and he willed it to slow down so that he could say the next words without sounding like a love-struck schoolgirl meeting her idol.

"You can live with me. I have a house and everything."

"Babe...I would love to live with you, but you have a housemate, remember? She might not like the idea of sharing her digs."

"Don't be a fool. My mother adores you." Mari shook his head at that argument. "She would be the first to insist you move in."

And I could wake up with you in my arms every day, he thought, warmed by the idea of it.

"Even if she did, it takes a lot of money to start a business, probably most of what I have put away. I can't just move in and live off you."

"Why not?" Mari asked him. "One more mouth to feed isn't going to break us. I earn a good living. And if you're keeping me warm, we will save money on the heating bills." He winked at Jake. "You know it makes sense."

Jake took his hand and led him over to the sofa, sitting him down. "Let's talk to Anni first. If she's not comfortable with this, it's a no go, okay? And if I leave the college, I'll still find a way to make a paycheck. I'm not going to expect you to support me."

Mari drew Jake down with him, sliding his arms around him enticingly. "Okay, but let me help you get there. I want to do this for you. I want to give you something in return for all you've done for me, something meaningful."

"You do that every day." Jake kissed him. "You don't have to do this, but...thank you."

"I never do things because I have to." Mari let his lips linger on Jake's for a few moments longer. "And I meant something more than just sex. I would be dead of frustration if it weren't for you." He touched a fingertip to Jake's nose, tracing his profile intently. "I owe you so much, Jake Chivis."

"You don't owe me anything, Mari."

Mari knew at once he'd said the wrong thing. Jake didn't exactly close down but the thumbnail crease he got between his eyebrows when he was worried had suddenly appeared.

"I don't want to move in together because you feel like you owe me something, Mari."

"I didn't mean it like that."

Jake looked at him hard for a moment, searching his eyes, then he sighed and raked his fingers through his hair. The frown line smoothed and Jake took his hand. "I know you didn't. Listen. I love you and there's nothing I want more than to be with you every night, but the idea of being dependent is kinda freaking me out. I'm not saying no, but just...be patient while I get used to the idea, okay?"

A spike of anxiety worried at Mari's gut. He'd not been anxious like this for ages. Having Jake in his life had relaxed him more than he could ever have imagined just a few short months ago. Hearing Jake say 'I love you' made him go weak inside and want to throw himself at his lover's feet in supplication. The balancing point in their relationship was often precarious, but just recently, things had seemed more stable between them, and he'd hoped that his offer would bring Jake and him closer together, not drive a new rift between them.

"I love you, too, Chivis," he said in a solemn tone, "and I don't want you to feel 'dependent' on me, whatever you mean by that. But I don't want you to be unhappy or feel unfulfilled, either. I would like us to be able to spend more time together, though. Look... I can't afford this while I'm paying for Mama's treatment, but...how would you feel about the idea of us maybe renting a place together, once I can be certain that she is going to be okay?"

"That's definitely something to think about. If I do this, start a business and everything, well... Who knows what the future holds, right? I mean, I chucked my career and moved across an ocean for a program that's still going through growing pains, with no idea if I'd be out of work in a month or not, so it's not like I'm afraid to take a risk. There's just one more thing."

"What's that?" Mari asked warily.

Jake cleared his throat. "How would you feel about being a part-time partner in the PI business?"

Mari blinked at him, taking a moment to wait and consider whether he had heard this invitation correctly. When he spoke, his voice sounded hoarse and he had to clear his throat to make a second attempt.

"You... You want me to be a PI? Don't I need to go to detective school for that or something?" It was a glib reply, he knew, but it covered his surprise for the time being. Mari remembered what Cordiline had once told him about Jake wanting to feel like he and Mari were partners, and how he thought Mari was pushing Jake away every time he tried to get closer. He wanted to think about the response before he gave it. Hurting Jake was the last thing on his mind.

"There is some training and a test you have to take to get your license, but it's fairly simple. Private sector work is not the same as going into law enforcement. I already know we work well together. It just seemed like a natural step. Since you're working full-time, though, I'd do most of the field work. I'd just need you to do what you do best."

"Keep you satisfied?" Mari joked.

"That too," Jake said, sliding his hand up Mari's thigh and kissing him.

"What? You want me to work overtime?" Mari snuggled into his embrace and returned the kiss with interest. Jake's powerful body fitted against his own beautifully. Rubbing up against him was deliciously good.

"Um, think of it as supplementary work. Besides, if you don't help me out, you'll only be annoyed that you don't find out everything that's going on."

Mari treated him to a small frown. "You are very manipulative, Jake Chivis. Did anyone ever tell you that?"

"It's not manipulation when it's the truth," Jake teased.

"In that case, I should be worried that you know me far too well," Mari said, and licked the tip of Jake's nose. "How on earth are you going to solve any crimes without my help? Of course, I'll give you the benefit of my experience and my...unique insights. You'd be floundering around blindly for weeks at a time otherwise."

Jake pressed his lips together and aimed a swat at Mari's ass, but didn't land it, presumably mindful of their adventures last night.

"Give me some credit here!"

"You get far too much credit already," Mari pointed out. "You come along and touch something, and everyone gets excited about what you might have seen. In the meantime, muggins here is doing all the cross-checking and making sure that you look the part."

He touched his mouth to Jake's again, lips lingering there for a good while as he kissed his handsome mate.

"Is that so?" Jake said when he was able. "Well, I don't have to worry too much about an inflated ego with you around at least. Are you staying tonight?"

"I can't stay all night." Mari sighed, cuddling up to him all the same because he loved to be entwined around his handsome Jake. "I have to start early tomorrow. They're sending me up to Oxfordshire in the morning. I think they have a skeptic up there that needs convincing I'm for real. I'll do some more digging on the train and message you if I find anything. In the meantime, you can kiss me some more. Maybe a little lower, huh?"

Chapter Ten

Jake had just shut down his laptop and was about to head for home when Professor Newberry came into his office with a man he didn't recognize. The stranger was average height and build, tanned and well dressed in a tailored suit. Jake couldn't rattle off the brand like Mari would be able to, but Mari had definitely influenced him enough to tell the difference between a quality cut and something off the rack.

Jake stood.

"Hi, Jake. I'm glad I caught you before you left," the professor said. "I'd like you to meet Tomas Garcés Arregui. He's from the Ministry of Internal Development in Spain and he's looking at the security work we've been doing here with a view to implementing new strategies at home. He has a few questions for you, if you have the time?"

Tomas Arregui. What were the odds that there was another man in central London right now with the same name as Mari's ex? Jake was betting on zero-to-none. Professor Newberry went on with the introduction without waiting for a response from him.

"*Señor* Arregui, this is Jake Chivis. He worked for the police in the US before joining us and he's become a valuable addition to our team."

She sounded particularly proud of that, as if it were an achievement to have brought him over from law enforcement into academia.

"*Encantat de coneixe't,*" Arregui said silkily, extending a well-manicured hand.

Jake inclined his head instead of shaking hands. There was no way he wanted to risk picking up a random memory from him. "I'll be happy to answer your questions," Jake said, because he couldn't force himself to say 'pleased to meet you'. Maybe this encounter *was* entirely random and the man didn't know who Jake was or who he was seeing, but Jake thought the odds on that one were zero-to-none as well.

Arregui surveyed him for a moment and dropped his hand. His eyes were the color of brushed steel and held just about as much warmth. He carried himself with the quietly confident posture of a man who knew exactly how much power he wielded and precisely how attractive that made him to many potential admirers. The stance was just a little too studied, and even though Jake didn't have an empathic bone in his body, he could feel the subtle vibe of intimidation he was trying to throw off.

Jake didn't know all the details of Tomas and Mari's relationship, but it *had* ended badly, and it was obvious that this man had hurt Mari. That was enough to make Jake hate him on principle.

Professor Newberry excused herself and left them alone.

When she'd gone, Arregui said, "You are the Elemental, the one that Professor Karden spoke of." He spoke in clipped, precise tones. His English was very good, only very lightly accented with the cadences of his homeland. "I have never worked with a psychometric before. A fascinating talent."

"What can I help you with?" Jake asked, not wanting to waste time on small talk.

"As Professor Newberry says, I am here on behalf of my government to talk with representatives of yours. Or rather, I should say, of your paymasters'. For many years we have looked into the use of those with unconventional skills and talents to improve our communication networks." Arregui paused and gave him a meaningful look. "Also, our security. I imagine that the university were very pleased to have you here, given your experience. How exactly does psychometry play into what you do here?"

"The security work I do here doesn't have anything to do with my being an Elemental, most of the time."

"But you are a part of the program here for Elementals? I thought they would have you working on projects using your ability?"

Jake clenched his jaw at the not so subtle implication that he was entirely replaceable. "A portion of my time is designated for research and testing related to psychometry and how it might be used to breach certain secure locations, but I also work on IT systems."

Arregui's expression was blatantly patronizing. "I see. Our people will be very interested in the work you've done, I'm sure. Have the programs you've worked on been tested against an interface?"

"An interface...or a specific interface in particular?" Jake countered.

Arregui hesitated for a moment. "I must confess that I hoped to meet with your fellow Elemental, too, but I understand Dr. Gale has moved on to bigger and better things. We worked together for a short time in Barcelona. Marijne was always ambitious."

The statement was innocuous on the surface but the tone fairly dripped with smug condescension. If Jake hadn't already known they had slept together, the emphasis on how ambitious Mari was certainly would have had him wondering.

"I don't think you and Ilmarinen have anything more to discuss. He's told you as much already."

Arregui raised one perfectly formed, mahogany-colored eyebrow in response. He glanced sidelong, in Professor Newberry's direction, but she was over on the far side of the office talking to another colleague and not paying them much heed.

"And why would Dr. Gale tell you such a thing, Mr. Chivis?" he asked in a smooth, atonal purr.

"Oh, I think you know perfectly well why. Listen… Whatever past you and he had, he's made it obvious that he doesn't want to relive it. I'd advise you not to keep embarrassing yourself by chasing him."

"Or you will see me off, Jake? Is that how it is with you two? What a surprise. I did not think that… Well, never mind," Tomas said. He did not seem offended by this hushed warning. "Let me give you a word of caution concerning Dr. Gale, Jake. Marijne's a beauty, and the brightest there is. But that one won't give you what you want, no matter how hard you work for it. Don't waste too much time chasing after that sweet tail, my friend."

Jake laughed at him. He couldn't help it. "God, you are as much of a pompous ass as I thought you'd be.

What Mari gives me is none of your fucking business." He should have left it at that but impulsively he added, "Just because you failed to perform doesn't mean every man he's with is destined to failure as well."

The steel in those observant eyes darkened but Tomas kept his cool. He pressed a humorless smirk onto his fine, ascetic lips and leaned close to whisper, "When you next bed your Mari, tell him that whatever he believes, he and I have some unfinished business, and if he doesn't man up and face that, he can speak to my attorney instead." He pushed away from the desk and, in a louder voice, said, "Most interesting to make your acquaintance, Mr. Chivis. Thank you for your most helpful information."

* * * *

Mari got back to London during the afternoon and, since he wasn't expected back at Trafalgar House, he decided to stop off at the British Library. On his way across the park from Marylebone, his phone vibrated in his pocket and he picked it up without checking, presuming it was Jake asking how his morning had gone. The message, when he opened it, was in Catalan, and right away he had a bad feeling about it that tightened his gut and left him with a sour taste in his mouth.

His mind translated the words all too easily.

It was good to see you again yesterday. I'd forgotten how hot you are, Doctor Gale. Can I buy you dinner tonight?
Tomas

He weighed the slender device in his hand for a moment, contemplating whether to ignore the message or just tell his ex to fuck off. Without breaking his stride, he sent a brief text back.

Too busy today. I have work.

He typed the word 'sorry', then deleted it, before pressing Send.

By the time he reached the British Library and found a quiet spot to log into their Wi-Fi, his agitation had settled, and he ran a quick search of the digitized local newspapers. His investigations into the social media profiles of the girls who had been attacked had indicated that one of them, Natalie Craig, was an aspiring fashion model. She posted a raft of professional-looking photos of herself on her various platforms.

Not long after four-thirty, he came across a small advertisement in the *London Evening Standard*, placed by Natalie, listing her mobile number and availability for work as an artist and photographer's model, including her terms and fees. He used his phone to take a snapshot of the ad, then packed away his tablet with the intention of heading over to the university to see if Jake was free.

He was just making his way into the Security department offices on Level Five—by way of a detour to deliver a bottle of tequila to Toby in dispatch, thanking him for the gossip the other day—when he got the shock of his life. As he came in sight of Jake's desk, planning to sneak up on him, he saw his current boyfriend apparently deep in conversation with none other than his bastard ex.

For a second he stopped dead in the doorway. He thought that he might be sick but the moment of nausea passed and, as Tomas turned away from the desk and called out his thanks to Professor Newberry, their gazes met. Mari swallowed hard and put his strictest business face on.

"Dr. Gale," Tomas said, almost tenderly, on the way out. "I understood you were working. *Ben capturat.*"

In the next moment, he was gone. Mari didn't even realize he hadn't been breathing until he needed to.

"What the fuck did *he* want?" he demanded, almost collapsing onto Jake's desk.

"Supposedly he wants to look into new security programs," Jake answered. His voice was too even, too calm, and Mari recognized the tone as the one Jake used when he was stomping on his temper. "I'd say what he really wants is you."

Mari felt all the blood draining from his cheeks. A shiver of apprehension went through him and he suddenly wanted to be as far from London as possible. "That's not what he wants," he said flatly. "He had his chance to claim me. He passed on it."

Jake didn't comment on that. Instead he picked up his jacket and they left the office. He put his hand on Mari's back as they walked. "You are what he wants, Mari. Not to claim you, but certainly to fuck you – or fuck *with* you. He made a not-so-veiled threat. Something about his lawyer dealing with you, if you wouldn't talk to him."

Mari exhaled a terse breath. His shoulder blades twitched under Jake's hand. "He's blowing hot air. He can set all the law experts he likes on me, but he won't prove that I sent his wife those pictures of us. And besides, she wouldn't leave him. He pays her too well!"

Jake stopped and pulled Mari to a halt. "You sent pictures of the two of you to his wife?" He looked floored by the utter vindictiveness of that move then burst out laughing. "No wonder he won't leave you alone." He shook his head, still chuckling. "That was very naughty of you, Mari."

"So, spank me!"

"That would be a reward, not a punishment."

"He'd just told the entire department that I was incurably frigid, which seemed like a coming-out statement to me. I figured it was only fair to inform her."

"Well, deserved or not, you've made an enemy of him, babe."

"What else did he say?" Mari grilled him.

"Nothing important."

Mari glared at him and Jake relented. "He tried to warn me off you, saying you wouldn't ever 'give me what I wanted'. So, I told him to fuck off and it was none of his business." Jake paused for a second then added, "I may also have told him that just because he's shit in bed doesn't mean every guy you're with is…or something along those lines."

Mari actually managed a weak titter of laughter. He was still shaking inside but something about Jake's down-to-earth humor settled the anxiety in his belly. He made him feel warm and safe in a way that Tomas never had.

Why do you still want to please the bastard so badly? his conscience chided.

He didn't have an answer for that.

"You are amazing," he told Jake, because it was true. "I'm a very lucky boy. He told me you were a nice catch, by the way, on his way out. I think he's jealous."

"If he's angling for a threesome, you can tell him to go fuck himself. That's one snake we don't need in our bed."

Mari winced. "My word, no! Just the thought of it would kill my hard-on. I think you're more than enough for me, Jake Chivis."

He could not stop thinking about the way Tomas looked at him or the text message still sitting in his phone.

I'd forgotten how hot you are...

But why was Tomas throwing his weight around? Making threats? It made no sense.

What had Jake said? *"What he really wants is you."*

Tomas had a funny way of showing it, if that was the case.

"Are you trying to stroke my ego?" Jake asked.

Mari pulled himself together, determined not to let Tomas spoil this for him.

"I didn't think you needed stroking, Chivis. You seem to do pretty well without encouragement."

"Aaaand, the second I start to think he likes me... *Bam!* Shot in the heart. Well, at least with you around I don't have to worry about getting a big head."

"There's only one kind of big head that does it for me," Mari reassured him, drawing him in close to put his arm around Jake while they walked. To his satisfaction, Jake eased an arm across his back, too.

"Let's get something to eat," Jake suggested. "We have work to do tonight."

They grabbed a takeaway from the Indian restaurant on the corner near Jake's apartment and were soon curled up on his sofa together with dinner spread out on the coffee table. Mari had his laptop open.

"Two of the girls are students but at different colleges," he said as he put a piece of onion bhaji into his mouth. "The second girl, Natalie, went straight into shop work from school, though. And she doesn't know the other two socially in any way that I can see."

"The police haven't been able to establish any connection between the three, either," Jake confirmed. "There's something, though…something we're missing. We need a wall."

"A wall?"

"A case wall. Pictures of the victims, facts, maps… That kind of thing. It helps to have a visual overall picture."

"Like the map I made of Helen March and her phone trails?" Mari nodded to himself, recalling how mapping the movement of the woman's GPS signals had led to the discovery that she was not where they'd believed her to be when the lover she'd shared with her husband had been murdered. It had been their first case and he was still proud of that success. "That's a good idea."

He opened a screen on his tablet and made some notes, then saw that Jake was watching him curiously.

"What?"

"You know, you use that thing for everything. It's like a comfort blanket," Jake said, reaching out and taking it from his hands firmly. "We can make a real wall, here, in the flat."

"But we can't take it with us," Mari protested, trying to retrieve his tablet. Jake held it just out of reach.

"Put it down. You look tired. Just let me do things the old-fashioned way for once. Trust me. We can do it together. I don't have to sit and watch you all the time, not that I don't like watching you."

Mari tamped down on his frustration and flopped onto the sofa, tucking his bare feet under him. Jake was not wrong about him being tired. It took a lot out of him to interface and when he was using his ability at work as well, it just compounded the situation. Lately he seemed to have a low-grade headache all the time, not that he would admit as much to Jake. He stole a samosa from Jake's plate and took a large bite. When he had swallowed the mouthful, he said, "Okay, Detective. Show me your way."

There was only one good place to set up, and it happened to be right across from them, where the small kitchen table was tucked up against one wall. Jake opened the apartment door, pushing the tiny bistro-style table and two chairs that went with it out onto the landing.

Mari watched him with a bemused expression.

"We hardly ever use it anyway," Jake told him.

With most of the furniture gone, they had a blank wall to work on. Jake went around the counter that was the only separation from the kitchen and rummaged in a drawer, eventually finding a roll of masking tape.

For the next fifteen minutes or so, he took the copied pages of the police files and worked on taping them up in a fairly organized way while Mari observed from the sofa.

"I love how focused you are when you're working," Mari said, picking up a piece of naan and nibbling at the edges of it as he sent things to Jake's printer on the kitchen counter.

Jake took a step away and surveyed the wall with his hands on his hips. Mari wasn't sure how this was supposed to help, considering that Jake's backside was the only thing his eye kept being drawn to. After another few minutes of Jake studying the wall in silence, he turned around.

"Let's see if the first victim, Emily Redbridge, is home. See if she has anything more to say when she's not talking to the police."

Chapter Eleven

Emily Redbridge was not only the first victim, but she also lived the closest to Jake. Her apartment block was on the other side of the college, on Harrison Street, within easy walking distance. She lived with two flatmates in a cramped one-bedroom apartment that was just as small as the one Jake inhabited. After Jake explained who he and Mari were and how they were working with the police, she let them inside. Her flatmates were a couple and both eyed Jake and Mari warily, but Jake thought that had more to do with the lingering smell of pot smoke than suspicion.

Jake laid photos on the coffee table of the second and third victims, Natalie Craig and Tamara Leyton-Skipp. "Take your time, Emily. Are you sure you don't recognize them? Never seen them before?"

Emily played with her hair and studied the pictures while Mari watched her quietly from the doorway. Jake sat at the opposite end of the bed-settee from the girl, deliberately not crowding her and giving her as much time as she needed to make up her mind.

"I'm not sure," she said at last, touching the picture of Tamara. "I don't think so. Maybe she came in the shop but a lot of people do." She looked up at Mari shyly. "He does. He has a sweet tooth."

Mari's lips twitched, but the answering smile reached his eyes.

"You wouldn't guess it to look at him, would you?" Jake remarked to lighten the mood.

Emily sighed, though. "I'm sorry. I'm not much help."

"You are plenty of help, Emily," Jake assured her. "It was a very long shot that you'd know each other somehow. It's much more likely that your attacker stalked each of you separately. You've just confirmed that."

"Who sells you the weed?" Mari asked, making Emily's eyes widen. She started to shake her head but he held up a hand to forestall her. "Don't worry. I'm not interested in what you do in the privacy of your own home. We're just looking for a common denominator to you and the other two girls. All of you were doped in some way before he attacked you. This guy has access to drugs. We're not about to bust your dealer, Emily. We might need to talk to him, though."

It was one of her flatmates that answered the question, eventually. The other two girls had been looking at each other warily since Jake and Mari had come in and it was Tess, initially the more vocal of the couple, who volunteered the information. She picked up the weed, and anything else they might need, from a guy called Faze who hung out at the Good Mixer sometimes.

Mari rolled his eyes. "That figures. Does Faze have another name?"

Bex, her smaller, shyer partner murmured something that sounded like Faisal. When Mari looked a question at her, she shrugged.

"I went to school with 'im."

"What school?" Jake asked her.

"And how long ago?" Mari added.

Bex turned nervous eyes on her partner but Tess just nodded. "It was The Grove Academy in Kentish Town, but it was a few years ago, five or six."

"Is Faze a friend of yours, Emily?" Jake asked her.

"He comes to the club sometimes, at the White Horse. We go to a music thing there at the weekends, but I don't know him well," she said, too carefully.

"No one is judging you, Emily," Mari told her, his tone surprisingly gentle. "We just need to establish who might have been in a situation to take advantage of you and the other girls."

She looked at him gratefully, though Tess, her flatmate, muttered, "Like blokes that come round our flat making out they work for the bizzies, you mean?"

"We're not taking advantage of anyone," Jake said calmly. "I used to be a detective. I want to be sure that whoever did this to Emily is locked up. The DI working on this has other cases, too. We don't. We can devote all our resources to finding him." He did not add that, since the man who had attacked her had taken her purse and ID, he knew where she lived. It was a fact, and a damn good reason to find him fast, besides preventing him from doing this to someone else, but he didn't want to scare her any more than she already was.

"Do you think it's someone that we know?" Emily asked, some of the color leaching from her face.

"It's a possibility, but since you're not aware of the other victims, it makes it less likely," Jake said. "We still have more work to do before we have a good suspect in mind."

"We'll talk to the other girls as well, if we can," Mari assured her. "Once we've got a clearer picture of the patterns of your lives, it will help us to look for the man who is doing this. If anything occurs to you in the meantime, you can contact one of us. I'll leave our details. Feel free to check up on us, if it helps set your minds at rest." He hesitated, then added, "You use a couple of dating sites... Are you...? You *are* being careful when you meet with strangers, aren't you?"

"Are you blaming her for what happened?" Tess said at once.

"No, he's not," Jake answered before Mari could.

Mari sighed but he didn't argue. Tess glared at him, though. "You reckon she was asking for it?"

"No," he said, "I didn't say that and I didn't mean that. But Emily is putting her personal information out there where men, like that animal that attacked and buried her, can find it. And if she can do that, so can a lot of other 'potential' victims. It's one avenue of inquiry. That's all. Do you use the — ?"

"Stop asking her stuff like that! It's creepy," Bex interrupted.

"You're her manager?" Mari narrowed his eyes at her.

"Okay, easy... Take it easy, everyone," Jake said, standing. "He's not creeping on her Bex. I promise," he soothed. "It's a legitimate question. Scum like that often use dating sites to stalk people. Mari's just trying to determine if that's possibly what happened to Emily."

"I'd not been on a date the night it...happened," Emily said hesitantly. "I was just out with the girls. They went on to a club but I had work in the morning, so I went home early."

"On your own?" Mari asked, which earned him another double-pronged glare from Tess and Bex.

"Obviously," Emily replied in a weary tone.

Jake sat down and ignored the glares Mari was receiving from the other women. "You told the police that you hadn't been approached by anyone that you could remember. Since you've had more time to think on it, is there anything else you can tell us from earlier in the evening on the night of the assault? Anyone you might have talked to or that seemed odd to you?"

"I told the police lady everything—everything I could remember properly. It was weird, like I said. There were a lot of people at the pub that we knew. I had a Cherry Coke because I was working. I didn't leave it anywhere. I left on my own and started walking home and I started to feel weird. After that, I don't remember anything until waking up and it was dark. There was something over my face. Then I realized there was dirt on me...like...I was underground."

"Did you buy your own drink?" Mari asked, sensing that she was beginning to get edgy about the memories of that night and wanting to take things back a way.

"Yeah...no. Bex got them in. She'd just got her giro so she was flush." Mari noted that he and Emily turned their gazes on her flatmate at the same moment.

"What you suggesting?" Tess, the more bolshie of the pair, demanded when Bex said nothing.

"Emily was probably drugged at the pub," Mari said evenly. "It makes sense that someone put something in her drink. If it was Rohypnol or GHB, it acts fast, so she was either drugged at the bar or very shortly after leaving. She says she didn't stop anywhere else on the way home or talk to anyone, which implies someone at the pub roofied her, Tessa. That's what I'm suggesting. Do you want to think about that again and tell me if you noticed anything suspicious, or do we have to start looking closer to home?"

"Fuck you, you lanky piece of shit! Em is our friend. Why the fuck would I give her anything, huh? Fucking tosser, you can get the fuck out." Bex gestured angrily toward the door.

He held his hands up again, looking at Jake quickly, though it was not a helpless look by any means. There was a flicker of annoyance in his eyes.

"Anyone would think you didn't want her attacker to be caught, Rebecca," he said icily, making a point of using Bex's proper name, as listed in the police report. "Because that's what this looks like to me. Someone in your group of friends put something into Emily's drink between the bar and your table. That drug — which was only useful for one thing, incapacitating the person drinking it — could have been meant for any one of you. Think about that for a while. Tell us, or the cops, if you've remembered anything useful."

"Get out! Both of you, get the fuck out!" she screamed at him.

Jake got up with a sigh. He didn't bother telling Emily to call if she thought of anything. Out on the street again, he waited until they were a half block away before he conceded, "Well, that was a disaster."

Mari chewed on his lips.

"I'm not good with people, I told you. One or both of those mouthy cows knows something," he said. "If she's such a good friend, why wouldn't they tell us?"

Jake shrugged. "Maybe they do, maybe they don't."

Mari glanced at him. "How can you be so blasé about it?"

"Because there is no proof one way or the other. You're assuming they knew the drink was drugged or that they did it. Granted you're using the facts as you see them to make that deduction, but there are too many unknown factors to hang your hat on it and call it a done deal yet."

"Is police work always this bloody frustrating?" his lover grumbled. "And how the blazes do you stay so calm if that's true? She was only there for an hour, tops. Her drink must have been spiked in the last fifteen-to-thirty minutes or she'd have been on the floor in the pub, but nobody saw anything suspicious."

"Yes, it is usually this 'bloody frustrating'," Jake mimicked him. "And I know how long it takes for a roofie to take effect. The thing you have to keep in mind is, people only think they have good memories. They think they remember what happened, but more often than not, eyewitnesses are completely wrong about what they recall. Questioning them is a starting point, not an end point."

"Where do we go from here then, Sherlock? Talk to the others and get some more useless answers? I hope they're friendlier than those two bitches back there." Mari bristled. "Could have offered us a coffee, at least. Anyone would think we were working for the enemy."

"Mari, you kinda accused them of playing a hand in the drugging and rape of their roommate. No matter how logical your conclusion might have seemed, telling them that wasn't likely to earn you any points." Jake heaved a sigh, though he wasn't angry. "As to where we go from here...? Home. We'll put up what we found with the rest of the stuff and take another look in the morning."

"I don't think I'm going to be any good at this." Mari exhaled, looking glum. "Maybe I should stick to my strong points."

"You will be good, if you remember to keep your cool and try not to wind people up."

"I was asking reasonable questions, given the circumstances. Their friend had been horribly and violently assaulted and you'd think they'd want whoever did it to be brought to justice. Instead, it seemed to me they were happy to have another reason to hate all men. Pair of Rottweiler bitches!" Mari huffed.

"Maybe you brought out the Rottweiler in them?" Jake said.

"I can't imagine why. I was perfectly polite." He sniffed. "Would they have preferred it if I was insincere, do you think?"

"Yes. Probably. I'm pretty sure I would have preferred you just smiled and nodded at them," Jake teased.

"Well, you're no fun at all," Mari said. "You're supposed to be on my side, Detective Chivis."

"I am on your side. I wouldn't give you such great advice if I wasn't on your side," Jake told him.

"I won't lie, not even for you," Mari said, his lips twitching around a half-smile.

"I would never ask you to lie, Mari. But my grandmother used to tell me, just because something is the truth doesn't mean you have to say it—which I think was her way of telling me to not be an asshole."

"You think I'm an asshole?" Mari sounded wounded. "I'm sorry. I don't mean to be."

"I don't think you're an asshole. But I do think you speak too plainly for some people," Jake responded. "I like your honesty. It's a relief not to have to play passive-aggressive bullshit games all the damned time. But most people are just not prepared to handle that level of reality. Not about themselves, anyway." Jake stopped walking for a moment and when Mari stopped beside him, he brushed his hair out of his eyes and kissed him. "You use your words like weapons sometimes, babe. That's not necessarily a bad thing. I'm just saying you need to be aware of it."

Mari reached up for him and returned the kiss, stretching out that sweet touch of lips. "I'm used to having to fight for the things I want," he said, and bumped his nose against Jake's. "I am not above fighting dirty. But if you're on my side, I promise I will try to tone down my dirty tactics, for you."

Jake chuckled and nuzzled him. "Thank you. I will try and warn you in advance when it's okay for the claws to come out."

"Teamwork, huh?" Mari smiled up at him. "I think I like the sound of that."

Jake put his arm around Mari's waist and kissed his cheek. They started walking again. "You want to get to the bottom of things. You have a strong sense of justice and want to prevent people from hurting other people. The rest is all technique. You'll learn."

Mari's sharp eyes met his own, sidelong. "You just don't want to do this on your own. Don't think I don't realize."

Chapter Twelve

Just over two weeks after their disastrous interview with Emily Redbridge, Mari was sitting in the day room, trying to eat his breakfast and watch the news while Mama was hustling around with the Dustbuster, tidying up in advance of Imogen coming in to clean during the afternoon. He hiked his feet up onto the sofa cushions and stuffed half a slice of toast into his mouth before she could take his plate away. Tonka sat at his feet, tongue out, begging shamelessly for leftovers.

"Why do you even have a maid if you clean before she arrives? And after she leaves?" he asked, putting a hand over his mouth so that he didn't spit crumbs everywhere.

Annabel fixed him with a disapproving glare. "I don't want her thinking we're slobs, Ilmarinen. And she's a cleaner, not a maid. There's a difference. Good domestics are like gold dust in this part of town. I don't want anyone poaching her."

Fortunately, he was saved from having to point out that their neighbors never spoke to them and no one cared what the house looked like except for her, when her expression changed to one of puzzlement and she gazed past him toward the TV screen.

"What on earth is Jake doing, standing in a cemetery in wellingtons at this time of the morning?" she wondered out loud.

Mari took in the blue-and-white tape and the small white forensic tent in surly silence. He already had a good idea why Jake was there. What he wanted to know was, why hadn't he been told?

* * * *

"It was four in the morning when Cordiline called me," Jake answered that question later in the afternoon when he came over. "I knew you'd been working late and I didn't want to call and drag you out of bed at that hour."

"You looked very striking up there in your boots and everything," Anni chipped in from the breakfast bar where she was applying eye makeup in a standard mirror. "We recognized you right away."

"Mama, hush," Mari exhaled. "He's a cop, not a Hollywood movie star."

"Ex-cop... I quit," Jake said. "And thank you, Anni."

Mari examined the ceiling briefly.

"I'm sorry. Next time — if there is a next time — I will call and you can come, too," Jake promised.

"Was the report right?" Mari asked more solemnly. "They said police found a body. Was she dead?"

"No, she's not dead." All trace of Jake's good humor disappeared. "She's in intensive care, though, and they aren't sure if there will be brain damage. She was buried deeper than the others and they're worried about the lack of oxygen she suffered."

Mari chewed on his lips for a moment. "You were right. Sooner or later he's going to kill someone. And all we have so far is a lot of pin-ups and a tangle of pins and string on your wall. How do you catch an invisible man?"

"It's not all we have," Jake said carefully and glanced at Anni. "This is confidential info, understood?"

"I wouldn't tell anyone, even if there was someone to tell," she confirmed.

Jake nodded. "This girl was a student at UCL, just like the last victim, Tamara Leyton-Skipp. Emily doesn't go to school there but the Bun Shop is just across the street. We have a connection, I think. Natalie Craig isn't a student, but the modeling you uncovered? She's posed for classes at the university."

"The killer could be you," Mari teased him, though his gaze remained sober.

"A college employee or even another student?" Anni suggested, capping her mascara and popping it into her makeup bag.

"Yes. Faculty, staff, students… Could be any of them, or none."

"Jake, that still doesn't point us at anyone in particular," Mari said.

"No, not yet. But it does tell us where he's hunting."

"The police are watching all the park areas in his patch but he still managed to do what he did last night. He's aware of how to hide his tracks," Mari mused. "Someone must know something about him."

"Maybe. A sick fuck like this…" He stopped and glanced at Anni again. "Sorry." She waved off his profanity easily, so he took a breath and went on. "It's hard to say what his profile might be. He could be the angry loner type, hating women and wanting to punish them. Or he could just as easily be a Bundy or Gacy type. Seems perfectly normal socially, has friends, maybe even a family, and lives this sick double life. We have precious little information about him. He doesn't leave anything behind on the victims, and what they all remember could fit on the head of a pin."

"He isn't making a statement, which means this isn't about making a name for himself," Anni suggested, looking from him to Mari and back again. "Not yet, anyway. The way he hides their bodies... Could be that he's trying to keep something for himself? You know, the way a dog will bury a bone? A loner, maybe?"

"Victims, Anni, not bodies," Jake said. His grim expression added an unspoken 'not yet' onto the end of that statement.

If she was offended by his comment, she didn't let it show.

Mari changed the subject. "You look nice. Are you going out?"

"I have an appointment. Solana is coming over at half ten," his mother replied.

"I'll go for a run then," he exhaled with a scowl.

"I'll go with you," Jake said. "I need to clear my head."

"Good. You can give me the gory details."

"I beg your pardon, children. I have worked in more war zones than you've had jobs. A bit of gruesomeness is not going to faze me," Anni said tersely.

"Jake isn't allowed to talk to members of the public about it. I'm his partner. I don't count," he reminded her. He blew her a kiss when she frowned at that.

Jake gave her an apologetic look as well and a sheepish shrug.

"You aren't working for the Met, last I knew," Anni said to Mari.

"Jake is, though, and he told his pet policeman that he wouldn't help if I couldn't be his glamorous assistant." Mari tipped his head to look at Jake. "Isn't that right?"

"That isn't exactly how I put it, but close enough. Speaking of, I turned in the last of the required paperwork to the ABI. Since I'd already had my level three security training through the university, it's just a matter of them finishing their background checks. I should have my PI registration cleared within a week or two."

Mari sat up and faced him with a radiant grin. He planted a kiss on Jake's mouth then murmered, "You are so smart and sly. You're going to be a private detective. Am I seriously more excited about this than you are?"

"Congratulations, Jake," Anni said with a warm smile. "Is this something you needed to work in an official capacity for the police?"

Jake hesitated just a moment before answering, "No, not exactly. I will continue working as a consultant for the police...but this is so I can open my own business."

"How exciting." She beamed at him. "I'm sure you'll be very good. I hope my son isn't going to get in your way too much."

"I'm not five years old, Mama. I will provide Jake with technical assistance when he needs it. I do have a job already." Mari sniffed and flopped down on the sofa but he turned his head to wink at Jake, unable to hide the delight in his eyes at the news.

"Exciting is one word for it," Jake said. "It's kinda daunting, too."

"Any new enterprise can feel that way to start off with." Annabel surveyed them both proudly then put her makeup bag away in one of the kitchen drawers. "Did you boys say something about going for a run?"

"Are you trying to get rid of us?" Mari pushed himself upright again, turning around to look at her with a thoughtful frown. "Are you sure it's just a healing session you have booked? You look very glamorous."

"Go and get changed," she told him, refusing to rise to his baiting. "And take Tonka out with you. He needs a walk."

"You *are* trying to get rid of us," Mari declared with a note of triumph.

"Solana has been telling me that I need to think and behave like a woman who expects to live. And that includes making more of my appearance," she responded primly, though she did hold out her hand to show them her nails, which were very neat and French manicured. "And I thought you didn't like her. Surely you'd jump at the chance to not be here when she arrives?" She tried and failed to suppress a smirk.

Neither of them said anything for a heartbeat, then Jake moved to her side and put an arm around her, kissing her temple and letting her go again. "I agree with Solana on this, and you look lovely, Anni. Let's go for that run," he added, before Mari could pass further comment.

"I'll just throw some sweats on," Mari said in a casual tone, which fooled neither of them. He never simply threw anything on when he was going out, for any reason. A good fifteen minutes elapsed between him going upstairs to get changed and coming down looking pristine in his snug black leggings with the green piping and an acid-green mesh vest that clung to his torso under the matching black and green hooded track top. The doorbell rang as he was pulling his running shoes on and Tonka set up a howl and went racing down the hall to meet the new challenge.

Annabel followed more sedately, and Mari and Jake shadowed her into the hallway as she caught Tonka's collar and put his leash on before opening the front door. The burly Staffie stared up at their visitor with a tentative twitch of his tail and barked once. Mari smirked, but only for a moment as, to the surprise of all of them, the dog strained forward and snuffed at Solana's maroon-colored pea coat then licked the hand she extended to him.

"I think he likes you," Anni said, looking pleased. "That's unusual."

"I love dogs," Solana told her in that rich, deep, musical voice. "I'm not allowed to have one, though. It contravenes the terms of my lease. Such a pity. Hello there, what's your name, handsome?"

She bent, her long hair tumbling forward and screening her face as she made a fuss over Tonka. In turn, the dog wagged his whipcord tail furiously and yipped like a puppy.

Mari swore under his breath in Suomi and zipped his track top up so ferociously that he broke the pull tab.

Jake tried his best to keep a straight face and coughed to hide a laugh. Mari glared at him but Jake ignored it. He extended his hand when Solana finished rubbing Tonka's ears. "You must be Solana. I'm Jake."

Anni's healer shook the proffered hand without hesitation and smiled at him with genuine warmth.

"Hello, Jake. You must be the boyfriend I've heard so much about. Well, Annabel, your boy has good taste, I'll give him that."

Anni handed Tonka's leash to Mari. "Jake and Ilmari were just heading out to the park. Weren't you?" she reminded them.

Mari managed not to pout or scowl. He nodded a curt acknowledgment of Solana's presence and her offhanded compliment.

"We were just going. Don't get herbs everywhere this time. Imogen only just vacuumed."

"Have a nice jog," Solana said. "Remember to stretch."

Mari bristled, on the verge of turning, but Jake gripped his shoulder and nudged him out of the front door before things could escalate.

"Smug bitch!" Mari exhaled furiously once they were outside and beyond earshot. "If my mother wasn't so taken with her, I'd show her how to fucking stretch!" Tonka looked at the house, whining, and he added, "Oh, don't you start! Bad enough that I have Mama mooning over her."

Jake took Tonka's leash from him. "C'mon, mukwa. You can keep me company. I'll take him for a walk while you run and meet up with you after, at the apartment, okay?"

Mari told Tonka to behave himself and headed off with a wave of his hand. He'd only got around the corner as far as Lancaster Gate when his mobile buzzed in the pocket of his hoodie and he tugged on the zip and swiped the screen to accept the call without looking.

"*Hola*, Marijne, I didn't actually think you'd pick up," Tomas said in Catalan.

Mari jolted to a standstill, his heart suddenly thumping in his throat as he contemplated just hanging up.

"What do you want?" he asked at last, forcing Tomas to speak English, which he was perfectly capable of.

"I wondered, if you're not still desperately busy, if you had time to meet me for dinner? Professor Karden has recommended a very pleasant restaurant to me. I hate to dine alone. I'd be delighted if you could join me, Marijne. It's been a long time since we spent any time together."

Mari quivered with a combination of rage and silent incredulity at the barefaced smarm of that invitation.

"There is a perfectly good reason for that, *Señor* Arregui," he said breathlessly. "As well you know. I don't have any desire to meet you for dinner. And besides, I have a boyfriend, who has already made it clear that he'll break your legs if you keep on sniffing around me."

"I bet that idea gets you hot." Mari could hear the smug note in Tomas' voice. "You always did like a forceful mate. Perhaps I was not rough enough with you."

Mari stared wide-eyed at his phone for a moment then stabbed the disconnect icon and switched it off. He pushed himself harder than usual on his run through the park and by the time he got to Maple Street, he was slick with sweat and breathing hard, but icy chills still chased up and down his spine.

Chapter Thirteen

Jake knew Mari was disappointed he didn't offer to go change to run with him but he would make it up to him later. At the moment, he was curious about this Solana person and why Anni was so eager to be rid of them. Jake was not quite as quick to rush to a judgment about her as Mari, but he was not one to give his trust right away, either.

He took Tonka around the block and, about ten minutes later, let himself in the front door again. He didn't try to sneak in at all. His intention wasn't to startle them or—god forbid—catch them 'doing anything'. He just wanted to make sure whatever it was they were getting up to was safe.

In the sunlit day room, Annabel was lying on the cushioned chaise facing toward the window and he almost ducked out of sight, into the hall, before realizing that her eyes were closed and she wouldn't see him anyway. Solana walked around the lounger at a sedate pace and he could hear the soft thrumming of music, not new age stuff but something jangly, from the Eighties, he thought. The Elemental healer was talking to her as she walked and Anni's lips twitched upward at the edges at something she said. Solana touched her patient's pale hair as she passed around the head of the chaise. Her touch lingered there but the casual caress seemed chaste enough.

Jake watched for a moment more, but it felt too much like spying, and he unclipped Tonka's lead and turned away to hang it on the peg by the door. He was just about to slip out when Solana's voice, almost directly behind, stopped him. "You can come in and sit down if you like, Jake. I can work either way. Anni and I don't mind if you stay."

Jake held up his hands. "I didn't mean to disturb you. Just bringing the little mukwa home. I'll be on my way."

Tonka trotted out and jumped up, putting his forepaws on Solana's thighs and woofing a curious greeting.

"You have competition, Jake," Anni said fondly.

"Don't count on it helping to win Mari over."

"Ilmarinen will come around," Solana said with a confident smile. The healer moved to sit in Anni's favorite armchair while she played with Tonka. "He just needs time to reconcile his mind. Once he realizes I am not here to challenge him, we will be fine. It's good that he is dating another Elemental. That will help him."

Jake narrowed his eyes. "He's not worried about a challenge. He's worried you're a scam artist."

That came out as blunt as he had intended but Solana just tossed her head with a hearty laugh.

"He should have no worries on that count," she said once her humor abated. "I thought that, living openly as I do, he found me an affront to his masculinity."

Jake frowned. "That's not likely."

She raised one perfect eyebrow. "You don't think so? Interesting."

Anni interrupted with, "Jake has been very good for Ilmarinen. He is a very polite and patient young man. I approve of him, wholeheartedly."

Jake looked from Solana to Anni and back again. Anni was trying to be complimentary, he knew, but he heard the note of nervousness she was trying so hard not to show. Why would she want to reroute the conversation?

"Look… I don't like games or cryptic comments. If you have something to say about Mari, spill it."

"If he hasn't told you…" Solana closed her mouth but, for the first time since he had come back to the house, she looked uncomfortable.

Jake scowled. "Don't start a sentence you're not going to finish," he warned, his patience starting to wear thin.

Annabel rose to her feet in silence as they faced off, but she crossed behind Jake to the busy, blond-pine shelves and cabinets on the wall across from the kitchen. On the bottom shelf were photo albums and she selected one. Opening it, she flipped a few pages until she found what she was looking for and handed it to him.

"This is what she means. It was the year Mari got his PhD," she said, quietly. "We were all so proud. I told him that I would love him, no matter what he did."

Jake blinked and refocused on the image before him. Anni he recognized right away, though she was tanned and her hair was shorter, worn in a bob like a halo of sunlight. She wore a trouser-suit that showed off more generous curves than she currently sported. The taller, older man on the right looked so like Mari in his features, he knew without asking that this was either his father or an uncle. Between them stood a statuesque blonde girl.

The mortar board and cape looked too dark on her. That was his first, confused thought. It made her features appear ghostly.

Long, fair hair was pulled back in a tail that hung from the crown of her head and spilled down one shoulder. The subtle eye makeup drew his attention to beautiful, ice-blue eyes and he saw the shadows of overwork beneath them, the strain in her expression as she put on a faux cheerful face for the camera. The fragile curve of her mouth was what gave it away. He had come to love that hopeful smile during the last year or so, and even with long feminine hair and makeup, he knew he was looking at Mari.

Jake hurt inside, like something was grabbing and twisting at his lungs, leaving him short of breath. Not for the reasons that Anni was anxiously dreading, given the look on her face, though.

The long gown under her cape was the same ice blue as her eyes. She looked like a Disney Princess on the verge of a nervous breakdown, elegant and beautiful, brittle and almost terrified. He ached to hold her and tell her...him...tell him that everything would eventually be all right.

"Ilmari was eighteen years old," Annabel said, coming to his side and gently resting her hand on his arm. "He'd been living and presenting as female for about a year and a half. His father was angry with us at first, but when he came over and saw how well Ilmari was doing socially, he mellowed. Troy could never say no to him. Usually it was me that wound up putting my foot down.

"My poor boy was desperately unhappy during his teens, Jake. I never saw a child so ill at ease with what nature was throwing at him. I understand that it's not easy for any child, but Ilmari was at university. He was far away from both of us. He grew up behind our backs and there have been days when I thought he genuinely hated us for making him go through that alone." She kept her eyes on the photograph, her expression fond and sorrowful.

"When he called me — and Mari never called me. It was always me, or Troy, calling him to find out what he was up to — but when he called, I came up to Cambridge right away and we went to see his therapist together. Ilmari seemed very composed. He knew what he wanted. Troy and I were both aware that he liked men, though he had a girlfriend at that time. He said that he felt awkward and uncomfortable as a man, and since puberty, he'd never been at home in his body. He wanted to transition. The therapist asked him a lot of questions and told him that he needed to try out living as a woman for a year, at least, before anyone would even consider letting him take the next step."

Anni sighed deeply. Her expression was one of profound grief. "That night he told me that he wanted to die. He was broken and unhappy, Jake. And I couldn't fix it for him. We went shopping together the next day and I helped him to choose clothes that he was more comfortable in. He got a makeover in one of the shops. We both got our nails done and went out for dinner. That was the happiest I ever saw him at any point in his teens. I convinced myself that he knew what he was doing."

"He changed his mind? Or it was changed for him?" Solana asked. The Healer had been listening to all of this in silence and she looked as if something pained her.

"When he went to Barcelona, he was still presenting as female," Anni replied. "He told me before he left that he was getting estrogen injections. I know for a fact that he didn't get them through his regular doctor in Cambridge. They were making him ill. He didn't seem unhappy when we spoke, but he told me that his specialist believed he was clinically depressed and wasn't prepared to recommend him for surgical intervention. He was too thin and he wasn't eating properly. I was concerned for him, but he was an adult. I couldn't tell him how to live his life."

Jake's head was spinning in a thousand directions but his hand was steady as he put the photo album back into her hands. "I need to go."

He turned toward the hall and Anni called after him, "Jake... I'm sorry. It isn't my place to tell you, but you have the right to hear this if you're serious about him. And I think you are. He's stable at the moment, Jake, but...he's seemed that way before."

"I'm not angry. I have to go. I'll talk to you later." He didn't like leaving her upset but he didn't have it in him in that moment to give her any comfort, not until he'd had some time to think or until he'd talked to Mari about this.

"Don't be too sharp with him," she called after him as he headed for the door. "He loves you, Jake. He just doesn't always understand how to express who he is and what he feels."

She was wrong about that, Jake thought as he closed the door behind him and took the steps down to the street. Their relationship might have taken Mari longer to come to terms with, but once he had, he'd not left Jake wondering for very long. Still, he understood why she'd say that. Mari could be very direct but it wasn't easy to get a handle on the workings of his mind or his emotions.

Currently, he'd settle for simply working out his own feelings. They kept slipping through his head and he was unable to settle on just one.

He thought of himself as fair minded and progressive when it came to topics like sexuality and gender. He got how nature, biology, the complexity of the human mind and all that stuff was not clear-cut, black and white like some people wanted to believe. He understood all of that, on an intellectual level anyway, but he'd never questioned his own gender and he'd only gone through a very brief period of confusion about his sexuality. He had hidden his desires for a long time, but he hadn't been confused about being gay since he was a very young child.

He supposed if he was upset about anything, it was not being sure if this changed anything. It certainly didn't change how he felt about Mari, but Jake had to wonder why he had never told him about this and what he would do if Mari ever decided he'd made the wrong decision. In his own mind, he was pretty sure that Mari was comfortable being a man, but what if he was deluded about that?

"Okay, don't make problems where there are none, Chivis," he muttered to himself. He debated heading into the park to see if he could find Mari there, but he wasn't dressed for a run and Mari had enough of a lead on him that it was probably a safer bet to just go home and wait for him.

Chapter Fourteen

Jake was surprised to find that his boyfriend had beaten him to Maple Street and was shivering outside the door to his flat, hugging himself through the thin, thermal sweat top, like he'd had as much of a shock as Jake. As Mari set eyes on him, relief flickered in his gaze for a second, then gave way to concern.

"What's wrong? You didn't lose my dog, did you?" The jokey nature of the question didn't disguise his anxiety well enough.

"As if he'd wander off without me," Jake said. "I dropped him off at home." He put his arm around Mari and landed a quick kiss on his lips before opening the door and letting them both inside.

"You didn't answer me. What's wrong?" Mari asked again, once they were out of the chill damp London air, in the comparative warmth of the hallway.

"Nothing's wrong. Nothing to be worried about anyway. Let's go upstairs and talk."

Mari trailed him up to the tiny apartment on the first floor in silence but, as Jake knew, if he was quiet for too long, there genuinely was a problem.

"Talk about what?" he asked when the door was shut behind them and they were in the snug privacy of Jake's living room. "What happened when you took Tonka home? Was that conniving bitch up to no good?" His eyes widened. "Is Mama okay? Does she need me?"

"Anni is fine. You think I'd leave her on her own if something were wrong?" Jake soothed him. Turning, he rested his hands on Mari's upper arms, looking into those anxious eyes, which took him right back to the photograph. "Okay, I don't want you getting worked up, I'm just going to spit it out. This is…awkward. Somehow — I don't even understand how — but when I dropped Tonka off, your mother ended up showing me a picture of you…from when you were about eighteen. And it…it um…surprised me."

Mari opened his mouth. Behind his eyes, Jake saw him doing the math. He closed it again and pulled away, putting a hand over his lips like he was afraid he might be sick. Jake gave him as much space as he needed, which was not much given the size of the flat and the speed his thoughts tended to run at. Jake felt sick too. When Mari came back to face him again his expression was harder, somehow. More guarded.

"You were there for a few minutes and she just…what? Showed you? *Why*? Why would she do that to me? Fuck it… It was *her*, wasn't it? That Solana bitch! She's been needling my mother, putting her up to this. Damn her! Jake… I *would* have told you, I swear."

As the words fell from his lips, his face ran the gamut of emotions, from bewilderment to dismay, through shock and defensive rage, settling finally into a kind of distraught despair. Jake kept his expression and his voice very neutral, though his heart was thumping.

"I'm not mad, Ilmari. Were you afraid to tell me?"

Just for few moments, Mari's eyes glistened with emotion then he blinked it away. His breathing hitched in his chest but he composed himself. He looked like he was sentenced to death, though, and his head bowed.

"No. I just... I didn't... I thought... Fuck it! I didn't know *how* to talk to you about it." He waved his hands vaguely then put them behind him like a child. He lifted his face again, chewing on his lips, and his eyes met Jake's. "You're *really* not mad about it?"

"No...not mad. Worried, maybe. That might be a better word." Jake couldn't stand the way Mari stared at him, like he was facing a firing squad. Like he expected Jake to be disgusted and tell him to go. "Mari, please don't look at me like that. It doesn't change the way I feel about you."

Mari took a step, leaning into him, and Jake wrapped his arms around his shoulders and pulled him close. That was better — warm — holding him tight.

"I wasn't sure..." Mari mumbled into his collar, snaking his arms around Jake and clinging on to him like he would never let go. "You told me once that you weren't into girls, not one bit. That scared me. I thought that if I told you about me, you might not... You might not want me anymore."

Jake closed his eyes and breathed in the scent of Mari's hair, hugging him tight. "You were afraid? I suppose I would have been, too, if I thought I might lose you over something that I couldn't change. I'm not..." He caught his breath, choosing his words carefully. "Seeing that picture... I can't honestly say it didn't freak me out a little, Mari. I had a pile of questions in my mind. But it didn't make me want to stop being with you. It didn't make me love you any less. You wanna tell me about it, maybe?"

Mari pulled his 'aww shucks' face but he mellowed and kissed Jake's nose.

"I'm all sweaty... Let me have a shower. You can scrub my back if you want. And I'll answer your questions as best I can." He scowled briefly. "But first, tell me the truth. It was her, wasn't it? That Solana woman? She started all this, I'd bet my kidneys. She has been stirring things since we first went to see her. I can't believe Mama told her about me."

Jake sighed. "I don't even recall how the conversation started. Something about how you might see her as a challenge to your manhood. And when I said I didn't think so, that's when Anni showed me the picture. Your mom said that you wouldn't tell me yourself but she figured I needed to know the truth."

Mari's stare was incredulous. "Unbelievable! I bet Solana's a fucking hypnotist or something," he exhaled at last. "Damn her! I tried my hardest to find some dirt on her but she's squeaky clean. Even when she was plain old Andrew from Weston-super-Mare, she'd not got so much as a caution for shoplifting. What is she trying to do to me? I hate her!"

"Hate is a waste of energy, babe," Jake told him and kissed his forehead. "It doesn't matter. It doesn't change anything. But I'd still like to hear why you didn't... Why did you stop?"

Mari leaned forward, touching his brow to Jake's as if he could somehow transmit all the truth that way and circumvent words. He closed his eyes for a moment or two then looked directly at Jake again, his face very serious.

"It wasn't fixing anything for me, Jake. I was at a crossroads in my life. I didn't know what I was supposed to be. I'd spent the previous six years, while I went through puberty, in an academic environment away from home, and my whole world changed during that period. I grew a foot taller in the first three years and I gained about thirty pounds. My voice dropped like you would not believe and I didn't understand why this was happening to me. I hated it. I thought I was some kind of monster. I was surrounded by desirable older boys, and they were all hooking up and getting off with girls, but I just…couldn't. I'd gone from being cute and adorable and…loved, to…some kind of gothic nightmare and I couldn't handle it. Even my parents didn't want me around." His voice cracked and he looked down, shoulders slumped, damp hair tumbling around his face like a curtain. Jake lifted one hand, brushing his cheek with his fingers.

"I can't imagine that," he murmured tenderly, though his heart was aching.

"Why would they pack me off to university when I was barely more than a child?" Mari buried his face in Jake's sweater and cried, unable to hold the tears in any longer. Jake had no answer to that question, so he just held Mari close and stroked his hair until he had his sobbing under control. Then he touched Mari's wet cheek again.

Mari leaned his face into the caress. His words were soft and hoarse. "It was beyond imagination, trust me. And the guys at my college in the States? Oh my stars! Some of those guys made Nolan and his cronies look like sissies. And I wanted to get fucked by them real bad. But even as a kid, I knew that if I so much as looked at those bastards the wrong way, I would be chopped liver. So, I concentrated on girls, but the girls my age either wanted to be with football players, or just players, or with older men — guys with cars and money. And the few boys who were openly queer wanted something more...*manly*? Not me, anyway." He stopped for breath and sniffed rapidly. "I'd tried so hard at Albany. I worked myself half to death for that degree. It was a sporty college, so I started to run there, too, in my last year. I worked out and lost loads of weight, mainly trying to impress a guy. Surprise, surprise! I got some definition out of it. Amazingly, I even got laid.

"And when I got to Cambridge, I hoped it would be different. I'd read about it and seen it in movies. I figured it would be cultured and all the men would be these amazing dandies and I'd find myself there. I'd bought some nice clothes and come all the way to England. I figured I could start again, in a new place, where people would get me. But it was no better here. People were...kinder, but I was still way out of step. I hung out with a group of women at my student halls and I felt safer there. More natural. And I thought...it felt right and that must mean I was meant to be a woman. I looked good in androgynous clothes and I wore my hair long, which not many guys that weren't in bands did back then. So, I told them when I registered for my PhD that I wanted to change my name. The bursary staff were all very sweet. They called me Marijne and made a fuss of me. Mama came up from London and went to my early therapy appointments with me and she was always supportive. Papi was livid at first, I don't think I ever saw him angry with Mama like he was that week. It took him a long time to come around to it, but we got there."

Mari heaved a sigh and stared into space for a while, as if he were composing his thoughts. In quieter tones, he said, "I managed to get a boyfriend, though it didn't last. He wanted something I couldn't give him. Nothing else went right for me."

"You got your doctorate. Something must have worked out," Jake said tenderly, though he was still confused. It astounded him that Mari was capable of using so many words and still not telling him what he wanted to know.

"Yes," his lover breathed. "*Academically*, I was a fucking genius. But *socially* it was like wading through sewage. I hit a point at Cambridge where I just wrote everything down because I didn't dare say the words to people. For two years I worked right next to a guy and we communicated solely by email. I was terrified of attracting more attention. Everyone thought I was crazy, but there were a lot of crazy genius people there. I wasn't on my own, at least." Mari looked down toward his clenched fists, then relaxed them and flexed his fingers. "I have never told anyone any of this. You are practically the only person, outside of family, that has ever treated me like I'm a human being, Jake Chivis."

Jake had listened to this breathless, tearful tirade with his heart in his mouth, almost glad that Mari was desperate to talk because he didn't have the words to express just how much this story kicked him in the chest. He kissed Mari's hair.

"That's a damn shame," he whispered. "No one deserves to be treated that badly. Your mother said she thought you were happy, though, when you started to live as a woman. It seems like some things got better for you at least. So, what happened? What made you change your mind?"

Mari got that harried look on his face again — there for an instant but quickly wrapped away behind his faux confident smile. "Maybe my therapist was right. The idea of surgery terrified me. Then I got sick and I had to stop taking my estrogen. And without it I didn't feel…complete enough. So, I quit. If I couldn't be perfect, I didn't want to try. No one loves a freak." The muscles between Mari's shoulders twitched under Jake's hand and his voice took on a bitter edge on those last words. There was more to that decision than Mari was telling him.

"Those aren't your words," Jake said, not making it a question. "This would have been after you'd graduated, right? And moved to Spain, started a new job. Then got involved with a manipulative older man that didn't tell you he was married."

"Jake, there was more to it than that. You've seen how I am. You knew what pushed my buttons within a month or so of being with me." Mari shrugged off his hoodie and peeled the sweat-damp vest away from his lean, run-toned body, letting it drop to the floor. "I need a strong hand. I always did. And trying to be a man but needing to be with someone stronger…someone who could manage me like that. It was hard for me. I'm not small and cute. Hell, you're the only man I've been with who was anywhere near my height."

"Uh-huh. You were what, twenty, twenty-one? Used to feeling like the misfit, uncomfortable with your body, socially awkward and sexually inexperienced. And your boss turned out to be a shithead who preyed on those insecurities."

"It wasn't like that," Mari said in a dull tone. He wriggled out of his tight leggings. Mari may have convinced himself his decision not to transition had nothing to do with his disastrous affair with Tomas Arregui but Jake could practically feel the discomfort radiating off him and knew he wasn't that far off the mark. He recalled the smug expression on Arregui's handsome face and wished wholeheartedly he'd wiped that look off when he'd had the chance.

"I don't want to talk about him. I feel filthy just thinking about it," Mari said, unwilling to even meet his eyes. "Every time I get a moment in the sun, something comes along to make it dark and horrible for me. I need to get clean." He looked up at Jake with soulful eyes. "And I need you to whip me."

Chapter Fifteen

Jake crossed his arms and tried not to grind his teeth. He debated pushing Mari some more because he knew he still wasn't being entirely truthful, but he let it go for the time being. "If that's what you want, you can take a shower afterward."

His lover made a small sound in his throat but he didn't contest the condition. Instead he went to the archway between the living area and Jake's bedroom and raised his hands, wrapping them around the bar Jake had put there for his pull-ups.

"Go on. Do it. I deserve it. Beat me." His voice was quiet, soft and husky, but not submissive.

Jake moved to stand behind Mari, reaching one hand up and placing it over the top of where Mari was gripping tightly. With the other he traced a finger down Mari's side from his shoulder to his hip.

"You think so? You think this is what you deserve?" He murmured the words along the curve of Mari's neck and into his hair.

"Jake…"

"Shh. No more talking. The only thing I want to hear from you is 'yes, sir', or 'no, sir'. Understand?"

"Mmmhhh…oh, yes, sir," Mari crooned, sounding happier already.

Jake slid the hand at his hip around and over the bulge at Mari's crotch. He cupped him through his skimpy briefs and gave him a friendly squeeze. "Good. Now tell me how beautiful you are."

Mari tilted his hips, pushing against Jake's hand eager for his attention.

"I'm yours, everything you want me to be," he groaned, wriggling in Jake's arms. "Everything, sir."

"Mmhm, that's right. You *are* mine." Jake told him, stroking him slowly. "But that's not what I told you to say. You are fucking beautiful, Ilmarinen. I want to hear you say it."

Mari half-turned and touched his mouth to Jake's. "You make me feel beautiful," he whispered at last.

Jake slid the hand covering Mari's down to his wrist, gripping him there while the other released him. He gave him a hard swat on the ass. "Repeat after me, Mari. I."

Mari hesitated and Jake spanked him again.

"I…" Jake prompted.

"I." It came out as a huff of sound.

"Am." Jake purred the word into Mari's ear and this time there was only a slight hesitation before he responded.

"Am."

"Beautiful." Jake said the word tenderly.

Mari shivered in his embrace and turned his face away. He was silent for a while and his voice caught like a plucked string as he whispered, almost inaudibly, "B-beautiful."

When Jake brought his hand up to caress Mari's cheek, he shied from the touch and Jake's fingers came away salty wet.

Jake kissed his neck and caressed his chest and belly for a moment before stepping away and taking off his belt. Mari needed his head space, and he needed this release, so Jake would give it to him.

He doubled the belt over in one hand and put the other on the back of Mari's neck, forcing him to lean forward, with his arms still stretched up over his head. He could tell Mari was holding his breath as he slapped him with the belt across his buttocks. The suspended gasp came out of him in a rush as he was struck, and he quivered under Jake's hand but did not cry out.

"Again," he whispered, at last, when his tremors subsided.

"Say it again," Jake instructed.

"Jake…"

"Say it again or we stop."

Mari keened softly. "B-beautiful. Please…do it again."

Jake did, landing the polished side of his belt firmly across Mari's backside. He made him repeat it each time he strapped him, until Mari got the idea and said it on his own before the belt fell.

"Beautiful… Beautiful… I'm beautiful. Oh, Jake… I'm beautiful. That feels so good. Tie my hands and fuck me." The last exhortation came out in a heated rush. Mari was clinging to the bar and his lean body shook with need, his sexy ass striped scarlet from the slaps of Jake's belt. If it hurt, his hard cock didn't seem to indicate as much.

Jake dropped his belt on the floor and reached up with both hands to take Mari's off the bar. He turned Mari, keeping his wrists pinned behind him as he kissed him hard. Mari responded eagerly, pushing up against him, tangling his tongue in Jake's mouth, and Jake walked him backward through the narrow archway into the bedroom. He kept going, a few more paces, until Mari's knees hit the side of the bed and he spilled down across the mattress, uttering a breathless moan as the material rubbed his tender backside.

"Unzip me."

Mari's fingers fumbled in his eagerness to obey. He snatched at the zip and tugged and wriggled it down, then tried to pull Jake onto him.

Jake kept his balance and pushed his fingers into Mari's hair, pulling his head back and bending to kiss him. "Get your underwear off and scoot up on the bed," Jake told him. He opened the drawer in the nightstand next to the bed while Mari complied and took out a bottle of lube and a plug, dropping them next to Mari.

Jake stepped clear and let his jeans drop to the floor. He was hard and wanted nothing more than to spread Mari's legs and dive between — but not yet.

"Put the pillows up behind you, baby. I want you to give me a show."

Mari's eyes glistened in the sudden flush of his normally composed face. There was no reluctance in his gaze, though. His beautiful Mari snuggled into the nest of pillows and hooked his arms under his knees, leaning back at once and opening himself to Jake without a moment's hesitation.

"I do love you," he breathed in that husky tone that made Jake's cock even harder.

Jake pulled his shirt off and dropped it. "I love you, too, sweetheart. My beautiful Mari. You've got me so hot, baby."

"I love it when you get that look in your eyes, like you could melt me just by staring at me." Mari sighed. "I wish…" He closed his mouth and looked away, unsure of his words.

Jake knelt on the edge of the bed and leaned over him, giving up on the game they'd been playing. He put his hands around Mari's hips and pulled him down the mattress. Jake kissed him, a slow, leisurely kiss meant to put him at ease.

"You wish what?"

Mari's solemn eyes met his and did not shy away. "I wish I'd met you sooner."

Jake kissed him again, just a soft brush of lips this time. "I wish you had, too." He pressed a warmer kiss to his lips and slid his arms around him, rolling his lower half until they ground together.

"We need to make up for lost time," Mari gasped when they broke the kiss.

"Mmm…" Jake purred in agreement. He combed his fingers into Mari's hair, tugging at the nape so he lifted his chin and kissed his way down Mari's neck, nipping at the base. He'd been in a kinky frame of mind, but Mari's mood flipped that around on him. He sucked the tender skin at the base of Mari's throat and caught one of Mari's knees with his other hand, pushing it up. The press of their bodies rubbing together was incredible.

Mari looped around him easily, locking his fingers at the nape of Jake's neck and drawing him close as he writhed against him. He made a growling noise as Jake's mouth roamed lower.

"Uhhhh…yes. Like that."

Jake rocked his hips and his cock slid down between Mari's cheeks. He let go of his knee long enough to snag the lube and uncap it, drizzling a clear stream over the crown and letting some run down the valley of Mari's ass crack.

"Turn me over," Mari breathed. "Take me on my knees, Jake. Hold my wrists and don't be gentle. Please."

He was shaking as he spoke, running his fingers up into Jake's hair and looking at him like he was some kind of miracle.

Jake knelt up and ran his hands down Mari's arms to his wrists. He pinned them both to the bed above Mari's head and kissed him passionately. When Mari was panting and breathless and grinding his hips up to meet him, Jake looked down at him seriously. "No. Not this time. I want to watch you. I want to see your face when you come."

Mari uttered another growl — of frustration. His long, lean body arced up from the mattress and he rubbed against Jake's belly frantically, locking his legs around Jake's strong thighs and bracing himself there as he wriggled and squirmed.

"Please! Get inside me!"

Jake almost laughed at the urgency in his voice but he didn't tease him. He was too eager to do exactly that. Mari lifted up and Jake tilted his hips, taking aim and tapping the head of his cock on his tight hole. He held there a moment, pushing steadily until the slight relaxation in his lover's muscles let him inside at last.

"Ohh…" Mari exhaled raggedly. He didn't say anything else though, just flopped against the pillows and stared up at Jake, drinking him in with his wide, blue eyes.

Jake might have refused the position change, but the rest of what Mari wanted he was more than willing to give him. He sank into him about halfway, pulled out again, then thrust in deeper, watching the shock and pleasure mix on Mari's beautiful face the whole time.

Mari clenched his fingers into fists as he surrendered to the pressure swelling inside him, his body curling up again as he struggled to ride each thrust, pinned as he was to the bed.

"Mmmh…yes…harder!" he keened as Jake pulsed out and in again.

Jake spread his knees wider and gripped Mari's wrists tighter, driving himself smoothly to the root. When Mari's breath caught, he withdrew inch by inch and did it again, moving faster and thrusting harder each time. He curled his spine, arching over Mari, loving every moan and every flicker of desire that crossed his face.

Mari's eyes closed and his dark gold lashes fanned his cheeks as he turned his head from side to side, growling and purring with ecstasy, occasionally murmuring something under his breath that Jake did not understand. It was like a familiar song but with the lyrics transposed.

Jake let go of one of Mari's wrists and brought his hand down, guiding it between them. "This feels amazing, Mari. I love the way you feel, the way you look, the way you sound…"

Again, Mari growled something urgent and alien, translating as he reached for Jake with his freed hand. "Need to feel you. Take me hard, please!"

For all that he could sometimes look delicate, in bed he gave rein to a stronger will and in the throes of passion he was anything but a wilting flower. Sex with Mari often bordered on violence but that never seemed to bother him. Mari thrived on the thrill of their often-frantic lovemaking.

Jake hooked his hands at the backs of Mari's knees and bent them higher, spreading his legs and leaning forward. The lube made them slide together easily and Jake picked up a driving rhythm, pounding into him until they slapped together on the down strokes. Sweat beaded on his neck, beneath his hair, and he tightened his grip on Mari's legs, folding him nearly in half so every single stroke slammed balls-deep into him.

Mari reached down, gripping and stroking his cock in time with Jake's rapid pounding. The breath being driven out of him came in tiny, whimpering cries as Jake edged him up, higher and higher. Mari's nude body was like wet silk under him, snug and hot around his cock, and it was going to be a near thing which of them got there first.

"Mari...baby...oh, fucking... Come for me..." Jake panted.

Mari barely needed the encouragement. His fingers flew faster over the glistening head of his cock. For just a handful of rapid-fire heartbeats, he fell very still before exhaling a low, wordless groan that was almost a cry of pain. He tightened reflexively around Jake's erection as he shot again and again, blasting long, creamy ropes of semen over his chest and belly.

Jake hit his peak only a second or two after him. Watching Mari shudder and moan through an intense climax pulled his trigger like nothing else could. He drove into him hard and held there, letting go of Mari's legs, bending over him and burying his face in the crook of his neck. He wrapped his arms around Mari and held on tight as each hard spurt shook him.

Finally, they both stopped gasping and trembling and curled around each other more comfortably. Mari tilted his head to look into Jake's eyes.

"You are so damn good for me," he murmured. "Thank you for that, Chivis. I don't understand what I did to deserve you, but I wanna keep on doing it."

Jake kissed his temple and stroked his fingers through his hair. "You are beautiful. Beautiful and amazing. I wish I could make you believe it."

"Hush," Mari admonished softly, hooking the back of Jake's skull gently and drawing him in for another kiss. "There's more to life than looking pretty, Chivis? When you look at me like that, I never feel like anyone else matters."

"There's more to life than being pretty?" Jake made a theatrical gasp. "And here I've wasted all this time thinking everything I'd done was meaningless because I'm not a supermodel?"

Mari swatted at him. Jake caught his hand before it landed and kissed him again.

"Truly," Mari whispered when his lips were unoccupied again, "no one has ever made me feel so worthwhile, Jake Chivis. You might think I have a long way to go, but from my point of view, I've made that journey — and that is thanks to you."

Jake looked into his eyes and brushed his thumb over Mari's cheek tenderly. "I'm glad. I'm glad I make you feel that way."

"I can't stand the idea that anyone could do anything to damage that," Mari told him seriously. "I can't face the idea of being without you, Jake."

"I'm not going anywhere. I'd still like you to tell me, though. Did it ever seem like you made a mistake? Stopping the hormones, I mean?"

Mari's gaze dropped for a moment and Jake's heart beat faster.

"Honestly?" Mari sighed, shaking his head once. "Jake...I've no idea. It was taken out of my hands. My consultant psychiatrist said that I wasn't a suitable candidate for gender reassignment. He— He questioned my mental stability, if you must know. Do I think he was wrong? I'm not sure. I guess I've always had my own style, my own way of doing things. If you want a proper answer, I don't truly feel like I fit in either sex. And I'm not sure what that leaves me."

Jake caught a of lock of hair that had fallen across Mari's forehead and smoothed it into place again. "It leaves you...yourself. Okay, you might not be the most masculine guy, but if someone has a problem with that, they can go fuck themselves."

"I don't care what most people think anymore, Chivis. I stopped all that that years ago." Mari looked up with a humorless smile. "I only care what one person thinks. And if he's going to fuck anything, I'd rather he fucked me."

Heat pooled in Jake's belly at the thought of that but he only rolled over, taking Mari with him so he was tucked under his arm. "All right, all right, I get it. I'll let it go. I just want you to be happy. Safe, healthy and happy. You play your cards so close that sometimes I just need to ask to be sure."

"You're not going to dump me?" Mari looked up at him, worrying his lips with his teeth.

"That never crossed my mind. Would I be planning on moving in with you if I were going to dump you?"

"You're planning to move in with me?" Mari pretended surprise. "You were still thinking about it last time I listened." He mellowed and winked at Jake, though there was still more than a shadow of sadness over his ashen features.

"I haven't been thinking about it. I've just been waiting to make sure you didn't change your mind," Jake teased him gently in return.

Mari's eyes narrowed, though. "Was that supposed to be a joke?"

"Sort of." Jake was suddenly less certain of himself. "I mean, we haven't talked about it since that first time it was mentioned."

"You still think I don't want to? Or that I'll decide I'd rather be a woman?" Mari said succinctly.

"Perhaps," Jake admitted.

"I'm not planning to transition, Jake. But if I did… Down the line, if I did decide that I wanted to look more femme, would that be a problem for you?" Mari curled up on his side, facing Jake, his expression suddenly very serious.

"Do you think that's a possibility?" Jake asked.

"That I might not always want to be this butch? I'm afraid so." Mari's eyes twinkled for a moment, sobering just as quickly. "But if you're asking would I physically become a woman? No. I'm coming to terms with the idea that I'm not a man *or* a woman. I'm something in between — or neither. Even if I thought, now, with a different doctor, I might get a different prognosis, I wouldn't want to put myself through those hoops again."

Mari sounded very sure of that and relief washed over him. Moments later, Jake felt bad for thinking that way. Yes, he liked Mari just the way he was but if he *forced* him to be like that, wasn't he just as bad as Arregui?

"You've got to understand that I've never been conventional," Mari said, his voice soft and uncertain again. "I like nice clothes. And yes, sometimes I like to look pretty. You've seen me wear makeup. Would it make you uncomfortable, if I *was* more androgynous? I need to know, if we're going to live together."

"If you had asked me a year ago, I would have told you yes. It would definitely make me uncomfortable." Jake sighed and folded his hands together so he wouldn't be tempted to touch Mari.

Honesty was important to him. It always had been. If he hedged, it might turn into something bigger later, and he didn't want anything to come between him and Mari.

"I have known since I was a kid that I was gay," Jake told him. "I didn't have that word for it, but I knew that I didn't get crushes on girls like my friends did. Instead, I got crushes on *them*. I pretty much knew, right away, that this was not okay, and that idea was reinforced daily. Friends, teachers and especially my father hammered home the idea in no uncertain terms, that being anything less than uber-masculine was wrong, disgusting, something to be ashamed of. I hid what I was feeling and got rid of any trace of anything in me that wasn't completely, one hundred percent, hetero-male. It actually wasn't that hard for me. I just had to keep my thoughts about guys to myself and I could 'pass' for hetero.

"I didn't feel safe enough to explore any kind of sexuality until after my father went to prison and I was on my own. I had some hook-ups, and even a couple of flings that lasted longer, but I kept it all a secret. I don't know what I was afraid of at that point — maybe it was just a lifetime of habit. Then, I decided to become a cop and it seemed important to keep my sexuality a secret there, too.

"I didn't think about things like having a 'type'. The guys I dated were all just regular guys. I fucked guys that were more, um…out, I guess. Like the way they looked and dressed and talked, there was no doubt they were gay. I fucked them, but I didn't see any of them more than once, and I guess I'm not so proud of how I treated them. Because if I was with them, it didn't matter how straight I looked, I'd be guilty by association. I was really, really stupid, Mari."

Jake took a breath and let it out. "Then all the shit went down with Alex and everyone finding out about us, and I panicked and left, but it was a good thing. I came here, and I met you, and I acted like a jerk and you put me in my place for it. I decided I didn't give a shit about hiding who I was anymore. I admired who you were, and it wasn't just that I didn't care who knew. I wanted people to see that I was with you. You changed me for the better in a way I never thought possible. I'm in love with you, Mari Gale — with who you are, not how you look. No matter what you choose to wear or how you choose to express yourself, I'll always be glad to be with you."

Mari had lowered his eyes when Jake was talking about how he'd fucked men in the past then walked away. He only looked up again when he said the part about admiring him. There was a shimmer in his pale eyes that had not been there before. He uncurled enough to wrap his hands around Jake's, holding them tight.

"I love you, too. I promise that I will always try to make you proud," he said in a small, husky voice.

Jake shifted so he could put an arm around him and pull him close, kissing his forehead. "You don't have to try, Mari. You already do that."

Chapter Sixteen

Natalie Craig lived in Blackheath, in a two-bed flat above a dry cleaner, shared with two men and another, older woman. Jake had called her ahead to set up the meeting, but at the last minute, he'd gotten a call from DI Cordiline and had asked Mari if he could keep the appointment with Natalie without him. Mari already imagined he knew her well, thanks to his research, but that hadn't helped when they'd interviewed Emily. He got the tube down to Greenwich, and because he needed to calm his nerves, he walked across the park and down Tranquil Vale to their block on Lee Road.

Like most English street names, Tranquil Vale was mostly optimistic. It formed part of the Blackheath Village high street and was bustling with traffic and shoppers. Even so, it was less frenetic than central London. He was conscious that, in his perfectly tailored Paul Smith suit, he drew the eye of passing shoppers and the attention brought a brief smile to his lips.

To his relief, Natalie was alone when he got to the flat. He wasn't sure he could handle another interrogation by flatmates.

She looked ashen and drawn, without makeup but still pretty, and she assessed him quickly and deliberately through the gap between the door and jamb before taking the chain off and letting him in. He accepted the offer of coffee and resisted the urge to pass comment when it turned out to be instant. At least she heaped a couple of generous spoonfuls into the mug before adding the water. He waved away the offer of milk and sugar. Then she came to join him, sitting in a weather-beaten leather armchair and keeping the coffee table between his perch on the sofa and her seat.

"So…you don't look like a copper," she said, only a slight tremor in her voice.

"No. Well, I'm not, not exactly. My partner and I are working with the police, as consultants. My partner did explain when he called."

"Yeah," she acknowledged, though she still sounded skeptical. "You're, like, psychic sleuths or something. That sounds…cool. Kinda weird, but very cool."

"It is cool," he agreed, "and weird. There are things that Jake and I can do that the police can't. I'm trying to gather information to help us trace potential suspects. I can go places that the police can't, Natalie. But I could use some help. I need the right directions to look in."

"I told the lady from the police station everything I could remember while I was at the hospital," Natalie said, hiding her features in the large coffee mug cupped in her hands.

"I read what you told her," Mari soothed. "You don't have to go into the details. It's okay. If you remember anything else about the man that jumped you, though, you can tell me whatever way you prefer. I'll give you my mobile number and my email address before I leave. What I'm trying to find out is whether you have anything in common with the other girls that he's attacked. I'm trying to create a profile for him, based on his movements, on the likely ways that he picks his" — he swallowed the word *victims*, editing the statement in his head at the last moment — "targets."

Jake would be proud of him. He was learning tact.

"Can you tell me anything about your movements during the days leading up to the assault, Natalie? Where did you go? Who did you see?"

She thought about that for a while as she drank her coffee.

"I was working at the shop in the days before, except for Wednesday. I had a modeling assignment in the afternoon, so I finished at lunchtime and went over to Camden."

He was making notes on his tablet and looked up at her curiously. "Did you go out after work, or for lunch at all?"

She shook her head. "I don't get paid until the end of the month. Money is tight. That's why I do the Camden assignment. I can take leave and get paid twice."

"What's the modeling job all about?" he asked her.

"I model for a life class at a place on the high street," Natalie said, blushing. "It's not catwalk stuff, but the instructor is nice and the people that come to her classes seem okay."

He peered over his tablet at her. "You're an artist's model?"

Natalie nodded once. "Yes. It's quite respectable, actually. Mostly older ladies…and students."

"Do you have any contact with the artists?" Mari asked her.

Natalie gave another small shake of her head. "No. I don't talk to anyone, just the instructor, Solana. I mean, Madame Stellara. She pays me, cash in hand. Afterwards, I walk to the tube at Chalk Farm and go home."

He blinked. "Madame Stellara?"

That has to be a coincidence, right? How many Solana Stellaras can there be in Camden?

"I think she's forcign," Natalie said. "She's quite exotic, though she doesn't seem to have a foreign accent."

No, you don't, do you, Madame Solana? Mari narrowed his eyes and made several less than complimentary notes on his tablet. He couldn't quite stop his nerves from jangling, though. Like his mother, Natalie seemed quite won over by Solana, but the fact remained that the Elemental Healer had every opportunity to take advantage of that trust. He kept thinking of the way that Solana had begun their session with an innocent offer of tea. Was that natural hospitality or the perfect opportunity to dope a potential victim?

He ground his teeth in silent frustration before realizing that Natalie was looking at him rather oddly. Tapping the edge of his tablet, he diverted his attention back to the interview.

"Have you ever seen anyone from those sessions outside of the classes?"

"No," Natalie told him. "Like I said, we don't talk. I just pose and they draw me."

"Has anyone ever made you feel uncomfortable while you were posing for them?" he asked her, more seriously.

Natalie seemed to think about that for a moment. At last she shook her head. "No. They all seem…ordinary. I don't think about them. It's a time when I can think about my own stuff."

"What about at work? Is there anyone that you work with, or who maybe comes in the shop, that you've ever felt uncomfortable about?" he persisted, though he could not stop thinking about his mother's Healer. Again, that sense of disquiet left him restless.

"I work in a clothes shop. There's always strange people," Natalie said with a grim smile.

"You've never been aware that anyone followed you after leaving work before?" Mari stroked a finger around the edge of his tablet.

"No. I don't think so," she told him, sounding less comfortable.

"Okay, don't worry about it." He put the tablet away in his messenger bag and rose to his feet. "Thank you for talking to me, Natalie. You have my details. If there is anything you need to tell me or just if you want to talk to someone, you can get in touch. I can see myself out."

* * * *

The message was weird and Jake was not a fan of weird. Cordiline's text just asked him to come down to the station and that he'd explain when he got there. It wasn't like Cordiline to be cryptic. Oh, and it had said to come on his own, something he hadn't mentioned to Mari because he didn't want another round of scathing opinions. If they were going to continue to work with the detective, he didn't need to throw any more fuel on the animosity bonfire. John had better have a good reason for not including Mari, though.

When he got to Kentish Town, they were expecting him because the sergeant on the desk waved him through and he was allowed to make his own way up to the next floor where Cordiline's corner of the office was fighting for space with about four other desks. The DI had gotten his small space more organized today and he looked up with a tired, tight-lipped smile.

"Thanks for coming so quickly. We've had an interesting development and you need to be on board with it because it's rather close to home. I wanted to tell you in person. Don't take offense that I didn't invite your boyfriend. I figured it was up to you if you want to tell him about this, but it wasn't my call."

"What's going on?" Jake frowned. It wasn't like Cordiline to prevaricate either, and that this was something he might not want Mari to know about made him uncomfortable.

"We've had an offer of assistance, on the rape case." Cordiline paused. "But he's stipulated that he wants another Elemental to talk to."

Jake didn't bother trying to hide his surprise. "He's an Elemental?"

"Yes. You have history, Chivis." Cordiline sucked in a long breath and let it go irritably. "The call came from Wormwood Scrubs. Aled Mustatti. He saw you on the TV news coverage. He was adamant that he could help us so long as you were his liaison on this case."

An ice-cold chill ran down Jake's back, swiftly followed by an acid burn in his gut at the sound of Aled Mustatti's name. Jake clenched his jaw. The irony that Mustatti said he could help solve a serial rape case was not lost on him. The man had drugged him and molested him, and he'd had no qualms about injecting him with an experimental drug that had already killed several people. He was currently serving time for his part in stealing the classified information on EQ10, and the wrongful deaths that had resulted, and had nearly killed Jake as well. He was not, however, doing time for what he had done to Jake in the bedroom of the last victim's, house because Jake had not told anyone what he had done. Cordiline had figured it out after going over the evidence found at the crime scene. He'd pressed Jake to bring charges but when Jake had refused, Cordiline had quietly buried what he'd uncovered and let it go. "He said he wanted another Elemental, or he asked to talk to me specifically?"

"He asked for you, Chivis — by name. Maybe he's bullshitting and he just wants to pull your chain. Could he have some kind of gift that would help, do you think?" Cordiline steepled his fingers and looked at Jake over the tops of them.

Jake felt a prickle of sweat at the name of his neck. Not a good sign. He needed to get a lid on his anger. The temperature spike when he was hit with strong emotions, especially anger, was a side effect of the EQ10, something else that was Aled Mustatti's fault.

He focused on the here and now, and what he knew. "He's an Earth Elemental. Some of them have a gift for finding lost things. From what I understand of the talent, they use the connection between owner and item to trace what they are looking for. It doesn't work on people, because people are autonomous, so I don't see how he'd be able to find a suspect that way, much less figure out who you're looking for."

Cordiline wiped a hand over his face and sighed. "The only way to find out what he's offering then is to go talk to him. That's a neat ploy." Cordiline paused, working his jaw for a moment before he said, "You don't have to do this, Jake. We have plenty to follow up without chasing around after fantasists like Aled Mustatti."

"And if I don't, we won't know for sure. That's not going to sit well with either of us. I'll talk to him. If he's just throwing bullshit, I'd probably be the best one to figure it out without wasting a bunch of time."

"That's what I'd figured, too." The DI nodded. "Scrubs will set up the interview. See what you can get out of him."

Chapter Seventeen

Cordiline offered to go with him to the prison but Jake politely declined his company. The DI had arranged his interview for the half-past-three visiting hour. Jake got to the tube station at East Acton just after three o'clock and navigated via the GPS on his phone to the Visitors' Center on Du Cane Road. He'd seen the outside—and inside—of enough prisons to be pleasantly surprised by the leafy thoroughfares around Wormwood Scrubs. There was a genteel aspect to even the outer reaches of his adopted home city and he took his time, enjoying the first hints of spring in the afternoon air. Blossoms were already out on some of the trees and thin, misty sunlight filtered through the clouds. Too bad it couldn't warm the chill of premonition from his bones.

The Visitors' Center was accessed through a zigzag wheelchair ramp and a large sliding door in the high, yellow-brick wall around the prison perimeter. He entered the building and his ID was checked by two uniformed guards, then he was shown to the lockers, where he stowed his jacket and wallet before he was taken into a long room with a bank of cubicles. A floor-to-ceiling partition of inch-thick glass separated the public area from the inmate side with a speaker grill installed in each visitor's booth.

Jake was guided to one of these cubes and took a seat. The guard who had come with him remained by the door. A few minutes later, a door opened on the other side of the partition and a tall, dark-skinned figure walked through in uniform prison sweats, escorted by a pair of guards. He was not cuffed, but the guards did not let him out of their sight as he spotted Jake through the screen and came to sit across from him. He looked leaner than he had last summer, his hair trimmed close to his scalp. His spoke into the grill.

"Chivis, thank you for coming," he said in a rich baritone rumble, as if he'd invited him out for coffee. "I didn't think you would."

Jake's stomach churned and he could feel his upper lip wanting to curl but he controlled the urge and kept his expression blank. He got right to the point. "You've managed to convince some people that you can help on a case. This is your one and only chance to prove that wasn't a lie."

Mustatti was silent for a moment, watching him through the glass, statue still. "Corrie injected me with the formula," he said at last, his voice slow and careful, as if waking from a brief sleep. "It left me with a curious side effect, but I didn't realize it until they brought me here."

"You're lying. It only worked on Fire Elementals."

"We thought so, too." Mustatti laughed, a dark, humorless sound in that quiet space. "Of course, none of us exhibited side effects quite as dramatic as the Fire Elementals. For that reason, it was presumed that the drug was only effective on your kind. But that is not the case. While I was here, a guest of Our Majesty, something occurred that changed my mind about the failure of the drug to enhance the abilities of other Elementals. And, as I was watching you on the television yesterday, it occurred to me that what I am able to do as a result could help you."

"Right. Because you have such a generous heart. Are you going to draw this out much longer?"

"I get precious few visitors, Jake Chivis. I have every respect for you, my friend." Aled managed to make the words sound sincere. "You are a miracle. The only survivor of our experiments on Fire Elementals. It was a pleasure to work with you."

A muscle twitched in Jake's cheek at the double implication. "I'm not your friend and I'm not here for a visit. I'm here to find out if you're of any use, of which I have every doubt. I know how Earth Elementals work. They can find things, sometimes, if they know what they are looking for. Sometimes they can flip pens and paperclips across a desk with their minds. Neither of these abilities is of much use in finding a rapist."

Aled stared at him with soulful, dark eyes, the whites tinged faintly yellow. "Locating is indeed a common trait among Earth Elementals, for those that have ability. True telekinesis is less common and, as you pointed out, limited to small items, at least in this generation. If you know those facts, I presume you are aware of the rarest of talents reputedly attached to Earth Elementals? The kind that have been relegated to myth and unsubstantiated rumor? Or did you think that legendary gifts such as true pyrokinesis were only the preserve of you Firebugs?"

Jake gave him a hard stare and resisted the urge to shift his position on the seat or wrinkle his nose. He knew exactly what Aled was hinting at and had to work to keep his expression blank when his upper lip tried to draw back in disgust again. "Are you trying to tell me you can speak to the dead?"

A broad white grin split the gleaming darkness of his face and Aled sat back from the table with his hands on his thighs.

"Now the intrepid Fire Elemental is on the right track," he said with a glint in his eyes. "I heard you were a detective in a former life, Chivis. About two months ago, there was a violent assault in D-Wing. Some unlucky bastard got on the wrong end of a knife. No one saw anything, of course. Poor bugger snuffed it and wasn't found until he'd already bled out. I was there when he was found. As the guards were coming, the dead man turned his head and opened his eyes. I know what you're thinking, that he wasn't really dead yet. Believe me when I tell you I wish that were the case. I saw his spirit struggling within his shell, Chivis. I saw the milky film over his eyes, and his lips didn't move when his voice named the killer."

"And conveniently, there is no way to prove any of that. Even if I believed you, all of our victims are alive and none of them has been able to identify their attacker."

"I watch the news. The most recent victim is in hospital, at death's door." Aled looked at him, his features impassive.

Jake could no longer contain his disgust and spat out, "You're hoping she dies so you can pretend to talk to her corpse."

"No. I'm giving you an option, Chivis," Aled said. "If the woman succumbs, I'll prove it to you. You can be present and hear what she has to say for yourself."

Jake leaned forward. "You could have told anyone this information. Why me?"

"Who in the Met would have believed me? Which of those plodding bastards out there could even have imagined such a thing possible?" Aled chuckled, a sound so totally devoid of humor that it made Jake feel sick. "DI Cordiline might be open-minded enough to want to believe, but he would have gone to you for confirmation anyway. Why not go right to the source?"

"Why help at all?"

"Because I am not a bad man. I have been given a bad label. That's all."

Jake snorted.

Aled folded his hands on the table, his fingertips touching the glass. "Your people are looking for a man who has done bad things. If he kills and I speak with the deceased before she fades from this world, I may be able to discover more about him for you. This, in turn, will help my application for parole."

Jake sneered and shook his head.

"What? You did not expect honesty? You are young to be such a cynic, Detective Chivis."

"Why would you think I'd expect any honesty from you? You forget that I know what you are. Helping to put another pervert behind bars won't change that." Jake stood up and turned to go, not giving him an answer one way or the other on whether he'd recommend they accept his help.

"If the next one dies, no one will be able to help you as well as I can, Chivis," Aled called out behind him. "Their families will be very grateful."

Jake walked out without looking back. He didn't trust what he might say. He wanted to tell him he could rot in a cell forever for all he cared. He wanted to tell him to fuck off, that he'd not give him any opportunity to butter up a parole board. He'd be lying if he told him that, though. He would use any tool at his disposal to find the asshole hunting these women and stop him, even a tool as distasteful as Mustatti. Even if the thought of how Mustatti might be able to help made Jake's skin crawl.

There were severe taboos in his culture against disturbing the dead. If he hadn't already got a good idea what kind of creature Aled Mustatti was, this would have sealed it for him. He collected his things and slammed out of the building, new determination that it wouldn't come to that in his every step.

* * * *

When Jake got home, he found takeaway beef pad thai on the table and Mari curled up on the sofa, immersed in something on his tablet, in an open shirt and his blue boxer briefs. He looked up with a warm smile that faded as he saw the expression on Jake's face.

"What's wrong?"

Instead of explaining the most recent development, he went with a more literal list of frustrations. "We have no new information. We've got nothing connecting the victims except the college. The last victim is still fighting for her life, and all we can do is sit here and wait for him to target another innocent woman." Jake dropped heavily onto the sofa and scowled at their case wall.

Mari slid an arm around him and snuggled closer. "You are very, very sexy when you have a strop on. Here's something for you. Natalie Craig was a life model for my mother's so-called Healer. Solana teaches painting classes at her eyrie on Camden High Street. I told you there was something shifty about her."

Jake waited a beat, but when Mari didn't say he was joking, he scowled harder. "That's a weird coincidence."

"Isn't it?" Mari agreed, leaning over for the chopsticks and maneuvering food from the container to Jake's mouth. "Just what I thought. I reckon one of us should have a word with her."

"Mari, just because the girl modeled for Solana, it doesn't automatically make her a suspect."

Mari planted tender kisses along his jawline then mimicked a comical Estuary rapper accent. "She is well dodgy, bro. Trust me."

Jake rolled his eyes but he pulled Mari into his lap. "Bro? What have you been watching lately? And, even if she is sketchy, that doesn't make her a rapist. I'm not saying we won't look into it further, but don't hang your hat on her just yet. First, let's find out if Solana has connections to any of the other victims. Next, we need to find out where she was when each crime was happening. We can question Solana about her relationship with Natalie, but let's not tip our hand until we have more info."

"You're no fun tonight." Mari snagged a piece of meat with his chopsticks.

Jake leaned in and stole the bite from him before he got it into his mouth. He smirked at Mari's affronted look as he chewed and swallowed. "Sorry. It's been a long day. This is something anyway. We have one connection between them. We just need to find more. We can start with Solana if you want, see if any of the other victims knew her or anyone that was in her classes, and go from there."

"We can do that." Mari nodded. "So, what did Inspector Gadget want today? You've been very quiet about that since you came in."

"There is the possibility that we have a new tool to use," Jake said and explained to him about the meeting with Aled Mustatti at the prison.

It was Mari's turn to scowl, and Jake couldn't blame him. Mari had suffered months, right along with him, of waiting to see if he would suddenly burst into flames after Birthright had given him the drug.

"Why did he ask for you? Surely the police are more useful to him?" he asked.

Jake actually debated telling him a fib but if he started down that road with Mari, it would not end up any place he wanted to be with him. "He said he wanted to speak with me because he didn't think he'd be able to convince anyone that wasn't an Elemental that he could be of use. I have my doubts, both about his reasoning and his ability. But unless we find a body, it's all conjecture anyway."

"Would it be possible, if he is what he says he is? Could he talk to dead people?" Mari asked in a serious tone. "I never met an Earth Elemental before. My grandmother never said much about them, either."

Jake had tried very hard in his life to put superstition behind him. He embraced reason and logic as a detective and knew in principle as well as practice that evidence and deduction were by far more valuable in solving a case than any 'gut feeling', no matter how much stake novels and movies put in that. Still, he could not stop the grimy sensation that crawled across his skin and raised the fine hairs on the back of his neck.

"It's a very, very uncommon ability. One of the rarest, as a matter of fact. Research suggests a lot of doubts to the validity of those that have claimed to be able to speak to the dead, and there has been a lot of speculation as to how such cases could have been faked. I've never met anyone, Earth Elemental or otherwise, who could actually talk to the spirits of those that have passed. That said, there remain certain unexplained phenomena and some descendants of Earth Elementals who swear the gift runs in their bloodline."

Mari wriggled around to face him. "You don't believe him, do you? How odd. You supported that Solana woman's claims to be able to help. Why is he different?"

"I didn't say I don't believe him. He claimed he's already done it and is willing to prove it if given the chance. I've no reason not to believe him. It's just…" Jake hesitated. Trying to explain the strongly ingrained cultural taboo to Mari was bound to make him feel ridiculous. The truth was, half his disgust at the idea was due to early and repeated indoctrination about the heinous nature of the act Aled proposed to do. The Christian concepts of Heaven and Hell, God and the Devil, absolute good and absolute evil, did not exist among the beliefs Jake had been raised with. But disturbing the dead was just about the most profane act one could commit.

"It's just… It's wrong, okay. The dead should be left in peace," Jake finished lamely.

"If they've been murdered, they're not likely to be in much peace," Mari pointed out. "How interesting. I mean...clearly he's a hideous man, but if he's not lying, maybe he can help."

"I'm not a very spiritual person, Mari. Logic says, this shouldn't bother me, and if it stops this depraved scumbag from hurting any more people, I will do what has to be done. That doesn't mean I have to like it. It's...disrespectful. To make the dead speak, to force his will into the body and hold their spirit here. I find the thought of that repulsive."

"It is rather horrible," Mari agreed, wincing. "If he can help them, will they be able to pass on? It could be a horrible thing for a good reason, is all I'm saying. I'm glad that's not my gift, though."

"I'm not sure I would call it a 'gift'," Jake said. "And, I have no idea what he can and can't do. My research tells me there is only a narrow window of time that the dead can be made to speak, I guess he can't hold whatever is left of them here indefinitely."

"And he's kind of presuming that one of them, sooner or later, isn't going to make it." Mari shivered. "How gruesome. He seems to have been thinking about this case far too much."

"I don't think he gives two shits about this case. It's convenient for him. Nothing more. If he can prove this new talent he claims to have is helpful, it will look good to the parole board. Worse, if he can actually speak to the dead, it would not surprise me at all if his sentence was commuted and he was offered a job, possibly by your own bosses."

"I can understand you not liking him. I don't like those Birthright bastards, either, and I never met them properly. But after the things they did to you..." Mari leaned against him from cheek to hip, a warm line down the side of his body. "That's not a comfortable thought. I knew they had all kinds of Elementals working with them, I just never had much to do with anyone that wasn't Air until I met you. It's kind of weird to find out there are people who can do even freakier stuff. And while Ashcroft is a decent boss, I still wouldn't put it past him to farm me out to the highest bidder if the chance came up. It's rather disconcerting. For the first time in my life I'm happy and I'm trying not to be afraid, but what we do is always going to be on the edge, isn't it? There are always going to be organizations trying to use us."

He curled up and wrapped his arms around his knees, looking all of a sudden like a child contemplating a world without Christmas.

"Why do you think I came here and joined the Program? You're right. We are vulnerable to a lot of people who would like to use us. The more people discover we're real people, they more they learn what we can and can't do, the harder it will be for them to cart us off in secret." He put his arms around Mari and kissed the top of his head. "You know, Solana's gift is nearly as rare as Aled's supposed ability. Water Elementals with any sort of talent tend to either read auras or are empathic. Very few can truly heal people."

"We don't have any actual proof that she can heal people, yet," his lover muttered under his breath.

"Hypothetically," Jake said, and kissed him again, on the cheek this time. "Your own ability is pretty rare as well, though not as rare as the Air Elementals that are remote viewers. As far as I'm aware, all of them have been snapped up by various military organizations."

"Like Great-Grandmama." Mari gave a rueful nod. "Damn it. No wonder she went insane. If I didn't have you, I'd probably be on my way to following her. I wish I was as grounded as you, Chivis. You just seem like…you're bombproof, somehow. I have no idea how you manage that when your gift is potentially even more volatile than mine."

Jake kissed his hair again. "You're in a dark place tonight. What's wrong?"

Mari leaned back in his arms and touched his mouth to Jake's. "I think it's just this case, and the worry about Mama. I'll be fine. I always am. It was just bugging me today, talking to Natalie. She was trying to be strong and such a terrible thing had happened to her but she seemed like a smart, sorted kind of girl. I just thought it was unfair. I wanted to be able to string up the bastard that did that to her so she didn't have to feel afraid of him every time she steps outside her flat. No one should have to be afraid like that."

"Maybe you missed your calling. That's exactly why I became a cop. We'll get him, and we'll stop him. It won't change what happened, but at least he won't be able to do it to anyone else."

Mari kissed him again, letting his lips linger longer this time. He twined himself around Jake like a sinuous vine.

"Did you get wet?" Jake teased when they broke the kiss, knowing that it hadn't rained at all.

"I was warm when I got back from Blackheath. I took a shower. There didn't seem much point getting dressed again," Mari said, ever practical.

"No, I don't suppose there was." Jake slid his hands under Mari's shirt and kissed him again, seeking this time, inviting.

Mari was more than willing to accept the invitation. He was already tugging and popping the buttons out of Jake's shirt and he kissed the line of his exposed collarbone as he unfastened all the way to Jake's belt, getting to work on the buckle.

"Eat something," he said imperiously. "It will go cold and I already had some."

Then, as if he'd not just spoken, he unbuttoned Jake's jeans and worked the zipper down, his lips sucking and pecking a slow line down Jake's bared chest and belly as he did so.

Jake laughed. "Is this payback for the other day? I can't eat while you're doing that, Mari."

Mari knelt up astride his thighs like a mischievous imp, his pale hair tousled and wayward. He reached for the chopsticks and the takeaway carton and proceeded to feed morsels to Jake, ignoring his protests. "You need to keep your strength up. And I know you like this. I ordered it on purpose. I'm not going to do anything else until you've finished it. But when you have, I expect you to be very badly behaved indeed."

He managed to chew and swallow what was in his mouth and Mari seemed content to feed him and wiggle in his lap as Jake caressed him all over. There was something very sensual in being fed like this, and while Jake might have protested that he could eat later, he didn't, simply enjoying Mari's company and attention instead, allowing the teasing to build up to something more.

It wasn't the first time they'd somehow made a mealtime into a more sensual experience, but each time it happened, Jake had the sense that it was something of a ritual for his lover, that he enjoyed this small element of control before giving himself up to their lovemaking. Last time it had been him ordering Mari to eat, but even then, he'd had a curious sense that Mari was pulling his strings. Not that he was upset by that.

"You look very mysterious," Mari remarked. "Like you're plotting something secretive. Should I be worried?"

"I'm just picturing how you'll look on your knees with my dick in your mouth," Jake told him.

Summer-sky-colored eyes fixed on him and the thin cotton of Mari's underwear couldn't hide what that comment did to his lower regions. He didn't blush, though. Jake had never managed to embarrass him, no matter how crude he got. Emotions sometimes unsettled his lover, but sex never did.

"Eat faster," Mari said with a gleam in his eye.

They had the container emptied in record time, in part because Mari ate half of it while Jake was still chewing. Once they were done eating, Jake pulled Mari's shirt off and pushed his fingers down the waistband of his briefs. Mari was already hard and a few firm strokes had him moaning into Jake's mouth.

He slid one hand into Jake's underwear and kept the other on his shoulder as he reciprocated the sweet favor, stroking with his thumb pad up and down under the head of Jake's stiffening cock. His lips kept up a slow caress on Jake's mouth as they worked each other. After a few minutes, Mari slid down his legs and hooked his fingers into the waist of his jeans and boxers, pulling them down until they were around his knees.

"That's better," he murmured as he knelt up and gripped Jake's cock again. He wrapped his lips around the head and drew him into his mouth.

Jake let out a shaky breath. He slid the fingers of one hand into Mari's hair, caressing along his scalp. "Ooh yeah…"

Mari lifted his head and plunged down a few times and Jake tilted his hips to meet him in small thrusts. "Mmm…that feels so good."

Mari's response was a muffled exhortation to go faster.

"Ah, fuck…" Jake moaned back. He tightened his fingers in Mari's hair and controlled the nod of his head because he knew how hot that got Mari, and it got him hot, too.

Mari's low growl shivered through the sensitive shaft of his cock and he shoved his pants to his ankles and wriggled between his knees. Jake bucked his hips in time with the bob of Mari's head. The feel of Mari's hot mouth on him, the way he took him down deep then shallow and fast, had him so hard it was only minutes before his peak was very close. He tipped his head and closed his eyes as the first sweet spasm hit and flooded Mari's delicious mouth.

When Mari came up, he wiped his lips on the back of his hand and planted soft kisses on Jake's belly. He slid back onto the couch, draped himself around Jake and rolled up against him. His body was beautiful, lean and hard and perfect, the muscles well defined under his pale golden skin, jeweled with sweat.

"Touch me," Mari implored, his voice shaking. "Stroke me."

Jake wrapped his fingers around Mari's turgid shaft without hesitation, stroking him with a slow, firm hand, his thumb sweeping to and fro over the silky crown, spreading the slippery spill of his pre-cum. After a minute or two, he jacked him faster and moved his lips to Mari's neck, nipping and sucking small kisses there.

Shivers rippled through Mari's muscles and he let out a hungry groan, rolling his hips and thrusting into each downward stroke of his fist. Jake wasn't sure what was hotter, having Mari blow him or watching him inch up slowly toward his climax, knowing he was responsible for all the pleasure on Mari's pretty face.

"Mmhhhhh...ohhh...Jake! *Jake!*" he yelped. "Yes... Yes!"

Jake sucked harder at the warm, silken skin of his neck and pumped him faster to bring him off. His cock grew even harder, just before a spurt of creamy semen spattered on his stroking fist.

Mari curled around him, burying his face in the curve of Jake's neck and shoulder, panting like he'd just run a mile at speed. Frantic whimpers escaped his throat and he shuddered, restless in the throes of his ecstasy.

"Ohhh...you are so good at that," he crooned at last, lips close to Jake's ear. "Thank you."

Jake uttered a contented rumble and kissed him. "Dinner and a blow job. You are the best boyfriend ever."

"Don't you forget it," Mari whispered into his mouth. A fond smile twitched at his wet lips as he pushed himself to his feet. Naked and glistening, he took the empty cartons over to the trash and dumped the utensils in the basin.

"Shower?" Mari asked.

"Shower," Jake agreed, and levered himself up.

Chapter Eighteen

Mari stayed the night at Jake's, so he didn't get back to his own house until later the next day. In a way, he had been avoiding going home since the other morning. He was still angry about the photograph and the way Mama had outed him to Jake without even consulting him. He hated arguments, especially with her, and it had been easier just to stay at Jake's place until he'd cooled down.

He spent the morning at work with a young woman from the Foreign Office, trying to show her how he could still get into their computer files, even after they'd thought they'd put a fix on their database to keep him out. She was a smart girl, very chatty and enthusiastic, but he got the impression that she was scared of him, too. Mindful of Jake's warnings about not being an asshole, he was sweetness and light with her for the entire morning, and she went away with a list of recommendations for upgrading her department's security and a smile on her face.

Ashcroft was pleased and he gave Mari the afternoon off.

The downside of that was, after a pleasant walk along the embankment and a tube ride up to Camden Town, he was facing a confrontation with Mama again. Mari went shopping first to put off the inevitable for as long as possible. He bought a woven silk scarf in dark red that he thought would look good on Jake and a pair of elegant, dark blue boots for himself from one of the shops on the high street. On the way home to Albany Street, he also bought a large bunch of flowers, figuring that apologizing in advance was his best approach.

Tonka barked and skittered down the hallway to greet him as he let himself in, and he pushed the door shut behind him and juggled his purchases in one hand while trying to subdue his enthusiastic dog with the other.

"Shushhh…yes. Yes… I love you," he promised as Tonka bounced all over him and tried to lick him. "Slobbery dog! Settle down!"

The door at the far end of the hallway opened wider and he lifted his head as Mama peered out at him. She looked tired, he thought, and worried.

"Is everything okay? You're home early," she said, a wary note in her voice that put him on guard again.

"It's fine. I'm finished for the day. I brought you some daffodils," he said, holding up the bouquet as evidence. "If Tonk doesn't try to eat them, that is."

Mama called to him and Tonka gave Mari a last proprietary swipe with his tongue before he turned and trotted back to her, tail wagging.

"Someone is pleased to see me, at least," he observed, under his breath.

His mother took the flowers without a word but dipped her face into the blooms to inhale the spring sweetness.

"They're lovely. Thank you. You didn't need to bring flowers," she said at last. "I was just wondering if you were going to come home, or…" She shrugged, uncharacteristically lost for words.

"Are you going to tell me you're sorry, or shall we just keep pretending it didn't happen?" he asked her. Straight off, he saw an image of Jake in his head, holding up a sign reading 'Asshole!'

"Were you ever going to tell him yourself?" she responded, neither apologizing nor answering the question. He silently congratulated her on using his own favorite tactics against him.

"In my own time. Maybe." He put the bags down, shrugged out of his coat and draped it over the back of the sofa, but Mama took it out into the hall, hanging it where it lived, by the door.

"Do you want tea?" she asked on her return.

"Is that it? We're going to sweep it under the carpet?" He folded his arms and tried to look serious.

"If that's what you want." Mama put the kettle on and spooned leaves into the glass pot without even glancing at him. "I take it Jake was gentle with you, since you're not here shouting and screaming at me."

"Jake is always a gentleman," he reminded her.

"Yes. He is," she agreed, finally looking up at him with tenderness that warmed some of the chill from his heart, but twisted it, too. He pushed aside the idea that she cared more for Jake than she did for him. This was not the time or place for that argument. Mama said, "You're a very lucky man, Ilmari. Not many partners, of either sex, would have taken that news so well."

"You still had no right to tell him," Mari pointed out, frowning irritably as the doorbell rang and Tonk went racing up the hallway. Only then did he observe that she'd set out three teacups. "You're expecting visitors. I'll go up."

"No. Stay," she said in a firmer voice. "Make the tea. I'll get the door."

He did as she'd told him, a frown still creasing his forehead. In the hall, Tonka uttered a single sharp bark as the door opened, but only the one. Usually that meant Jake, but Mari didn't hear him and there was no reason why Jake would have come around here at this time of the day.

When Mama returned to the day room, it was her healer who was beside her, talking to Anni in a soft voice and tickling Tonka's head, between his ears, as if she had known him for years. A hot spike of annoyance poked at Mari's gut and he whistled sharply, calling the dog to heel. Tonk proved reluctant but he came, at least, nosing Mari's fingers and sitting by him. The terrier looked at Solana with a sorry whine.

"What's going on?" Mari demanded, prey to a sudden shiver of anxiety. They both looked so serious that his first thought was the treatment was going badly and Mama was getting sicker. That was enough to push their disagreement right out of his head for the time being.

"Good afternoon, Dr. Gale." Solana said, ignoring his rudeness. "I was hoping I might see you again. I'm afraid I owe you an apology."

Mari blinked at her, wrong-footed again by her polite response. It took him a few moments to respond.

"You most certainly do," he declared at last, still half-paralyzed by the cold dread that something was terribly wrong.

"Ilmari!" Mama chided him, shaking her head.

Solana smiled at her, an expression that didn't quite reach her eyes for once. "No, it's all right, Annabel. He has a right to be angry." She returned her attention to Mari. "I'm sorry, Dr. Gale. I assumed, given your close relationship with Mr. Chivis, that he knew of your…fluctuating status. It was my indiscretion that prompted your mother to reveal your past to him."

Mari digested that while the spike of ice inside him slowly turned to a white-hot flame.

"Given your profession, I might have assumed that you'd exercise more caution when speaking of private affairs to a stranger," he snarled, furious with her. "Just because you choose to parade what you are in the public eye, you shouldn't assume that we all do."

"Ilmarinen!" his mother exclaimed in horror.

He opened his mouth then closed it again, wishing he could take the words back already, even though a darker part of him wanted vengeance. He wanted Solana to hurt the way he was hurting and didn't care how he made that happen, so long as he managed to penetrate the cloak of cool assurance she wore. Instead of saying more, he ground his teeth in frustrated silence.

To her credit, Solana didn't flinch in the face of Mari's rage. She took a deep breath and let it out slowly. "It was a mistake to speak to Jake about what I'd seen in your aura. I admit that," Solana said, her words steady and her voice still calm. "However, if I choose to present as the same gender I know I am, that is not 'parading', nor should I be ashamed of it."

"That is not what this is about." Mari pointed one finger at her like a pistol. "I'm not ashamed, Solana, I'm angry. You had no fucking right to bring it up. You did it on purpose, to mess with me. I have no idea why, but you can think yourself lucky that my partner is a good man. If your indiscretion had cost me Jake, I would be making you pay for it."

Solana shook her head in denial. "It was not done on purpose. It's very clear to me, just by looking at you, that you're…fluid. You have aspects of both sexes – or perhaps neither. If it was obvious to me, a complete stranger, I was sure someone you were intimate with would be able to see it plainly as well."

Mari bit down on what he wanted to say. His cheeks were suddenly too hot and he felt confused and foolish under her unwavering stare. Her quiet self-assurance was painful in ways that he could not even begin to analyze. Jealousy warred with the need for retribution in his head.

"That's utter sh—r—rubbish," he faltered, conscious of Mama's furious glare. "Jake doesn't… He's not… It doesn't matter to him. He loves me for who I am. But you still had no right to tell him!" He lost his stammer as he got back onto more certain ground. "You ought to respect a person's confidentiality. I love him, too. That's all that matters."

Mama touched Solana's arm with gentle fingers. "Ilmari was not in a good relationship before he met Jake."

"Mama!" he protested. "Must you?"

"I'm only trying to help, darling," she sighed. "And it's true. He did not sound like a nice man, that married fellow you were seeing in Spain."

"It's none of her business!" Mari pointed at Solana.

"You're right that I shouldn't have said anything in front of Mr. Chivis," the healer conceded, again. "I have admitted that, and I am truly sorry. I can't undo it, and I very much hope it's caused no lasting harm. I may be a healer and an Elemental, but I'm human, too, and I own up to my mistakes." She patted Anni's hand, where it still lay on her arm, and said, "Perhaps we should continue our sessions at the Retreat?"

"Perhaps you should. I don't want you in my house," Mari said, more than a shade ungracious, he knew, but he couldn't hold back. "And I don't care what you think you're doing, but I don't want my mother to continue her association with you."

"Ilmarinen! That is not your decision to make," Mama snapped at him. "Solana is doing me good, better than a lot of my conventional doctors."

"You know nothing about this person," Mari shouted, making Tonka whine again. "She could be a mass murderer for all you know. I don't trust her and I don't want her here. And I'm perfectly entitled to make that decision, thank you."

"That is quite enough, Dr. Gale," Solana said in a firmer tone. "I've apologized and you are of course under no obligation to accept it or to welcome me in your home, but you will not cause Annabel this undue stress. I can heal her. I can cure her. I've already made progress and I will not allow a petty disagreement between us to interfere with that."

"*Petty*?" Mari wanted to strangle her but he restrained himself. Still, he struggled with his conscience. Jake had warned him already not to act without evidence but he so wanted to see Solana's true face.

"Natalie Craig," he said at last, forcing calm into his voice. "How did you protect *her*? Oh...forgive me. I don't think you did, did you? And since it happened, she's been too scared to leave her house. I don't want my mother going anywhere near you, do you hear?"

Solana looked perplexed. "What are you talking about? What does Natalie have to do with this?"

Mari hesitated, thrown by her confusion. He wanted to hit out but he was less sure how to lead her where he wanted her.

"She modeled for your art group. And someone took it on himself to do something evil to her. I don't know who he was yet, but until we do, I don't want my mother to see you. Understand?"

"Ilmari, you're being paranoid and utterly unreasonable," Mama said in her most disapproving tone.

"Something happened to Natalie? When? Is she all right?" Solana asked with apparent concern.

If she was lying about her ignorance of what happened, she was a damn good actor, but Mari wasn't willing to let go of his suspicion just yet.

"No. She isn't. She's putting on a brave face but she's scared to go out in case that maniac is still around and scared to stay in alone in case he knows where she lives. She doesn't sleep well because of the dreams of being trapped underground. She's still waiting for the results of tests for sexual diseases that I'd rather she didn't have to think about. In a nutshell, she is *not* all right. She is very, very far from all right." His voice was trembling as he closed his mouth and he took a couple of quick, hard breaths.

"Jake and Mari are involved with the police investigating the Cemetery Rapist case," his mother added.

"Mama, that makes it sound like we're suspects," he protested. "Jake is a consultant on the case. I'm…assisting. And you may have just compromised the entire case."

"I think you've done that already, Ilmarinen," his mother retorted.

Solana's eyes were wide and misty with emotion. Her face had gone pale. "Annabel, if you'll pardon me, I would like to reschedule our appointment. Natalie is a friend and I had no idea this had happened to her. I need to offer my support to her."

"I think it's better that you don't have anything to do with Natalie until this case is solved," Mari said, still angry and unable to keep that fury out of his voice. "The police have spoken to her and taken evidence from the crime scene. If she's your friend, how come you had no idea? Leave her be. Let us try to catch the man that nearly killed her."

Up until that point, Solana had remained calm, poised, initially contrite but shocked by his news. She finally snapped at Mari's last shot.

"I didn't know because I don't see Natalie every day. That doesn't mean I don't care about her. I have no intention of interfering with what the police are doing, but I will see her and I will offer any comfort she wishes because that's what friends do when something terrible has happened. If you don't understand that, there is more wrong with you than even I can fix. I don't like your tone, Dr. Gale, and I don't like your insinuation I'm somehow responsible for what happened to Natalie. If this is how you conduct an investigation, accusing people of something vile just because you don't like them, perhaps you're not cut out for this type of work!"

With that, she swung around and took Anni's hands, kissing them briefly. "This is in no way your fault. Please rest and call me when you are ready."

Solana released Anni's hands and headed toward the door without another glance at Mari.

"Good riddance," he murmured under his breath, bending to fuss with Tonka's ears. When he straightened up, Mama had returned from seeing Solana off and was glaring at him from the doorway.

"Do you and Jake have even a shred of evidence that connects Solana to these crimes? Other than her happening to be a friend of one of the victims?" she demanded.

"Possibly. We have to cover every eventuality. She had the opportunity to connect with other victims. But Natalie modeled for her on a regular basis. Statistically victims of sexual assault and violent crimes know their attackers prior to the incident."

"That would be a no, then. You don't. And yet you felt compelled to accuse and insult her, the one person who has helped me to feel better and not sicker — in case you hadn't noticed." The clipped sentences told Mari well enough how upset she was. Worse, she didn't sound angry, so much as profoundly disappointed. He folded his arms and tried to look penitent.

"Mama, I just don't want to take any risks around you. You're too important to me for that. The rapist could be anyone. And just because Solana presents as female doesn't mean she's incapable of being the attacker." He was careful to moderate his tone this time, aiming for rational and concerned rather than all-out defensive. "Yes, I want you to get well. But how many times do you read in the papers, when someone is arrested for assault or murder, his family and neighbors all saying 'oh no, it couldn't be him, he was such a nice chap'? I'd rather not take the risk."

"Well, that's too damn bad, Ilmarinen. It's not your risk to take."

He stared at her, helpless and angry. "Mama, please… I can't lose you. If anything happened and I hadn't tried to protect you…it would kill me."

There was a slight softening to her features and she sighed. "I believe your anger is clouding your judgment, Mari. Solana had nothing to do with those crimes. I'm sure of it. Does Jake share your opinion that Solana is a suspect?"

Mari chewed on his lips for a moment. At last he shook his head, defeated. "Not as much as I do. No. But his mother isn't taking herbal baths with her, is she?"

His mother's expression flushed angry again. "There is absolutely nothing inappropriate going on in our sessions, and, even if there was, it would be none of your business."

He threw his hands up and Tonka stared at him and uttered a startled bark in response.

"I didn't say there was. Did I say anything at all about inappropriate? I just pointed out that the opportunity was there if she isn't to be trusted. *If*. That's all."

"I am done with this conversation, Ilmarinen. I don't want to hear another word about Solana until you're ready to make amends with her."

Mari's heart kicked against his ribs at that. Mama had always listened to him. Even when she'd believed that his decision to transition had been hasty, she'd listened and given him the benefit of the doubt. Hearing confirmation that she would support a complete stranger first hurt more than he was willing to admit.

He turned away to hide his dismay. "I'm going to take Tonka out. He needs a walk. So do I."

Chapter Nineteen

Jake had been concerned when Mari had called to tell him he just wanted to stay in and get an early night, so his first thought when his phone rang at three a.m. was that something terrible had happened.

Something terrible *had* happened, just not to Mari. The last victim of the Cemetery Rapist had succumbed to her injuries. Cordiline sounded exhausted, his voice raspy and tired on the other end of the phone as he told Jake to get down to the morgue as soon as he could.

He was out of bed and pulling on clothes as he rang Mari. "The Jane Doe in the hospital died tonight. Do you want to come to the morgue with me?" Jake asked.

"You're such a romantic." Mari's voice was husky with sleep. "Give me the coordinates and I'll meet you there."

Mari was there first, in a button-down shirt and dark blue two-piece suit, looking ridiculously smart for the time of morning and the short notice. His tousled hair was the only giveaway, and even that was artfully rumpled rather than 'just crawled out of bed' disheveled.

Jake greeted him with a quick, tired smile. At least one of them appeared somewhat professional. His own suit coat was expensive and tailored but needed to be pressed and the rasp of stubble on his chin needed to be scraped off.

Cordiline was waiting for them in the lobby.

"Dr. Gale," Cordiline said in a mild, polite tone, "I wasn't expecting you."

"Nobody expects the Finnish Inquisition," Mari murmured, and Cordiline glanced oddly at him. Jake saw the way that both men's lips twitched at the joke before the DI turned back to him. *Will wonders never cease? Common ground.*

"I thought I could use another Elemental's opinion," Jake said.

"You almost have a full set, Inspector," Mari told him. "Are we here to witness miracles?"

Cordiline sighed. "I have no idea. I suppose we'll see pretty soon if this is all just a con to get Mustatti out of his cell for a few hours. Will either of you be able to tell if what he says is the truth?"

"You'll find out for yourself if he's telling the truth about his ability," Jake said.

"What do you mean? I thought the 'séance'" — Cordiline made air quotes with his fingers — "would be Mustatti telling us what he's hearing 'from beyond'." Again, he quirked his fingers.

"You're thinking of movie psychics. An Earth Elemental that can make the dead speak does so literally."

"He's the last word in spectral ventriloquism," Mari elaborated with less subtlety. "At least, one would hope so, having thrown oneself out of bed at such an ungodly hour. If he's faking, I'm going to be very annoyed."

"You'll know if it's fake or not, believe me." Jake grimaced. "If he's for real, you'll see a talking corpse." He felt dirty just saying it and didn't want to go beyond the solid-looking doors at the end of the hall. He clamped down on the urge to say 'fuck it' and run out of the building. He wasn't afraid, not of dead bodies or ghosts, but the thought of what Aled would force that body to do made his skin crawl.

Perhaps Mari sensed it because he was the one to make the first move, touching his fingers to Jake's upper arm, light as snow, when he drew level. There was forced cheeriness in his voice now.

"Shall we see what Jane has to say for herself?"

The three of them moved down the hall and through the heavy modern double doors that had been retrofitted into the old bricks.

The autopsy room was as chilly and antiseptic smelling as any hospital OR, but the patients that landed here were unlikely to lodge any complaints. Three uniformed constables, including PCSO Ladley stood in a cluster near a metal table upon which the body of their Jane Doe was laid out. A few paces from them, wearing the standard prison garb and a set of handcuffs, was Aled Mustatti. He was expressionless until he spotted Jake, then he flashed a sardonic grin. Jake kept his own expression blank.

Cordiline made introductions and Jake and Mari shook hands with the officers.

"Detective Chivis, I wasn't sure you would come," Mustatti said.

Jake kept his game face on. "I would be a hard man to refuse, wouldn't I."

Aled's mocking smile widened. "I suppose you would. Shall we see what this poor tragic soul has to tell us?"

Jake's gorge rose but he gave no outward sign. "Time is ticking."

"Right, that it is," Aled agreed and held up his cuffed wrists. "Would you be so kind?" he said to the constable nearest him.

The man didn't seem happy to be here, and appeared even less happy to remove the cuffs, but he didn't question it, either.

Aled stepped up to the table and pulled back the sheet to the woman's waist. Jake guessed she had been pale enough in life. In death she was waxen, her skin pasty except for the livid bruising around her chest and throat. She was dark-haired and small. Jake would have guessed she had been in her late teens, far too young to be lying in this cold room.

When he looked up, Aled was watching him.

"Ah, there's an emotion. I was starting to think you didn't have them," Aled said.

"You think this is funny? There's a dead girl on the table — or hadn't you noticed?" Jake snapped. The cold of the room was sharp against his skin as his body temperature rose with his anger.

"No, I don't think it's funny. Not at all, Detective." He glanced at Mari. "You can come closer if you want. I can see you're curious, and I'll wager you won't witness anything like this again in your lifetime."

Mari hesitated, inching closer at last, so that he was standing adjacent to Jake on the opposite side of the mortuary table from Aled. His face was pale but his eyes glittered beyond his long, tawny lashes, the only hint of any emotion in his features.

"Can she feel anything?" he asked, his gaze moving from the silent body of the fourth victim to the tall, dark-skinned stranger across from them.

"She is beyond feeling," Aled said in a gentle tone.

Jake knew it was meant to sound soothing but it just rang false to him. He had to struggle with his temper for a moment. He heard more mockery in that response than was probably there, and he wanted to punch the man for lying to Mari, with his tone if not his words.

He had time to do neither as Aled put one hand on the girl's forehead and the other on her sternum. In the movies, there might have been flickering lights, a ghostly wind, perhaps some eerie music. None of that happened. In fact, nothing at all happened for almost a full minute.

Out of the corner of his eye, Jake could see Mari watching intently. He didn't look disgusted. His expression conveyed more of a detached fascination to Jake.

Aled opened his eyes. The dark brown was obscured by a milky film and his features were slack. He lifted his hands from the girl's body and her eyes opened as well. There was a gurgling, choking sound coming from her throat and her tongue protruded between her lips.

"Jesus H. Christ…" Jake heard Cordiline murmur behind him.

"Speak. Tell us your name," Aled commanded.

The girl's head lifted then slammed against the metal table. Her throat worked and her tongue darted in and out from between her blue lips.

"Speak!" Aled demanded again.

"Christa," the girl rasped. "Where am I?"

Aled ignored the question and focused his milky eyes on Jake. "What do you want me to ask her?"

"Last name. Address. Did she know her attacker?"

"What was your last name?" Aled said.

The girl, Christa, twisted her head back and forth but the rest of her body was quite still. Her breath sounded labored, and a greenish fluid was leaking from the corner of her mouth. One of the PCs stumbled away, retching.

"Burns," she said at last.

"Where did you live?"

"Do you have to ask in the past tense?" Jake said.

"She's dead, Detective. It doesn't matter," Aled said. "Where did you live?" he asked again.

She gave the address and Jake saw Cordiline scribble it on a pad of paper.

"Do you remember what happened to you?" Mari asked.

"She won't answer you, Dr. Gale," Aled murmured. In a more strident tone, he said, "Christa. Tell me what you last remember."

For a short while, her head turned slowly from side to side, as if she were denying him, but at last she wailed, an anguished sound that hurt Jake's ears.

"Choking. I can't breathe! I can't *breeeaaathheee!*"

"Stop! Who choked you?" Aled's voice cut through the wail and for a moment she was silent. There was no resentment in her face but, to Jake, it seemed as if she tried to deny him every step of the way.

"He did."

"Who? Give me a name."

Her head shook for a longer time.

"He did," she repeated, her words atonal.

"Who choked you? What was his name?"

"He did," she said again, without elaboration.

"Ask if she knew him," Jake prompted, his police instincts kicking in and overriding the disgust that made him want to puke right here on the mortuary floor. The cold, sweet stink of death and the sharp tang of disinfectant and embalming fluids filled his senses and he thought he would never be rid of them.

Aled asked the question and Christa answered.

"Yes."

"Where did she see him?" Jake asked and, like an automaton, Aled repeated the question.

"Home."

"Did he live with her?"

"Near."

The corpse started to make choking sounds that soon resolved themselves into soft sobs, although her eyes remained open and tearless.

Mari's fingers were at work on his tablet already, taking notes, searching for information, though his horrified gaze returned periodically to Christa's face. His wide eyes glittered with unshed tears.

"Let her go," he said, his voice no more than a hoarse whisper. "I've got her social media feed. We can track her from here."

"She can't or won't give us a name. Ask her if she knew his name," Cordiline said.

Aled asked the question.

"No. No name," came the strained answer from blue swollen lips.

"If you have any more questions, ask them fast," Aled said hurriedly. Sweat was beading on his brow and his dark skin had an ashen cast to it.

"What did he look like?" Jake asked.

Aled repeated the question and there was another long pause before Christa said, "Through the camera."

"Ask again," Jake said with more urgency.

Aled did, but after a moment or two, she went completely still, her wide-open eyes staring up at the ceiling. Aled asked twice more but there was no response and he stumbled back from the body, closing his own eyes and gasping for breath.

"That's it. That's all I can do," he said and if he was feigning the exhaustion, he was a better actor than Jake gave him credit for.

No one spoke, no one moved. The room was filled with the sound of harsh breathing. After a moment, Jake reached over and gently closed Christa's eyes, then pulled the sheet over her again with careful hands. He moved away from her and from Mustatti. Aled was right about her being dead, beyond sensing their words or touch, but that didn't do anything to erase the uncomfortable idea that they had violated her again.

"Detective..." Aled called to him but Jake didn't turn. "Jake, I'm sorry. I hope this makes up for what I did to you."

Jake swung around. He grabbed Aled by the throat and slammed his head against the wall before anyone else moved. The taller man flailed at him, trying to break his grip, but Jake was stronger.

Cordiline and the other male police officer were on them both in moments, prying them apart. Mari was seconds behind, having stopped to place his tablet on the edge of the stainless-steel mortuary table. He focused his attention on Jake, undeterred by his partner's efforts to shake him off and go for Aled again.

"Sshhhhh… Jake…no. Let it go. He didn't have to help us," he said, his voice low but still hard edged. "Leave it. Come away. We've got enough."

"You should watch your temper, Jake. You can't afford to get this angry," Aled taunted him.

"Whose fucking fault is that?" Jake shouted at him.

Aled looked surprised. "You're still angry about the drug? But it was worth the price, wasn't it? I figured you were only mad about the other thing…"

Jake lunged at him again, somehow getting an arm free from Cordiline. He threw a right hook and his fist landed square on Aled's jaw, sending him reeling back into the arms of the PC that was more holding him up than holding him back.

"That's enough! Get out of here!" Cordiline barked, grabbing Jake again and shoving him away. The strength behind that push was controlled. He could feel that, if it came to blows, they would be well-matched. "Go home, Jake. Now."

Jake saw red, but he was not so crazed that he was willing to end up in a cell next to the scumbag who was still holding his face and moaning. Nor did he want to fight with John over this. He turned around and stalked out through the double doors before he did something he knew he'd regret.

Mari hesitated only long enough to grab his tablet and stuff it into his messenger bag. He flashed Cordiline an apologetic look.

"Thank you. That was truly fascinating. I ought to…" He waved a hand in the direction Jake had gone.

Cordiline nodded but said, "I want both of you in my office, at Kentish Town, at eight a.m. sharp. Understood?"

"Perfectly." Mari was already heading for the door.

"Tell your boyfriend that if he pulls a stunt like that on me again, he's off this case," Cordiline shouted after him.

The door banged shut and Mari hit the steps up to street level at a run. There was no sign of Jake when he got out of the building, so he turned for home, following his instincts, moving at a brisk trot, since he wasn't dressed for a full out sprint. When he rounded the next corner, he caught sight of Jake's familiar, tall figure, brooding shoulders hunched against the light morning drizzle that had begun to fall while they were inside. He stretched to a run to catch up with him but gave Jake some space once he had drawn level. The reasons for his anger were hardly mysterious. Aled Mustatti's organization, Birthright, had abducted Jake and injected him with an experimental drug that subjected him to the risk of bursting into flames if he got too stressed. But he wasn't currently doing his stress levels much good, in Mari's opinion.

"Are you okay?" he asked at last, when Jake failed to acknowledge him after they had matched strides for a whole block. "I mean...apart from the obvious. You know, the girl. Aled being a prick. Apart from all that."

"I don't think I'm about to combust, if that's what you asking," Jake snapped. He came to an abrupt halt and took a deep breath. "I'm sorry. That wasn't fair." He reached out and pulled Mari into an embrace. "I'm okay."

After the day he'd had, to be held was nice. Mari slid his arms around Jake, glad that his anger wasn't anything else that might come between them. He curled his fingers around the back of Jake's neck, drawing him closer, with his cheek on his shoulder. In this position, he could rub his face in Jake's hair and breathe in his familiar, comforting scent.

"What he did was horrible, but it will help us catch her killer," he promised, his voice gone husky with the emotions he'd struggled to restrain in the morgue. "Isn't that worth playing nice with him for a while?"

"He's a disgusting sack of shit," Jake said.

"I agree. But he volunteered to do this thing. I can't imagine that it was a pleasure for him. It certainly wasn't for the rest of us," Mari whispered into his hair.

"He doesn't care that she's dead. He's trying to get early parole. That's all." Jake fumed.

Mari let him go and stroked light fingers down Jake's unshaven cheeks once they stood facing each other again.

"What's wrong, Chivis? It's not normal for you to fly off the handle like that. He's paying for his crime. Isn't that enough?" he asked, choosing his words with care. "And what did he mean, 'you were only mad about the other thing'? That wasn't to do with the drug, was it? What was he talking about?"

"Nothing." Jake started walking again.

Mari turned and followed. "Jake..."

"Goddamn it. I knew it was a bad idea to put you in the same room with him," Jake seethed.

"If you don't want to talk about it..."

"No. I don't. He's a fucking pervert. That's all that needs to be said...*ever*," Jake responded in clipped sentences.

Mari stopped in his tracks, perplexed by this. For the second time in twenty-four hours, he had no idea what was going on. It was not a feeling he wanted to get used to.

"Don't you start blaming me for everything as well, Jake Chivis," he warned, raising his voice, since Jake hadn't stopped walking. "If you didn't want me there, you shouldn't have called me. Don't feed me half a story then stomp off like it doesn't matter."

Mari broke into an automatic trot to keep up with Jake because it was that or shout to be heard, but he stopped again, cursing under his breath. After Barcelona, he had promised himself that he wouldn't go chasing after guys who strung him along, yet here he was again. Only with Jake, he had let himself hope it could be different.

Damn it! It *had* been different. What on earth was wrong? His temper was piqued, though.

"Cordiline says if you play up like that again, you're sacked!" he yelled at Jake's retreating back. "I'm going home, to bed. We have to be at the cop shop by eight o'clock!"

Then he turned and stalked off the way he had come. There would be no trains at this unholy hour and it was going to be a long walk if he couldn't find a cab.

Chapter Twenty

Jake knew he should go after Mari, explain, or at least apologize for barking at him. He couldn't bring himself to do it, though. Instead he headed home to change, then went to the gym. There was no way any amount of talk could help him calm down. This was one of those rages where he needed to pound something until he couldn't move, then afterward he might be able to think.

It had been many years since he'd needed to do that. The fact that it was Mustatti who'd driven him to that point only fueled his anger. The gym was almost full, all the early birds getting their workout done before heading off to their day jobs. Even so, most of them took one look at Jake's dark scowl and gave him a wide berth.

After he had lifted enough weights and done enough pull-ups to make his arms ache, he beat the heavy bag until his knuckles were raw and bloody and he was drenched in sweat. There was just enough time left to shower and change before heading to the station.

Jake was calmer, having burned off most of his angry energy, but it hadn't helped clear his head any. He was going to have to tell Mari what Aled had done to him. Even if Mari didn't push him for an answer, the evasion would settle between them like an uncomfortable wedge otherwise.

First, they needed to deal with Cordiline and whatever Mari had unearthed. Jake knew his lover well enough to guess he wouldn't have gone back to bed. Mari had probably figured out more about the girl in five minutes than Cordiline's crew had found in two hours.

Jake was prepared for a dressing down as soon as he set eyes on John's stormy face. Mari already sat across from the DI, one knee crossed over the other, his expression composed. Jake took the empty seat next to him and braced himself.

"Mustatti decided he didn't want to press charges," Cordiline said without preamble.

Jake nodded.

"I'm giving you the benefit of the doubt, Chivis, because I think he deserved what he got and more, but I'm sticking my neck out for you and I'd damn well appreciate it if you'd remember that."

"Understood," Jake said.

"Good." Cordiline turned his attention to Mari. "What have you got for us, Dr. Gale?"

Mari's limpid eyes were still on Jake and he mouthed one word. "Okay?"

Jake gave him a nod, torn again by the combination of worry and frustration in that gaze. He knew Cordiline would have kept his secret, more so the harder Mari pushed him for the truth. There were no fears there, but he hated the concern it put in Mari's eyes.

To all intents satisfied—if not happy—with his response, Mari returned his attention to the slim tablet in his left hand. He tapped the screen with his index finger.

"Christina Jayne Burns, aged nineteen, Scottish father, half-Italian mother. Youngest of five children. The only girl. She had lived in London for eighteen months—the rest of her kin are in the North East. Her brothers are already stirring things up online, so the family has presumably been notified." He looked at Cordiline, who confirmed it with a grim nod. It was every cop's least favorite job, informing the next of kin. At least John Cordiline had been spared that task by lack of proximity.

Mari dropped his gaze to the screen with a wry, humorless twist of his lips. "Christa was another student. She wanted to be a fashion designer but she modeled on the side, for extra money, and worked for a supermarket in Earl's Court. Her modeling assignments were interesting. Some of the photos are on her social media pages."

He tapped the screen again and showed them a montage of images, most of which showed a small, pretty girl, half-dressed or naked—it was often hard to tell—and smeared in mud. Or paint designed to look like mud. That was also difficult to distinguish from the photographs.

"Do you know who took these?" Cordiline inquired.

"The photographer is someone she calls 'Stella May'." Mari frowned.

"That could be a name and a date?" Cordiline suggested.

"Maybe?" Mari didn't sound too sure, though. He scrolled through the photographs. There were a lot of them. At last he hit a particular image. "This one is shared from another source but the original webpage doesn't exist anymore."

He tilted the tablet again to show an image of Christina with wet hair, dressed only in a purple bath towel. The image seemed artistically blurry until Cordiline, astute as ever, remarked, "That looks like someone snapped it through her bathroom window on a long lens."

"Ten points to Kentish Town," Mari told him, without looking up. "Christa shared it with her friend by private message before it went public. She thought that a guy across the courtyard from her flat was spying on her. She found this posted on one of his social media pages. I think she re-posted it on her page to shame him."

"If it was the killer, he may have taken it as a challenge or a sign that she was interested instead," Cordiline mused, casting a speculative glance at Jake. "We've already pulled in a team to question the occupants of the flats where she lived."

"In that case, you should get them to check out flat four-oh-four," Mari said darkly.

They both turned toward him. Mari tapped his screen again and showed them.

"I've been running in and out of all the hits on her various pages all morning and one of the hits came from a user that called himself variously Sep, SG, Grace and one spooky-looking thing that just has a crux decussata—that's ah, a saltire or St. Andrew's Cross, you would say over here—with nails in it as his profile name. He appears to have been stalking her online. He uses different identities, as I said, but they all tie back to the same ISP. He never talks but he likes her pictures—especially the nude ones. He's been in and out, viewing them more than a few times."

"You presume the stalker is male," Cordiline said.

"His profiles claim he's male," Mari clarified. "In any case, I checked out some of his online presence and ran a trace to his phone company. He lives in Christa's block. Number four-oh-four—it's a bedsit apartment rented in the name of Joseph St. Andrews. Joseph has been registered as a student at Central St. Martin's for three years. He has a work permit and has been employed as a bartender and casual garden maintenance worker. He also draws an online cartoon that you both should see."

He gave the screen a final tap, turned it around and handed it to Cordiline with a sigh of disgust. For several moments, Jake and Cordiline studied the webcomic. The content depicted a number of women being stalked individually by a shadowy character. On every page the stalking led to a graphic rape scene, then finally to the women each being buried alive and struggling to escape the grave, all done with a keen sexualized horror.

"Considering that these were drawn by someone that lives across from a girl that was raped and buried alive, I'd say that's pretty damning," Jake murmured.

"We'll bring him in. Thank you. Both of you, for your help on this case," Cordiline said.

Chapter Twenty-One

"Well, that was a surprise," Mari said, as Jake slid an arm through his on the way down to the street. "Do you think that the other girls were practice for him? Was he building up for the attack on his neighbor the whole time?"

"I don't know, it's possible," Jake said. "I suppose they will find out, once they have him in custody."

Jake fell quiet again until they were outside. "I'm sorry I snapped at you earlier."

Mari tugged him closer to his side and turned his head to snatch a quick kiss.

"It doesn't matter. He riled you up, I understand. I just wish I knew why you let him get to you. Normally, you're laid back about everything, borderline horizontal."

They walked down the pavement together and Jake silently mulled over what he wanted to say for a few moments. Steeling himself, he said, "The experiment with EQ10 wasn't the only experiment Birthright was doing."

Mari frowned at the apparent non sequitur and Jake went on.

"After their first attempts with the drug failed, they decided that if they couldn't get a viable subject without the person eventually bursting into flame, that perhaps the enhanced abilities could be passed on through genetics. They were planning to breed a bunch of enhanced Fire Elementals."

Mari stared at him for a moment, eyes wide and incredulous. "I thought you told them that you weren't interested in women."

"I did." Jake wanted to look away but Mari's gaze had him pinned like a deer in the headlights. His expression slowly changed and Jake could almost see the cogs turning.

"That didn't matter to him, did it? He just wanted you to…donate? Is that why you're so mad at him?"

"Mari…when I came to from the sedatives they gave me, I was tied to a bed. Mustatti had his hands down my pants and was scooping my semen into a collection cup. That what he was talking about. That's why he makes me sick," Jake said plainly.

Mari blinked at him. "Why the fuck didn't you tell me this? I would have held him down for you to kick, and Cordiline and the cops could go screw themselves. I'm the only guy that gets to play in your pants."

He slid his arms around Jake and pulled him closer, planting a lingering kiss on his mouth.

"I didn't tell you because it wasn't worth telling. There was nothing that could be done to change it. I just wanted to forget about it. And I would have never thought of it again if I hadn't had to see him."

"Does he know?" Mari looked back in the direction of the police station and Jake didn't have to ask who he meant.

"I didn't tell him what happened, but yes. He was the lead detective that processed the crime scene. He asked if I wanted to press charges for the sexual assault and I said no. That was the end of it."

Mari looked perplexed. "Why?"

"If there's no charge, the police won't proceed," Jake said, keeping his voice patient.

"No. I mean, why didn't you press charges?" Mari persisted. "He molested you."

Jake just shrugged. "There are a lot of reasons, Mari. I'm gay, so I might not be believed. I'm male, so does it matter if another guy comes on to me? It would have been a circus and it was already that. It didn't seem worth it to go through the hassle when he was already on his way to prison."

"I want to hurt him," Mari growled, "and not in a good way."

Jake put his arm around Mari's waist. "Yeah. That's another reason I didn't tell you."

Mari leaned against him so that their heads rested together for a moment. "I hate that I have to go to work. I want to take you home to your place and comfort you."

Jake slid his hand up to the nape of Mari's neck, kneading there with gentle fingers for a moment.

"You can comfort me later." He gave him a brief, tender kiss. "You did good work today, Mari. If the neighbor is our guy, though, you might have to eat a bit of crow over Solana."

"There is that." Mari pulled a face. "I think I may have to eat the whole fucking crow, actually. Damn it!"

"It's part of the job. You get used to it after a while."

"I'm not sure I want to get used to it." Mari linked arms with him again and they walked on for a time. "I did a bad thing, Jake. I know you told me not to be an asshole, but I was worried. I told Solana I didn't want her to treat my mother. And Mama called me out on it. She kind of ripped me a new hole and said she'd do what the heck she wanted. I am going to have to swallow an awful lot of humble pie with her, and she is not going to let me forget it."

He looked crestfallen and rather lost, in spite of his more recent success.

"Yes, you will. But Anni doesn't seem the type to gloat, not for long anyway. I'm sure she'll be relieved enough that she won't take it out on you too badly."

"Maybe not, but Solana will. You can bet your life. She is going to love every minute." Mari ground his teeth with an irritable scowl.

"You're going to tell her that you're sorry?" Jake asked.

"By the time the real story gets out, I don't see that I'm going to have much choice. It's that or emigrate," Mari conceded.

"Chalk it up to a lesson learned, babe. Don't point a finger at someone until you're sure you're pointing in the right direction."

"How did I get myself such a smart, handsome man?" Mari wondered aloud, in a rueful tone. "I love you, Detective Chivis."

Mari went in to work after his meeting with Jake and Cordiline but he found it hard to pay attention to the job in hand. His concentration finally failed him at half past eleven when he received a call from Jake telling him that the raid on flat four-oh-four had failed to net their suspect. The property was empty. Their bird had fled. St. Andrews had quit the university and his Municipal garden maintenance job the week before.

At lunchtime, Mari signed out for the remainder of the day, telling Ghislaine that his mother had a medical appointment. He grabbed a coffee and texted Jake to say that he wasn't working. In his favorite booth at the British Library, he hacked into Holmes 2, again and ran a search for Joseph St. Andrews, the name on the lease for flat four-o-four Horrocks West Court. It came up empty. Tapping the edge of his laptop screen, he decided on a different approach and ran a search through the university lists of foreign students. There was every chance that Sep was either lying about being a student or he was a British National, but the search would be easier if he could narrow it down. There was no student on the list named St. Andrews, but there was a Josep Sant Andreu Garcés, who had come over from Viladecans in Spain eighteen months earlier to study art and design.

That tied in pretty neatly with Christina Burns' course in fashion. There was every possibility that he knew her through their college. More interesting was that surname, because it wasn't the first time he'd come across it. Sant Andreu was the surname of Tomas Arregui's late mother, Elodie.

Mari closed his eyes and touched the screen of his tablet, interfacing with Josep's file at the university, and from there, backward through any online document that might give him some genealogy on their suspect. When he reached the young man's passport, he knew that he'd hit gold. His mother, Arantxa, was listed as his next of kin. He went from there to the Spanish college files on Josep and discovered that he had been a student at the Universitat de Catalunya in Barcelona, the same institution where Mari had once been employed, and where Tomas Arregui still worked. Reaching further still, he found the sponsorship documents enabling Josep to come to England to study, under a grant from the UC. His sponsor was Tomas Sant Andreu Garcés Arregui.

Mari came up gasping from the prolonged interface and blinked for a couple of moments as his body reoriented and he remembered where he was. An old man in a nearby booth looked across and frowned at him and Mari lowered his head, staring at the screen in front of him. He was shaking. Tomas had a younger sister named Arantxa. He had taken Mari with him once to a family wedding in Sant Cugat, brazenly telling his distant kin that Mari was a cousin of his wife's. Isabel had refused to go, as she was not on speaking terms with most of Tomas' kin. Arantxa had been the talk of the wedding because she was pregnant, again, and refusing to name the father of her latest baby, though she already had two other children out of wedlock to different fathers.

That much fitted in with what he knew about Josep. In all the documentation he'd found so far, there was no mention of a father. Was that why Tomas had turned up here in London? He'd claimed he was here on business, but Mari knew how Tomas Arregui worked things. It would not have taken much effort on his part to negotiate a working trip to London to see how the English were using their Elementals. That had always been his brainchild, in Barca. He was their expert on Elementals.

You fool! He put his head in his hands. *You thought he was here chasing after you and all the time he was checking up on his sister's kid. Jake is right. You think far too much of yourself, Ilmarinen Gale.*

He closed his laptop and put his equipment away. If anyone knew where Sep St. Andrews had vanished to, it was his uncle, Tomas.

"You bastard," Mari exhaled as he fished out his phone and called the number Tomas had given him a few days ago. "You knew I would wind up doing this, didn't you?"

The line rang out three, four times and just as Mari was beginning to think it would go to voice mail, Tomas answered it.

"Ilmarinen. It's good to hear from you. Did you change your mind about lunch?"

Mari swallowed twice before he could speak. Tomas always had that effect on him and he hated it. His mouth was too dry and he found himself short of breath, an anxious intern again, desperate to please.

"I need to talk to you about something," he began, keeping things formal.

"Yes, you do. I have been telling you as much," Arregui said, his voice gone very serious. "Is that why you have been avoiding me? Are you afraid to deal with the consequences of what you did?"

"I'm not afraid. And what happened when I left Barcelona was your fault," Mari told him, recovering some of his composure.

"I'm just heading back to my apartment. Your university people have seen fit to house me in a very nice place on Manchester Square for the duration of my stay. Would you like to come over there and we can talk about whatever your fickle heart desires?"

He gave Mari the address and hung up, not waiting for a response. That was so like Tomas that Mari almost gave in to the temptation to leave him hanging. It would be easier to go to Cordiline with the information and let the police deal with it. He knew Tomas Arregui, though. If the cops came sniffing around, he would politely dismiss them with apologies and excuses. Maybe he would be more forthcoming with a familiar face, or maybe not, but Mari had to try.

In his head, Jake's voice said, *What if he's harboring the killer?*

"No one knows yet," Mari mused out loud, earning him the disapproval of the man in the opposite booth, who had already shushed him once when he was on the phone. It was true, though—the police had not issued a statement. Cordiline's theory was that if they went public with a manhunt, St. Andrews would go underground and they might never find him. There was absolutely no reason for Tomas to be aware of what his nephew had done.

Unless Josep told him, Jake's voice said.

Mari shoved the rest of his belongings into his messenger bag and set off at a fast walk for Manchester Square. En route, he texted Jake.

I'm going to see Tomas. Something has come up. I think he maybe knows more about the Cemetery Rapist than he's letting on.

The apartment was in a very handsome block close to the Wallace Collection, and as Tomas opened the door and invited Mari inside, he experienced some annoyance that it was considerably bigger than the tiny set of boxes the college had given Jake. There was a comfortable-looking sofa and a large flat-screen TV in the lounge and, beyond a set of louvred doors, he could see a well-appointed kitchenette. There was no sign that Tomas had another guest.

"What will you drink?" Tomas asked him politely, heading for a maple cabinet and retrieving a bottle of Spanish brandy. "You had quite a taste for this stuff, as I recall."

"Just a splash, and plenty of soda," Mari said, though he had no intention of drinking. He just wanted to get this interview over and done. "I need to ask you something, and it's not easy to talk about."

"Isabel wanted a divorce at first," Tomas said, without turning from the cabinet where he was fixing their drinks. His tone was cool, polite, as if they were talking about something as normal as work. "She wanted the house, of course. And if she'd had her way, I would never have seen my children again. It took a great deal of negotiation to change her mind. Naturally, we no longer share a bed — or even a property — but my work always meant that we spent a lot of time apart, as I'm sure you will remember."

He turned and handed Mari a tall glass, taking a sip from his own and setting it on the low table between them.

"You saved your marriage then." Mari clutched his drink like it was a talisman to ward off evil. "Good for you. Not so good for her, I'd have thought."

"She has what she wants — my money and the lifestyle my work can buy her. Isabel is not unhappy. Arantxa persuaded her, for appearance's sake. It was not as if we were in the first throes of passion when I met you, Marijne." Tomas swallowed a mouthful of brandy and came over to the sofa, running one hand over Mari's hair.

He ducked his head, shying from the touch automatically.

"I never even realized that you were married." Mari took a tentative sip from the glass to keep his hands busy. Tomas always mixed his drinks too strong, but this was fine, quite light with a hint of afterburn from the brandy. He gulped some more for Dutch courage and put it down on the table. "You don't wear a ring. There were no photographs in your office. It wasn't until one of the girls in the office mentioned that you spent weekends in the summer with your wife and kids in Garraf that I even thought about it. Have you any idea how that felt? I'm not a homewrecker, Tomas. I would never even have looked at you if I'd guessed that you had a family."

"You know as well as I do that's a lie." Tomas sat down beside him on the sofa. "You wanted me from the moment you walked into my department. The attraction was mutual, by the way. Although I confess, I was almost fooled. When you came to the interview, I thought you were a woman."

"I was a woman." Mari fought the urge to throw his drink over the man.

"Until you changed your mind."

"Until I wasn't able to take estrogen anymore, and that's when you started to be cruel to me. I hated you for that. I still hate you." Mari picked up the glass and took another, longer drink to settle his nerves. The emotion coursing through him made his voice shake and that annoyed him.

"You were always a sucker for punishment," Tomas said, ignoring the rest of his reply. "You needed a strong male figure in your life, and I was there for you. If your daddy had whipped you more often, you might not have grown up with so many issues. Still, I'm grateful. I'd never imagined how much of a turn on that would be until you showed me what you needed."

"That's bullshit!" Mari managed a huff of mirthless indignation.

"Really? So, if I put you over my knee right now and take my belt to you, it won't get you hard?" Tomas never took his eyes off Mari's face and the intense scrutiny made him even more uncomfortable, in spite of his resolve not to let the man bully him.

"It won't make me love you," Mari muttered.

"Who said anything about love?" Tomas said, his tone scornful. "Neither of us was looking for that, Marijne. You were looking for a sugar daddy with a big cock. I was looking for Marilyn Monroe. And one day she just happened to strut into my department, in six-inch heels, like she owned the place. Shame she turned out to have actual balls instead of just metaphorical ones."

Mari put the glass down with a bang and slapped him for that. Gratifyingly, Tomas was so stunned that he shut his mouth.

"I didn't come here to listen to your fantasies, *Señor* Arregui. I need to find out where Arantxa's son is," Mari said, reaching for the tumbler again because his mouth was suddenly too dry. "I need to talk to him about some…incidents at the university campus."

Tomas looked quizzical for a moment, a small frown creasing his forehead. "You knew Josep was here?"

"Was?" Mari repeated, not bothering to answer this question. "As in 'isn't here anymore'?"

"Josep's mother asked me to come out and speak with him," Tomas said in a neutral tone. "She wants him to finish his studies in Barcelona. I agree that it will be better for him there."

Mari wasn't certain how he knew it, but something about that statement didn't ring true for him. Tomas was lying and he couldn't figure out why. He emptied the glass but was still desperately thirsty.

"I need some water," he mumbled. His tongue had grown thick and parched and he was beginning to sweat.

When Tomas didn't offer to get him a drink, he leaned forward and tried to push himself to his feet. The room lurched and he almost fell. As Tomas caught him, steadying him, he realized that the man was on his feet but he hadn't seen him rise.

"It's okay. Sit down. I'll get you something," he said and walked into the kitchenette, where he banged around in the cupboards and refrigerator for a moment, returning with a tumbler of iced water.

Mari snatched and almost dropped it, gulping it down greedily. The room was spinning and he couldn't get his balance. Mari blinked hard. He could not be drunk, not from just a shot of brandy. Again, he tried to get up, this time making it as far as the hallway, where his legs stopped cooperating and he had to catch hold of the apartment door to keep from falling to his knees. Cold panic trickled down his spine.

"Where are you going, Dr. Gale?" Tomas murmured in his ear, hooking his hands under Mari's arms and pulling him upright, leaning against him, pinning him to the door. His body seemed too warm, a stripe of heat along the length of Mari's spine. His breath was hot, billowing across Mari's cheek.

"Do you remember the first time you invited me up to your flat? You wouldn't let me screw you up against the wall, the way I wanted to. But you went down on your knees fast enough, didn't you? You always were a fantastic cocksucker. It was your saving grace."

"Fuck you!" Mari slurred, forcing his hand along the wall until his uncooperative fingers were fumbling at the door latch. Whatever Tomas had put in his brandy and soda, it had started working fast. His only chance was to somehow get the door open and yell for help.

"Mm, I think you will do just that." Tomas yanked him away and turned him in the opposite direction, confounding his hopes. "I haven't shown you the bedroom yet. You'll want to lie down in a moment. You're going to enjoy the cocktail I mixed for you to the fullest, believe me. And I will enjoy sending your hot-tempered lover the type of photos you're so fond of sending to other people's wives."

Chapter Twenty-Two

At half-past-three in the afternoon, following the unsuccessful morning raid on the Cemetery Rapist suspect's flat, Jake got a call from Cordiline. There was also a message on his phone from Mari, saying he had skipped work.

"We're working on tracking St. Andrews down, but it might help speed things up if you could tell us what he was last doing before he packed up and skipped out," Cordiline was telling him.

"Sure," Jake said. "I'll meet you there. You know the drill, though. No promises. I'll see if I can pick up any memories, but it's not guaranteed."

"Yeah, yeah, I remember. Just do your best."

Jake hung up and grabbed his jacket. Conveniently, Cordiline had sent a car to pick him up and take him right to the flat.

There was still a cordon of police incident tape across the balcony on either side of the door but the uniformed officer on duty outside waved Jake through when he arrived, and he soon found himself in a deserted flat.

"St. Andrews must have figured we were on to him," Cordiline said with a scowl. "He cleared out most of his stuff before we arrived but there's some odds and ends left."

"Okay. Keep everyone out, if you would."

"I already told them," Cordiline said. "We've got the place to ourselves."

Jake gave him a sidelong look but didn't reply. He got to work, making his slow and careful way around the mostly empty apartment and handling the few items their suspect had left behind. There wasn't much, but Jake was extra thorough. After twenty minutes of drawing blanks, Jake was about ready to give up. He took a moment to focus, sucking in a deep breath and letting it out slowly. The whole concept of being able to control his ability was still so new that he felt foolish trying. Still, giving up was not in his nature. He visualized energy flowing through him, making him stronger, and, weirdly, he did feel different. Calmer. More confident. He ran his hand over the back of a kitchen chair and got sucked into a memory so fast he was dizzied for a moment.

He focused on the man standing across from him and was so confused he wasn't sure what was going on.

Tomas Arregui was yelling at him, apparently furious about something, but he was speaking another language and Jake couldn't understand a word, nor could he understand the words coming from his own mouth. That confused him less than seeing Mari's ex here at all. What the fuck was he doing here?

They shouted at each other for a few minutes until Arregui slammed his hand on the table and made a cutting motion with his hand that ended the argument. His words grew soft, though no less intense, and Jake turned and went to the bedroom. He took down a battered case from the wardrobe and started filling it.

Jake blinked and was standing back in the present. Cordiline was watching him intently.

"You got something?"

"Yeah… Don't get your hopes up. I didn't see him making travel reservations or anything. But — this is going to sound real weird — there was a man here arguing with him, and it was someone I've met before. Someone Mari knows."

"If you tell me that Dr. Gale has been investigating suspects on his own again, I am going to be very annoyed," Cordiline told him.

"No, not as far as I'm aware, anyway," Jake said. A slow chill was starting to creep over him. "I think…" He paused then made up his mind. What he'd seen wasn't definitive of anything, but his gut was telling him he was right.

"The man's name is Tomas Arregui. He's allegedly here to discuss some research. I met him at the university. He was in this apartment. He argued with the suspect in what sounded like Spanish then St. Andrews started packing. We need to find Arregui. Fast. Before he gets the kid out of the country."

And before Mari figures out Arregui has a connection to the suspect, if he hasn't already figured it out. A ball of ice dropped into the pit of Jake's stomach.

Cordiline knew better than to argue and he was already on the phone as they headed back to his car, instructing his team to find an address for Arregui, and if possible to bring him in for questioning. For good measure, he requested that Arregui's and St. Andrews' details be sent out to the Transport Police at all of the London area airports and international rail terminals. When he finished the call, he fired a dark look at Jake.

"How is Dr. Gale linked to this guy?"

"They worked together in Catalonia," Jake answered. It wasn't a lie. If Jake's hunch was correct, he wanted Cordiline to help him find Arregui as soon as possible, not waste time wondering if Jake was jealous over an ex.

Cordiline's phone rang and he took the call.

While he was talking, Jake's phone pinged and he fished it from his jacket pocket. The ball of ice in his gut spread icy tendrils outward as he read Mari's message.

"We need to go. Now, John," he said. "Mari's gone to meet Arregui."

Cordiline juggled the phone against his shoulder while he scribbled something down on his notebook and thanked the caller. "We have an address for him."

Jake started to head toward Cordiline's car with him and the inspector stopped. "Maybe you should head home and I'll ring you if we find anything, Chivis."

The tone, and the fact that he hadn't called him Jake, told him Cordiline suspected he was holding out on him. Jake shook his head. "Let me go with you. If Mari has already figured out the connection between Arregui and St. Andrews... I've got a bad feeling. I need to come with you."

Cordiline heaved a sigh. "I get a bad feeling every time your boyfriend gets involved with one of my cases."

"Can we discuss this while you're driving?" As he spoke, he pulled out his phone to give Mari a call. The line rang out and went straight to voice mail.

"Pick up, Mari," he said, trying not to let his voice shake. "Just let me know you're okay."

Traffic could be heavy in London at the best of times and four-thirty p.m. was far from the best of times. Jake drummed his fingers against the door frame as they crawled up Oxford Street.

"It would be quicker to run," he grumbled.

A message notification popped up on the screen of his phone just as he was contemplating reaching for the door and jumping out. He opened it when he saw that Mari was the sender, frowning at the contents. It was a picture, and he had to turn the phone around twice before he realized what he was looking at.

His lover was in full screen, lying on a sofa or a bed with his arms raised and his hands above his head. At first, he thought Mari was baiting him with selfies, something he'd never needed to resort to as, most times, a straightforward invitation to come around and put Mari over his knee was enough to get Jake running. There was something about the slack-jawed set of his features and the blankness in his eyes that made Jake's hot blood run colder, though.

His hands were visible and the camera must have been above him somewhere. He had obviously not taken the picture himself.

Jake's phone pinged and when he saw it was a second message, he almost didn't want to open it. Cordiline must have seen the look on his face because he leaned across to peer at the screen while they were sitting at a red light.

"Lover boy?" he queried. "Very nice. Good abdominal definition. Did you take that?"

The ice in the pit of Jake's stomach turned to lead and he thought he might be sick. He vividly recalled Mari's less-than sheepish tone as he'd admitted to sending Tomas Arregui's wife pictures of them in bed together, after Tomas had dumped him and humiliated him.

His phone pinged at him again but Jake didn't open it. "We need to get to Arregui's flat as soon as possible. Like *now!*"

The DI floored the gas in his beat-up VW Passat as the lights changed. "Are you going to tell me what's going on?"

"The picture was just sent to me, from Mari's phone. But he didn't take the photo."

Cordiline was silent for a moment before he said, "Jake, are you sure —"

Jake cut him off before he could finish the thought. "He texted to tell me he was going to Arregui's apartment, remember? He wouldn't have done that if he wanted to hop in bed with his ex, and he certainly wouldn't be careless enough to let the bastard get ahold of his phone to document it. He did not end up in that bed willingly. I'll lay any money on that."

Cordiline swore colorfully and pulled out into faster moving traffic. He hit a switch on the dash and the windshields, front and rear, were illuminated in flickering blue light.

"I don't get to use them much," he said as a gap opened up ahead and they roared through it.

Jake forced himself to sit still as Cordiline wove through traffic as fast as he could. He kept his teeth clenched and his lips pressed together so he didn't snap at him to drive faster.

"Chivis, whatever we find at this apartment, you had better keep your head on your shoulders," Cordiline warned him. "I can't afford to have you assaulting our suspects. Understand? If you punch this guy, it could jeopardize our whole case."

"Don't worry. I won't get in the way of you arresting him."

It wasn't a promise not to punch him first, but Cordiline must have sensed it was the best he was going to get out of him. As they turned off the main road into Manchester Square, a call came through on the radio to confirm that Arregui and a passenger named Sant Andreu were booked on a flight out of Heathrow to Barcelona that evening. Cordiline requested that the passengers were to be intercepted if they showed up.

He parked on double-yellows, a couple of doors down from the apartment. A gap had just handily opened up there, as a young man in a leather jacket jumped into a gleaming Range Rover with heavily-tinted windows, pulled out and sped away with a screech of tires. Cordiline muttered something about bloody trust-fund kids but Jake was already on his way up the steps to the building, ringing all the bells until someone buzzed him through.

Cordiline caught up with him on the first-floor landing and knocked smartly on the apartment door. A few moments passed while Jake drummed his fingers against the wall. When the door opened they came face-to-face with Arregui, pulling a small cabin case, a laptop bag slung over one shoulder. His eyes widened but he covered his surprise quickly.

"Tomas Sant Andreu Garcés Arregui?" Cordiline said, in his best cop voice, holding out his warrant card. Arregui spotted Jake at his shoulder, and his gaze narrowed again.

"Yes?"

"I'm Detective Inspector John Cordiline working out of Kentish Town and this is Mr. Jake Chivis who is a private contractor working with the Metropolitan Police. We have some questions for you, sir, in relation to a recent serious offense."

"I'm sorry. I'm in a hurry, Detective. I thought you were my cab driver."

"Too bad," Cordiline said. "You can answer some questions here, or I can take you back to the station. It's up to you."

"Can we talk in the car, Inspector? I need to be at the airport in less than an hour," Tomas said in a crisp tone. "I am booked on a flight from Heathrow this evening. You can check that if you wish."

"I am aware of your arrangements, sir. Please, may we go back into the flat?" Cordiline said, keeping his tone just the right side of cordial.

"You may check the apartment if you wish, but I must leave in the next few minutes," Tomas intoned, though he stood aside for them.

Cordiline took his time opening a notebook. The old-fashioned kind made of paper and requiring a pen, which he made a show of patting his various pockets for before beginning his line of questioning. If Jake were less angry or worried, he would have appreciated it more. As it was, he only half-paid attention as Cordiline outlined the barest details of their investigation and asked him if Joseph St. Andrews was his nephew.

Jake listened to the careful answers with one ear while he moved into the living room and let his fingers trail over the sofa cushions, a lamp, the coffee table. He picked up a book and set it down. The room was almost surgically clean. There wasn't much to hold a memory even if there were one to hold.

He moved on to the kitchen. Cordiline was asking when Arregui had last seen his nephew and whether he had been in the apartment. Jake ran his fingers over the countertop, the back of a chair, willing himself to pick up something, anything. He neither expected nor cared if he saw any trace of St. Andrews. He wanted to see whether Mari had been in this building.

His hand brushed a tumbler drying in a sink rack and he was sucked into a memory.

The world looked weird, distorted. He gulped water from the glass and he could see a blurry figure from the corner of his eye, then it was behind him, murmuring in his ear. "Where are you going, Dr. Gale?"

Jake was standing in the kitchen again, staring at the glass. He could hear Cordiline's low rumble and Arregui's impatient response. He made a slow turn and went out into the hall.

There was a bathroom off the end of the corridor and a bedroom through the door on his right. He looked in but the room was empty. The bed had been stripped down to the undersheets and there was no trace of either Mari or St. Andrews, but he recognized the bedroom as the one the pictures of Mari had been taken in. He checked the closets just to be sure, then looked in the bathroom again. There was a faint, sweetish smell of vomit, masked by cleaning fluids. The basin was jeweled with water and had been freshly used. He ran his fingers over the edges of it and was sucked into another memory.

Mari's face looked back at him from the mirror, pale and blurry around the edges. He clung to the lip of the washbasin to keep his balance, his stomach still churning as he washed the taste of vomit from his mouth. He heard the murmur of low, angry voices in the hall and at first was frustrated again because they weren't speaking in English. Then one of them switched and he caught a few words.

"No...you call me an idiot...take him...meet you at Heathrow..."

That was all he could make out before a tall, bearded young man appeared in the reflection at his shoulder. St. Andrews.

Mari's eyes were huge black pits of fear and confusion and he tried to twist away when St. Andrews put his hands on him.

"Time to go, mate. We've got somewhere to be, and we can't take you with us – "

The vision dispersed. Jake wiped his mouth on the back of his hand and stepped away from the sink. He had never gotten a memory from Mari, not once in all the months they had been dating. Today he had received two, in the space of a few minutes. The echoes of this one were still clear, right down to the taste in his mouth. He turned and strode back into the hallway as Cordiline was ushering Arregui back out, calling his name.

"St. Andrews was here. This piece of shit is planning on meeting him at the airport to get him out of the country before you can connect him to the rapes."

Tomas narrowed his eyes and glared at Jake.

"All conjecture, my American friend. Josep is my sister's son, as I already told the inspector. He has been a student here. I paid for his flight home. My sister wants him back there with the family. He has committed no crime."

"Then I'm sure he won't mind giving a DNA sample. Mari was in this apartment, too. He left with St. Andrews. Where did he take him?"

"So, it comes to this. UCL's celebrated Elemental banging down my door, desperate to put me in the frame for some misdemeanor. No, I am not surprised." He turned to Cordiline with an expansive gesture of both hands, a wry look on his face. "Inspector, Dr. Ilmarinen Gale was, some years ago, my research assistant. He was also my lover. When I ended our fling, he took it as a personal slight and attempted to destroy my marriage. He failed, and he has never quite overcome his frustration at not ruining me. Now he enlists his…boyfriend?" Tomas looked a question at Jake. "In the attempt to get his revenge against me."

Jake grabbed him by the lapels and slammed him against the wall, his promise to Cordiline be damned. "Listen, you fucking piece of garbage. You instructed your sick fuck of a nephew to take Mari somewhere and Mari struggled against him. You tell me where he took him or the next one buried in a shallow grave will be you. Understand me?"

"Take your hands off me! This is outrageous! You have no evidence for any of these lies!"

Jake shook him and cracked his head against the wall again. Cordiline grabbed his arm and a short, violent tussle ensued before the inspector pried him off Arregui, shoving him away.

"Enough, Chivis!" Cordiline roared.

"You are fortunate I have a plane to catch. I'll have my attorneys deal with you," Arregui raged at the same time.

"Turn around and put your hands behind your head, Arregui," Cordiline barked at him. "I am arresting you on suspicion of harboring a wanted criminal, in connection with cases of abduction, assault and murder. You do not have to say anything, but anything you do say may be recorded and used in evidence. Do you understand the charges, sir?"

Tomas stared at him, mouth hanging open. "You are joking! You have no evidence on which to hold me, Detective Inspector. The Spanish government, which employs me, will not look with favor on this situation."

"Save your threats and do as you're told. Her Majesty doesn't look kindly on people aiding and abetting rapists and allowing killers to escape her justice."

Tomas put down his case and put his hands behind his head at once, though he looked far from happy about it. Cordiline cuffed him, his jaw clenched so hard the skin was white amid the hectic red blotches in his cheeks. Jake couldn't blame him for his fury. John was already sticking his neck out big time for him, and he'd had to step in twice now to prevent him beating the shit out of someone. They had better find St. Andrews and hope to hell the DNA was a match. More importantly, they had to figure out where he'd taken Mari.

While Cordiline took Arregui outside and called for a uniform to come pick him up, Jake tried to call Mari again but it went right to his voice mail.

"What's the closest cemetery to here?" Jake asked Cordiline.

The inspector looked like he'd had it right up to his eyes but, to his credit, he didn't snap. He sat Arregui down on the pavement, ignoring his protests, and retrieved a plastic zip tie from his pocket to attach his cuffs to a signpost. He took Jake's arm and moved a few feet away. "Look— St. Andrews thinks his good old Uuncle Tomas is gonna save his arse and take him home. The MTPs at the airport are waiting for him. If the flight goes when Arregui says it does, he's not got time for fooling around in cemeteries."

"Mari must have figured out that Arregui knew what his nephew was up to, and he came here to confront him. Arregui took a leaf from his nephew's book and drugged him. I'm sure of it. The memories I picked up were distorted, blurry, and I smelled vomit in the bathroom. His nephew took Mari, and he'd have to leave him somewhere before he went to the airport. What if the bastard decides on one last hurrah before being forced to go home and buries Mari like he did those girls he attacked?"

"Jake, if Arregui sent you those pictures of Mari as revenge for what Gale pulled after they split, it doesn't make sense that he'd kill him afterwards. He'd have to know you'd figure it out."

"I doubt Arregui would tell his nephew to kill him, but that doesn't mean St. Andrews won't act on his own. John, Mari was in that fucking apartment and now he's with a man that raped multiple women and murdered at least one of them."

Cordiline glared at him in silence.

"He's fucking got Mari!" Jake erupted.

Cordiline sucked in a breath through clenched teeth and exhaled it in a testy sigh. "We've been here at the apartment for nearly twenty minutes, enough time that he could have dropped Gale off anywhere within at least a five-mile radius. Our best bet is to find St. Andrews, since we know where he's ultimately heading, and question him about Mari's whereabouts."

"I am not sitting on my fucking hands and waiting to see if he actually shows up at the airport." Jake brought up the map on his phone and did a quick search.

"Well, what's your plan, hot shot?" Cordiline flashed back at him. "You're just going to run around half-cocked, hoping you somehow run into them?"

"Let me borrow your car. Hammersmith Cemetery is directly between here and Heathrow. If that's where he's heading, it's the easiest place to try something. Mari said he was working for the Parks and Recreation Department, right? He'd know the best places to bury a body and he even has the tools for the job."

Cordiline's scowl was fierce enough to leave permanent lines, but he pulled his keys from his pocket. "I'll put in another call to have a patrol meet you there. Do not— Are you listening to me? Do. Fucking. Not. Approach St. Andrews on your own if you see him."

"I will wait for backup as long as I can," Jake said, the most truthful answer he could give.

Cordiline heaved a sigh but he handed over the car keys without a word. Jake didn't waste any more time. There would be time for thanks later, or recriminations, and they both knew it. He pulled away from the curb and headed into traffic, waiting until he was at least around the corner before he put his foot down to see how hard he could push the car. Detroit steel it was not, but it still had some pep, and if worse came to worst, he could always put the lights on.

Chapter Twenty-Three

"Time to go, mate. We've got somewhere to be, and we can't take you with us. More's the pity."

Mari stumbled and almost fell against the washstand as a young man appeared, reflected in the mirror behind him. His hands were strong and warm on Mari's shoulders as he turned him and steered him back into the hallway, still unsteady on his feet. Tomas helped him to get Mari back into his coat.

"Make sure you leave him where no one will find him before he comes around," he instructed, his tone sharp and edgy with irritation.

"Keep your hair on. It will be fine, Uncle," Josep said.

Mari was ushered down the hallway and into the lift, with Josep holding tightly on to his arm. His head swam and he grayed out for a moment, though he was trying to keep focused. In the bedroom, he had mercifully lost consciousness, but at the moment, he could barely feel enough to control his own body. Whatever Tomas had given him, it had robbed him of any resistance. He couldn't even make his tongue form words.

The cold air on his face, as they came out onto the misty street, roused him for a few seconds and he tried to pull away, but Josep was holding his arm firmly and steered him across the pavement to a waiting vehicle, a large, black SUV of some kind. He didn't see enough of it before the locks popped and he was heaved into the back. Josep pushed him down across the rear seat and strapped him in with both belts, then was gone. Moments later the driver's door opened and he climbed up, cursing, and slammed it behind him. The engine rumbled to life and his stomach rolled again as the young man pulled away at speed, still swearing under his breath in Catalan.

"Josep, please..." he managed to slur, though his tongue still felt as if it belonged to a dead person. He remembered the gray, lifeless features of the girl in the morgue and choked back the urge to spew. "Let me go... I won't...won't say...anything."

"Too right, you won't." Josep laughed, though it wasn't a particularly happy sound. "Where you're going, you won't have anyone to talk to anyway — just the worms."

"Don't be...stupid." Mari tried to struggle upright but he couldn't get his arms and legs to function properly. "They'll wor...work it...work it out. The cops...Jake."

Jake. Oh my stars, my precious, precious Jake. I am so sorry.

"Too bad I won't have time to draw you," Josep muttered as he drove. "I made sure the others could dig their way out, so I could capture the moment, but they never saw me. You? I can't let you get out. I've got a nice deep hole for you. You'll have time to think about things down there, I reckon, before the air runs out."

Mari sagged against the leather seats. Panic kicked in as his drug-addled senses darkened around him. He managed to free one of the belts then forced his hand across the upholstery and curled his fingers around the door handle, squeezing it for all he was worth. The rear door clicked open and a rush of cold air and petrol fumes washed over his sweating face.

He hissed an incoherent curse and struggled with the second belt as the car bounced to a halt amid a wave of irate curses and vehicles honking their horns. It was like trying to tie a knot in a stream of water. He could not make his fingers obey the desperate imperative of his brain.

But if he couldn't, he was going to die. No two ways about it.

I'm not ready. No. I can't die, not without apologizing to Jake first.

"Help! Help me!" he cried out, but the words sounded too frail in his mouth and he cursed himself again.

Then Josep leaned into the vehicle and dealt him a smack to the head that sent him reeling once more. He slammed the door shut and jumped back up behind the wheel, activating the central locking and wagging a finger at Mari as he glanced back between the two front seats.

"No need for that. If you wanna kill yourself, just leave it to me. I've got it all sorted out." Josep put the car in drive and released the brake and Mari felt them lurch forward again, moving off at speed.

For a little while he grayed out again, and when he came to his senses, the car was traveling more slowly.

Mari walked his fingers down to the pocket of his coat, checking for his phone. If he could just activate the keypad and dial nine-nine-nine, the operators would have to trace the call. Surely, someone would come after him. It was better than doing nothing at all. That was easier said than done, though. For one, his fingers were pretty reluctant to play ball and his slender Android was deep enough in his pocket that he was struggling to reach it.

He'd lost some motor control since Tomas had drugged him but he wasn't aware that his status had deteriorated during the car journey. His worst-case scenario was blacking out completely. If he did something monumentally stupid like fainting, he was pretty much screwed.

Mari figured he ought to be more frightened and – had he not been tranquilized to the eyeballs – he guessed he would have been. But, for the moment, he was just running on adrenaline.

Eventually the car rolled to a stop and Josep got out.

"Stay there," he warned, then slammed the door.

Mari just glared at the ceiling. *Like I have a choice!*

Sep's footsteps crunched around to the back of the car, then the boot opened up and the young man rummaged around there for a moment or two. Finally, with a metallic scraping sound, he dragged something out and banged the rear door shut once more. The locks clunked down and the alarm beeped as Josep left him alone in the vehicle.

He tried to calculate how long it had been since Tomas had drugged him. Back at the apartment, he had lost consciousness, and he could only guess at how much time he had lost. His mind, at least, was functioning now, even if his body didn't want to play along.

He managed to extract his phone from the pocket of his coat and juggle it up to where he was able to see the screen without throwing it on the floor or breaking it. That was an achievement and he congratulated himself silently, until he opened his call log, thinking to ring Jake and tell him where he was.

There were five photo messages in his log and his finger froze over the call icon as he registered them. He had a vague recollection of sending Jake a text before he set off to see Tomas, but he was pretty sure that he would have remembered sending him a picture message, let alone five of them. A cold sensation invaded his gut and he almost closed the message box and put the phone away, not wanting to know how he had managed to send Jake photos while he was gratefully unconscious.

When he opened the most recent image, a tiny, involuntary whimper escaped his throat.

"No. No. *No, no, no, no!*"

He shoved the phone back down into his overcoat pocket, not wanting to look at the results of his own stupidity. *Why did you go there alone? You should have just called Jake, or Cordiline, and got the police to check things out.*

Like a fool, he'd somehow believed that Tomas would talk to him. That what they'd once shared might, in some small way, have made a difference.

Well, you got that right. Jake probably thinks you deserved everything you got.

He closed his eyes for a moment because his head was spinning and he wanted to be sick again. That wasn't going to help him one bit.

Pull yourself together. You are going to die if you just lie here and then you'll never get the chance to explain.

It was heading toward dusk. If he was going to be found – if anyone was searching for him – they would need as much light as possible. That made his heart beat faster and he curled his fingers around the phone again, taking comfort from the small rectangle of warmth in his hand. He pulled it to his chest again and tried to make his fingers work to send a message. When that proved beyond him, he opened his mapping app and took a clumsy screenshot instead.

Come on fingers, blast you. Help me out here.

At the third attempt, he managed to send the screenshot, with its little blue location pin planted squarely in the heart of Hammersmith's Margravine Cemetery, to Jake's number. Then hoped fervently that his lover would understand what it meant.

He thrust the phone back into his coat as Sep returned from wherever he'd disappeared to with the spade and unlocked the car again. Rough hands grabbed him by the collar of his coat, dragging him out of the vehicle and, as he lost his uncertain footing, he was hauled across the turf between the plots and silent gray stones, into the bushes beyond them.

You are ruining a very expensive coat, bastard. You will pay for this, he cursed silently.

Even in his addled state, the sight of the disturbed ground and the yawning dark hole was enough to send a fresh surge of panic through him. He did struggle then, as much as he could, managing to get to his knees and plant both hands on the ground, pushing away from his would-be killer. Josep was stronger than he looked, though, and dragged him off balance, shoving and kicking him determinedly toward the lip of the makeshift grave.

From the way he was huffing, lost for wisecracks, Mari figured he wasn't used to his victims fighting back. That made him try even harder to wriggle out of the path he was being herded down. Sep swore at him in Catalan, dropped him hard and hurried around to grab him under the arms, hauling him back to the edge and manhandling him over it, even as Mari turned and clawed at him. The short drop took his breath away and he struggled to get air into his lungs, trying not to let panic take over and make him crazy. He scrabbled for the side of the grave with one hand, making every effort to pull himself to his knees, calculating that he was only about a meter down at most. He almost got there, then Josep grabbed the spade and swung it at his head, knocking him out cold for a few seconds.

When he regained his scrambled senses, the maniac on the surface was shoveling loose earth onto him as fast as he could. Mari could only haul his coat up over his head and he screwed his eyes shut to keep the dirt out of them. Shoving one hand into his pocket, he brushed his fingers over the screen of his phone, keeping it deep down where, hopefully, the soil couldn't jam its tiny components.

Chivis… You have every right to hate my guts. Really, you do. But if you have one speck of love left for me…please help me.

He took a last, long breath before pushing all his senses out into the web of communications that spiraled off from his phone and leaving reality behind.

It was like flicking a switch and illuminating a whole new space. Interfacing showed him a world within the mundane world he lived in — a world where he didn't need his body, at least, for the time being. He found his way back though the networks to Jake's mobile easily enough. The next problem was what to do with it. He was used to extracting information from another device, but putting information there was another matter. He was not a machine, just a ghost in the network. He wriggled his way into the messaging app and activated the ghost face emoji repeatedly. The message coming through would activate an alert, if Jake had his phone with him and switched on.

He triggered a couple of heart emojis for good measure. That had to help, didn't it?

His heart almost sang when Jake picked up the message. Of course, he had no idea how Jake was responding to it, but Mari saw him retrieve it.

He flicked into Jake's mapping app and woke it up, waiting until he knew it was on the screen of Jake's cell. A small blue dot identified Jake's position on the map.

If he had been in his actual body, he would have blinked for a moment because Jake was already heading this way — and at some speed. Mari pulled the signal from his own mobile, which was weaker down here in the ground but still active, and planted a second flag on the GPS map on Jake's cell phone.

Jake's phone pinged and he grabbed it, thinking it was Cordiline with some news. Maybe they'd picked up St. Andrews already. Maybe they'd found Mari. The message was from Mari's phone, though, and his heart started hammering double time as he opened it. He kept one eye on the road and the other on his cell. No words, just a screenshot of a familiar map image — Hammersmith Cemetery. Jake flicked the blue lights on as the traffic slowed. After a few frustrating moments of drumming his fingers on the wheel, a gap opened for him in the traffic ahead as drivers moved aside. He put his foot down and the car sped through the clearing.

His phone alert sounded again a few miles down the A4. He glanced at the message and frowned. Ghosts. Then hearts. Again, from Mari's number. Jake accelerated, glad of the warning lights as he had no intention of stopping.

His mapping app opened without any prompting from him and he swerved around a car that was slowing down for traffic lights. If St. Andrews had Mari's phone, he might send him ghosts and hearts to fuck with him, but only Mari would be able to open a map on his screen from within his own phone. He ran the light, and drivers blared their horns at him from all directions but he didn't care. A flag appeared on the map, in the middle of the cemetery. Ice cold fingers tickled down his back and Jake coaxed more speed out of the car than he'd imagined possible.

He took the turn practically on two wheels and got as close as he could to the cemetery before abandoning the car at the nearest entrance. Jake grabbed his phone and headed through the gates at a trot. He was so focused on the map and that small blue flag he nearly missed the vehicle sitting just off the shoulder—same color, make and model that had pulled off in a hurry from the curb in front of Arregui's building. His stomach churned at the thought of how close he'd been.

He scouted around but there was no sign of anyone, so he turned down a smaller trail through the grass between the plots, at a jog, moving past ancient gravestones, the undergrowth whipping his arms and legs. Just as he was starting to think that he was following an animal trail in the long grass, he heard the sound of a spade biting into dirt. As he came through a stand of bushes, he spotted a man with a shovel. The digger looked up when he heard Jake and they locked eyes.

He could only imagine what his face was like at that moment but whatever expression he wore, St. Andrews found it intimidating enough to stop digging and lift the shovel in a threatening arc. Jake kept his momentum. Surprise was gone but the fastest way to end a fight before it started was to tackle his opponent. St. Andrews swung the shovel at him as he came in range and Jake lifted an arm to protect his head.

The impact sent a shock of pain through his arm and Jake put his shoulder down, ramming into the man's gut.

St. Andrews grunted and dropped the shovel as Jake took him down. They grappled, both trying to get a punch in, but Jake had the advantage. He felt the pain in his arm only distantly. He landed a fist to St. Andrews face and blood instantly gushed from his nose.

"Fuck!" the man screamed and thrashed, switching from trying to fight to trying to get free. Jake twisted his fingers in the man's hair and got up, dragging him to his feet as well. He got an arm around his neck and lifted, putting pressure on the carotid arteries, bending him back nearly in half. St. Andrews struggled for about five seconds, then went slack, but within ten seconds he was out. If he really wanted to, Jake could give a final twist, and he'd never open his eyes again.

Instead, he dropped him on the grass and grabbed the shovel. There was a shallow depression of disturbed earth in front of him, about six feet by three, to his trained eye, with fresh clods of damp soil strewn all around. He glanced at his phone. He was standing right on top of the flag. Jake grabbed the shovel and started digging, frantic that he would be too late and sweating bullets that he'd accidentally drive the shovel into Mari if he went too fast.

"Mari! Mari!" He didn't expect an answer but if Mari heard, at least he would know that he had found him.

Dirt flew and, as he got deeper, he forced himself to go slower, more carefully. He prodded first before he sunk the business end of the shovel deeper and about a minute later he was glad when he nudged against something softer but not as yielding as the fresh earth. Jake dropped the shovel and started digging with his hands, throwing big clods out of his way and shoving as much as he could aside until he uncovered soft, sage green wool. Mari's coat.

"Mari? Oh my god, Mari… Mari…oh fuck, please be alive…"

Blue lights strobed through the foliage, looking eerie and alien in the gathering darkness as Jake straddled the hole. He pulled the coat back and was greeted with Mari's pale, still face.

"No…no, no, no… Oh spirits, no…please… Mari!" He tapped his cheek and got no response. He felt for a pulse and couldn't detect one. "Mari!" He lay down on the edge of the hole so he could reach Mari's lips without risking kneeling on his chest. He pinched his nose and opened his mouth before starting rescue breathing and chest compressions.

A few moments later he was surrounded by figures in uniform, police in dark blue and paramedics in green jumpsuits, all of whom set to work with their hands to excavate the rest of the shallow grave in the woods. Jake was barely aware of any of it. He only saw Mari's beautiful face, eyes closed as if he was asleep, his skin streaked with earth.

Finally, they removed enough dirt to free him, and one of the paramedics told Jake to stop CPR so they could get him out. The transfer from the bottom of the hole to the ground beside it took seconds and a set of paramedics took over CPR.

Jake stared, the feeling of helplessness the worst he'd even experienced. His chest constricted like it was in a vise and he was shaking hard enough to rattle his teeth. Time distorted in one long, torturous, never-ending cycle of chest compressions and breathing. The minutes felt like days going by.

One of the officers questioned him about the man lying on the ground a few feet away.

"He's Joseph St. Andrews, the Cemetery Rapist. I found him burying Mari," he said, on autopilot.

"Got a pulse," one of the paramedics said. Jake closed his eyes and swallowed.

Mari was transferred to a stretcher. As Jake started to follow, his phone pinged in his pocket and he pulled it out, finger poised to turn the damned thing off. The message was from Mari. A large heart shaped emoji, surrounded by smaller ones. Nothing more.

Jake wasn't sure if his own heart was still beating. Mari was still interfacing. How was that even possible?

"Hang on a minute," Jake told one of the paramedics as they were fitting an oxygen mask over his nose and mouth. "I need to find his phone."

"I think he's got more to worry about than losing his phone, mate," the medic told him with a good-natured grunt as he moved around to lift the stretcher.

His phone pinged again. Several times, in fact. A scramble of random images popped up on the screen.

A wide-eyed scream face, a box with a ribbon on it, another heart, a hotdog, a frustrated face. That one popped up three times.

Jake reached across Mari's torso, ignoring the objections of the nearest medic for one moment. Mari had one hand free but the other was still trapped in the pocket of his muddy coat, secured there by the restraining straps that held him on to the backboard. He flipped the buckle of the belt around his middle and slid his hand into Mari's pocket. The slim mobile device was still very warm, warmer than Mari's fingers, as Jake retrieved it and stroked his dirt-streaked hair in reassurance. "I've got you, Ilmari."

"We need to get him loaded into the ambulance," the other paramedic, an older man, told him in more strident tones.

"Okay…just one more second," Jake said. He moved the oxygen mask from Mari's face. "Come back to me, baby," he whispered, taking Mari's face gently between his hands and kissing him.

For a long moment, nothing happened. He pressed his mouth harder and brushed his nose against Mari's. It came away wet and he knelt back, wiping blood from his face. Mari's lips parted and he took one long, ragged breath then another. The blood was coming from his nose, and Jake remembered what Mari had once told him about backlash caused by coming out of a prolonged interface too quickly. He didn't have time to feel guilty. Long tawny lashes quivered and Mari opened his eyes, looking straight up at Jake like he'd known where he would find him.

"You're real," he croaked in a small, fragile voice. "I wasn't sure."

Jake made a choked sound. Some of the dirt must have gotten into his eyes and he blinked a couple times. "I'm real. I'm here. And so are you." He put the mask over Mari's nose and mouth again with careful hands and took a shaky breath himself. "They're going to take you to A&E. I'll be right behind you." He kissed Mari's forehead and the paramedics buckled him up again, got him onto the gurney and hurried him toward the waiting ambulance.

The scene was gruesome. An open grave, flashing lights, and more police and emergency workers had arrived while Jake had been focused on Mari. St. Andrews was handcuffed and had also regained consciousness.

"Jake." Cordiline strode toward him. He'd either just arrived or had been talking with the uniforms. Whichever, he'd spotted Jake now and came over, putting a hand on his shoulder.

"I thought I told you to wait for backup."

"You didn't really think I would?"

The hand on his shoulder squeezed then patted him. "No. I suppose I didn't. One of the patrol is going to give you a lift to A&E. I'd take you myself but…"

"It's okay. You got your man, now go make sure the case sticks."

Cordiline nodded and Jake gave him back his keys.

Chapter Twenty-Four

The world swayed around him as Mari lurched in and out of consciousness. Sometimes strangers loomed over him and asked him questions that he could not answer.

"Where's Jake?" he slurred, wondering if he had imagined the kiss — imagined seeing that beloved face looking down at him, golden eyes warm with love and concern. It felt like a dream and he closed his eyes again, letting reality slip away.

When he opened them again, he was in a bright, busy room. The light hurt his eyes and he kept shutting them.

"Hello there. I'm Ashley. Can you tell me your name?"

He risked a glance. A solid-looking man in blue scrubs that set off his short ginger hair and beard was smiling down at him. Mari swallowed hard and told him.

"That's a mouthful. What do you like to be called?" the nurse asked him.

"Just Mari will do."

"Splendid. What happened to you, Mari? Can you remember?"

He shook his head, but that made the room spin, so he closed his eyes again.

"Welcome back, I'm Dr. Stanley. Did you get a knock on the head, Mari?" A smiling, dark-skinned woman in a smart-looking business suit was standing over him when he opened his eyes again. He was not sure how long he had closed them for.

"Not sure...um, yes. I think he hit me with a spade," he mumbled as broken images of the last few hours began to slot back into place in his head.

"You have a nasty bump there but the X-ray doesn't show a fracture, so I guess that makes you a lucky chap," she said cheerfully. "Your breathing is better now and you've got a bit more color in your cheeks, so we're going to move you into a ward once we've got that cut on your head stitched. The police will want to talk to you, when you're ready."

He blinked at her. For a moment he wondered what he had done then remembered — the apartment. Tomas. Josep dragging him down from the car and into the bushes.

"Not yet," he managed.

"That's okay. No rush," she told him. "Is there anyone we can call for you?"

"Jake," he said automatically. "He said he would come with me."

One of the nurses said something that he missed but the doctor just nodded. "I think he's in the waiting room, I'll get someone to bring him through."

He closed his eyes again.

When he came to, he was in a quieter room in a bed with blue curtains around it. The light was softer and he sighed with relief. A chair creaked to his right and he turned his head. Jake smiled at him, pleasure warring with weariness in his dark, amber-colored eyes.

"I have never been so scared in my life," Jake told him softly, squeezing his hand then coming to his feet and bending over to plant a kiss on his lips. That was good, almost normal. "I thought I'd lost you."

"I thought so, too," he said, and the words were dry and rattled in his throat. "Can you get me some water, please?"

Jake reached over and poured from a jug by the bed into a small, plastic tumbler. He fiddled with the controls on the bed to raise Mari up into a position where he could drink without spilling the water all over himself, then sat on the bed beside him, stroking his face with shaking fingers.

"It's all right. I'm okay, Jake," he said in a small voice. "But I wouldn't have been, if it wasn't for you. Thank you."

Jake leaned forward and wrapped his arms tight around him. He buried his face in Mari's hair and his breath was warm and comforting as he whispered, "I never want to feel like that again."

That made him teary and Mari hated himself for it, even though he wanted to be held in Jake's arms more than anything. Someone had changed him out of his dirty clothing into clean hospital scrubs while he was out of it, but he still felt filthy and spent. Even if he took a shower for the next twenty-four hours, he wasn't sure if he should let Jake touch him. He wasn't strong enough to fight that comforting embrace, though, and the warmth of it melted some of the barriers he'd put up to stop himself thinking or feeling too much.

"I don't disgust you?" he whispered, his voice coming out small and cracked and entirely pathetic. "I disgust me."

"You could never disgust me, Ilmari," Jake murmured, his lips pressed to Mari's temple. "What happened was not in any way your fault."

"You're kind," Mari crooned, altogether overwhelmed by this gentle acceptance. He turned on his side, nuzzling his face up under Jake's chin and wriggling his arms around him. Utter exhaustion washed over him and, even after all that had happened, he knew he was safe in Jake's embrace. "Too kind. I should have waited for you. I ought not have gone in on my own. You've told me so many times. But I... I didn't think he'd actually harm me. Not physical harm, anyway."

They were interrupted by one of the nurses doing her rounds before Jake could respond. She clucked softly at Jake and told him off for sitting on the bed. Then, when she had checked Mari over and asked if he needed any more pain relief, she said, "The policeman still wants to talk to you. He's been very patient. Are you ready to have a word with him?"

He nodded, though he wanted to hide under the bed until everyone but Jake went away.

The policeman, to his surprise, was not Cordiline but a younger Asian man in a Met vest, who arrived in company with an older white lady in a skirt suit and a blue sweater. The lady had a clipboard and a small case with her.

"Hello, Dr. Gale. Thank you for seeing us," the man said. "I'm PC Azim Khan from Hammersmith Broadway and this is PC Charlotte Reitz. She's going to be your OIC. So, anything you want to talk about in total confidentiality, she's your Case Officer."

"Confid…" Mari looked at Jake, who lowered his eyes.

"I may have mentioned to the doc when they brought you in that you'd possibly been…" Jake stopped talking. Mari couldn't have said whether it was the expression on his face or just an attack of guilt. "I mean," he said at last, "I thought you would want to make a report."

Mari closed his eyes for another moment. He lay back and composed his thoughts. Then, without opening his eyes, he said, "The man who abducted and tried to bury me was Josep Sant Andreu Garcés. He also goes by the name of Joseph St. Andrews. He is wanted in connection with the Cemetery Rapist inquiry. He took me, by force, from premises in Manchester Square occupied by his uncle. They were planning to leave the country this evening."

"Can you tell me why you were at the premises on Manchester Square?" Khan asked.

"Certainly. I went there to ask questions of the gentleman who was staying there." Mari took a long breath.

The PC tapped his phone. "That would be the apartment of Tomas Arregui? Was he present when you were taken from the premises?" Khan pressed.

"I was under the influence of a debilitating drug and I don't recall what happened. I don't intend to press charges, Officer," Mari said simply. "Was there anything else?"

Even with his eyes closed, he could feel Jake staring at him. Those warm fingers gripped his hand a little tighter.

The police tried a few more questions. PC Reitz attempted to persuade him to let them take DNA samples. Mari lost his temper around that point and they left empty-handed.

For a while after they had gone, Jake was very quiet. Mari curled up on the bed with his eyes squeezed shut. He heard Jake swallow hard and his voice was husky when he finally said, "You should let them collect the evidence they need to prosecute him, Mari."

"No." His response was altogether too quick, and he knew it from the way Jake's hand tightened around his. Softening his tone, he repeated it. "No, Jake. I don't know what happened. I don't want to know. It's wrong, but if I have to testify in court, it will be horrible and I don't want to go through that. I don't want to talk to a roomful of strangers about what he did or didn't do to me. I don't want my mother to find out. And it won't change anything. It won't turn back time or magically make it not have happened. I don't want them poking and prodding at me. I just want to go home."

Jake exhaled but not in an impatient way. The sound of it was more accepting, or perhaps defeated. "Okay. I get it. And you're right. It won't change what happened." Jake cupped Mari's face with one hand and looked into his eyes. "But please let them treat you, at least. I want to make sure you're okay."

Mari forced a smile, though he did not feel it. He would do it, for Jake, because he loved him more than anyone, ever, and he wanted Jake to understand that. He still worried that things had changed irreparably between them as a result of those photographs. Jake was here, holding him, though. His beloved Jake had come looking for him...and that was more than he deserved after all the secrets and whatever had happened in that apartment this afternoon.

"I'll do it, if you promise not to leave me alone. But tell me something. How did you know that I needed you?" he whispered. "When I reached out to your phone, I could tell from the mapping app that you were already on your way. But you had no idea where I'd gone. You have no clue how much I loved you in that moment, by the way."

He looked up at Jake, feeling almost shy. Funny that it was still strange and exotic to admit it to him, even after all this time.

"I'm a detective. It's kinda what I do," Jake teased him in a gentle tone. He explained how, after he'd gone with Cordiline to St. Andrews' apartment and seen Tomas there in a memory, it had all started to fit together rather fast. When he told Mari about seeing him in a memory at Tomas' flat, he began to tremble and found himself fighting tears again.

"Damn! You knew...before I did. I didn't need to..." Mari broke off and swallowed hard. Sickness rose in his gorge at the realization that he could have avoided everything that had happened had he only waited and spoken to Jake.

He curled up tight on the bed, wishing he could stop thinking altogether.

Jake murmured, "Thinking about 'shoulda, woulda, coulda' isn't going to help anything, Mari. You're a grown-up. You thought you were doing the right thing going in alone. There's no way you could have guessed what that bastard would do."

"I need to tell you something, Jake." Mari unfurled and laid his cheek against his lover's chest so he could hear the comforting drum of his heartbeat. It thudded slightly faster at his words. He stroked his fingers in the open neckline of Jake's button-down shirt. "I don't want to tell you but you need to hear this from me, because I'm kind of scared. I'm clearly not totally immune to your psychometry. One day, maybe, you'll touch me and all of this could come spilling out, whether you want it or not."

"What is it, babe?" Jake asked, equal parts tender and worried.

"I..." Mari swallowed because his throat was too tight. "I didn't want him to do it. You have to believe me. I didn't go to his apartment for sex."

"I know, sweetheart. He drugged you. He took those pictures for revenge," Jake said. "I understand."

"No. You don't." Mari looked up at him, touching his lips with his fingers to silence him for a moment. "Jake...he gave me more than just the roofies. He slipped something into the water he gave me afterwards and...when he put me on the bed, before I lost consciousness, I was hyper, Jake. I couldn't control it. It was like a storm running through me. I was hard before he even touched me. I don't remember what I said or what I was thinking. And afterwards, when I saw those photos, I just felt really bad...and wrong. And I'm sorry. I didn't want to feel that way. Not for him."

"It...it doesn't matter, Mari."

He heard the slight hesitation in Jake's voice but, before he could turn away again, Jake took his face between his hands and forced him to look directly at him.

"It doesn't matter," he said in a firmer tone. "I *do* understand. I love you, Mari, that hasn't changed. Okay?"

"I... Jake, I love you too...more than I've ever loved anyone in my life," he breathed out, making himself say the words before he got cold feet and bottled it. He didn't tell Jake this enough and tonight it was his imperative. "If I can't be with you, I don't want to be with anyone. Ever."

"Don't worry. You can't get rid of me that easily."

"Does that mean we can go home now and pretend this never happened?" he asked hopefully.

"We could do that, if the doctors are happy for you to leave," Jake agreed. "How's your head? They were worried about concussion."

"I feel okay. The pills they gave me are keeping it quiet." Mari touched the bandage under his hair and frowned.

"Well then, if you're not going to cooperate with them, I guess I should take you home." Jake eyed him in a way he had come to recognize. It meant he didn't like what was going on but was willing to go along with it for the sake of a quiet life.

"How would you feel if it was you they wanted to stick their swabs and needles in?" he demanded.

"I know it isn't nice," Jake conceded, taking both of his hands and squeezing them gently. "But if it makes the difference between punishing him and letting him get off completely...?"

Mari touched his fingers to Jake's lips. "Sshhh. He will make my life a fucking misery, Jake. If I take this to Crown Court, he will make sure that we are both crucified for it. He's a powerful man and he has powerful friends. Better to let it go and walk away intact. He's got what he wanted. He humiliated me. We're even. He will let this go."

Jake looked thoughtful for a while—and angry. Mostly angry. Mari wanted to hold him and kiss him but he wasn't sure it would be welcomed right at that moment. At last, Jake said, "Okay. I'm not going to push you to prosecute him, but let them take the samples, even if they never use them. Call it insurance, in case he doesn't walk away."

"Jake…" Mari protested wearily.

"No, listen to me," Jake persisted. "If you walk out of here now and, for whatever reason, in three months' time you change your mind, you can never get your hands on the evidence you need. But if you let them take samples now, and in three months' time everything is going fine, you haven't lost anything, have you?"

Mari pursed his lips. He wanted to argue but his logical brain told him that his precious Jake was probably right. "Oh, damn it," he growled. "Can't I tell you're still a cop at heart?"

"Does that mean you will?" Jake lifted his hand and kissed Mari's knuckles tenderly.

"I guess I don't have any dignity left. I might as well," he sighed. "Go and find them. Let them know. But then we leave. I've had it up to here with today." His voice trembled a little on the final words and he lowered his head, not wanting Jake to see him weaken. Jake put a finger under his chin, though, lifting his head and brushed a kiss on Mari's lips, the tip of his nose, his forehead.

"Shh, it's okay. Everything is going to be okay." He pulled Mari in close again and held him tight, and for just a short time, everything was.

Chapter Twenty-Five

Two weeks had passed since Mari's release from the hospital. Cordiline had promised right after he was discharged that, in line with reporting regulations, he would not be identified in any of the press releases on the arrest of the Cemetery Rapist. Mari was grateful for that. He'd explained away his injuries to Mama by saying that he had been hurt helping the police apprehend St. Andrews, which was not entirely untrue.

He knew that she had sensed a lie, though. She was careful around him and that just put his nerves on edge once more. He'd visited the outpatients' surgery four days after his hospital stay, where he'd requested, and had been given, tranquilizers.

He'd hidden himself away as much as he could without being grilled about it. What his employers made of his absence he wasn't sure, but he couldn't find it within himself to care much. The hospital had given him a vague sick note that allowed him four weeks' grace to recover. No one had called to question this, so he sat at home and felt like a fraud.

He took Tonka out in the early mornings and late in the evening when the streets were at their quietest. All the same, he found he was looking over his shoulder constantly. If someone tried to speak to him, they got the brush-off, and he escaped at the first opportunity. Jake ran with him some days but most of the time he was up even before his lover, unable to sleep. When he did sleep, his dreams were dark and disturbing.

Twice, Jake had stayed over at the house. After the second time, when he'd come down to find Mari curled up on the sofa in the day room, Jake asked if he just needed more space and, despondent, he'd had to admit that it might be for the best. Jake had looked like an abandoned kitten and Mari had felt like a heel, but he didn't want company — not even from the man he loved most in the world, and the one he felt that he had committed the biggest betrayal against.

Mama had interrogated him after Jake had gone home with his tail between his legs, which had been embarrassing.

"What on earth is going on with you two? You've been odd since you caught that awful man."

"Nothing is going on with us, Mama. We just have our own things to do. That's all," he'd told her. It was his most constant lie. She never believed it.

"That's never stopped you before," she'd pointed out.

"Mama, I'm pretty sure I don't want to know what you mean by that."

"You know, all right. You boys try to keep things quiet, but I sleep just down the hallway and I'm not deaf." She'd narrowed her eyes. "Did you argue about this case again?"

"Mama!" Mari had thrown up his hands. "No. We didn't argue. I'm just tired. That's all. Not that I'm having a conversation with my mother about my sex life. This isn't happening. Right?"

Anni had just given him a tolerant smile, the way she used to when he'd been small and tried to fib his way out of homework. She'd let it lie, but he knew the peace would not last.

At least, this morning, he had some respite. She was meeting a friend for lunch and afterward she had an appointment with her professional oncologist, Mr. Barnard, to discuss some test results. Usually he went with her, but today he didn't have the heart for another round of discussions about her blood count and the latest expensive trial that she might be able to get onto. He was relieved that she declined his offer to come along and did not push her to relent. Again, that earned him a curious look, but he saw her off with a kiss and vowed to himself to get her some flowers before she got home.

Then he went to his bedroom, took a couple of his happy pills and crashed on the bed for an hour. He woke with a jolt from a vague dream where he was trying to escape from some unidentifiable threat by following Tonka up the side of a steep sand dune. The Staffie's paw prints suddenly vanished and he found himself sliding down the slope, clawing at the loose sand. When it came crashing down on his head, burying him, he returned to his senses, kicking and thrashing, tangled in the throw on his bed. The drumming of his heart was painful and his struggles woke a dull ache in his back muscles that had been off and on since that day in the cemetery.

Mari went down to the kitchen and made a cup of tea. He took some painkillers and curled on the sofa with his laptop but was unable to do anything more than surf for music. When the doorbell rang, he was sprawled supine, with the machine resting on his chest, listening to a nineties thrash metal playlist through his earbuds. Only the sight of Tonka rushing into the hall with his tail wagging wildly alerted him to the presence of someone at the door.

At first, he presumed it was Jake and got to his feet with a weary sigh to greet his lover, but when the bell rang again, he frowned. Even given their current lack of sex life, Jake would have let himself in by now. And he usually approached their house through the rear garden anyway.

He reached for the latch and, at the last minute, put the chain on as a precaution. When the crack between the door and jamb revealed the visitor, he was surprised to find Solana looking in at him, dressed in quite sober light-blue, boot-cut jeans and a chiffon blouse in gold and soft greens.

"Mama is out. She won't be home till gone two," he said, unable to keep the testiness out of his voice, while trying to tow Tonka out of the gap in the doorway with a couple of fingers hooked in his collar.

"Actually, I came to see you. May I come in?" Solana asked.

He blinked at her, rendered stupid for a moment by the cocktail of codeine and sleeping pills. His blood ran cold all of a sudden. "Why? Is there something wrong? Should I have gone with her to see the specialist? Oh fuck…"

He fumbled for his keys, taking the chain off the door. Tonka leapt up and put his small white paws on

Solana's knees. His tail flicked from side to side like a metronome. Solana patted Tonka's head and rubbed his unchewed ear with an affectionate smile.

"Nothing is wrong with your mother, Mari. She's doing very well. The fact that you haven't noticed is what's concerning to me. That, and you're high as a kite in the middle of the day."

Mari glared at her for a moment, caught between annoyance and guilt for the fact that it was true. He had been so wrapped up in himself that he'd barely paid Mama any heed at all the last couple of weeks—and because that was her way, she hadn't even chided him for it, using her gentle digs about his stuttering relationship with Jake as a lever to get him to open up instead.

"I'm not high. I'm just tired," he countered as she and Tonka followed him through to the day room. "I have a very stressful job."

"Which you currently aren't doing," was her pithy response.

Mari suppressed the urge to swear.

"Do you and my mother spend your entire therapy session discussing me?" he asked instead, switching on the kettle because it was clear that Solana was not about to leave in a huff, and he might sometimes be rude, but he had been raised to be hospitable.

"Not always," Solana said, sliding onto one of the bar stools across the countertop from him, "just when she's worried about you. She amazes me with her determination, your mother. The progress she's made in the short time I've been seeing her is extraordinary. I would not be surprised if we will be able to end our sessions in less than half the time I initially thought."

Mari blinked at her, lost for words, though not for long. "You believe that she's getting better? For real?" He amended that at once because it sounded impolite and he had promised Jake that he would not be rude to her. "That's...incredible. I don't... I don't think anyone would have fought for a cure as hard as she has. She's never given up hope."

He poured water over the tea to hide the fact that he was mildly embarrassed to be caught gushing about his mother to a virtual stranger. It must have been the drugs, loosening his tongue like that.

"It's still too early to say that, but she's stronger. We'll have to see what the tests say about her blood count. Eventually the scans will either confirm the cancer has left her or not, and you'll have your answer as to whether I'm a fraud. I'm not, by the way. I know you won't believe that, yet, but...I wish you would, so that I could help you." Solana accepted the tea cup Mari passed to her and took a delicate sip. "Thank you."

"I don't need your help, thank you very much," he said, watching the quiet grace of her movement. Once, he might have envied her that fluidity and confidence. He wasn't so sure anymore. Until recently, he would have said that he was happy as he was.

Solana lifted her eyes from the tea to look at him and Mari refused to drop his own gaze, though he wanted to more than anything.

"You haven't told Annabel what happened, and I understand you not wishing to worry her more than necessary, but she is well aware that something is bothering you. I don't believe she suspects how badly hurt you were, though."

Shameful heat rose to his cheeks but, even so, he did not look away.

"I've no idea what you're talking about. There is nothing wrong with me. My mother worries too much."

Her expression did not change but he still knew she wasn't convinced. Lowering his eyes, Mari laced his fingers around the glass mug in his hands. He suppressed the urge to shudder at the memories he had struggled hard to just file away and forget about for the last couple of weeks. For some peculiar reason, he found himself thinking of the case he and Jake had dealt with before the Cemetery Rapist. One of their suspects, Ed, had been a Water Elemental who'd professed to be able to read auras, like Solana. Some of the things he'd said about Mari had been dangerously accurate.

In that instant, he wanted to chase her out of the house and lock all the doors. But he held still and stared into the golden pool of his teacup instead.

"I didn't say there was anything wrong with you. I said you've been hurt by someone. You might be able to hide this from your mother, but I can see the damage that was done. It is as if you were standing in front of me with open wounds still bleeding." She said this in a quiet, matter-of-fact tone, pausing to take another sip of her tea. "In all honesty, I came here today to ask you to resolve whatever anger issues you are having with your mother because it was upsetting Anni, but the moment you opened the door, that ceased to be my concern. Your aura is... I've helped people recover from very bad situations with their partners. Your aura is currently the same. Did Jake hurt you?"

A surge of bile rose to the back of his throat as her words sank in and he took a gulp from his cup to keep himself from being sick. At first, he misunderstood what she was trying to say, and when he caught on, he wasn't sure what he wanted to deny first.

"No… That's ridiculous. Jake would never— He's never laid a hand on me. I mean, well, obviously he *has* but he would never hurt me!" he blurted out, unable to quell the trembling in his hands. He put the mug down before he dropped it and pressed his palms flat to the counter to keep them still.

"Good. I'm glad. He seemed a very honest and loyal person when I met him. I'd hate to think that had changed. Does Jake know that you were…assaulted?"

Mari drew in a breath, but before he could unleash another protest, Solana held up her hand to stop him. "I know something happened to you. I *know* it, Mari. You saying otherwise won't change that." Her words were quiet and intense, not hysterical in the least. "If you won't accept my help, at least see someone else. Please. There were shadows of an old pain around you before but nothing like this. The hurt in you is massive, and if you ignore it for very much longer, it will grow to hurt everyone around you as well."

He wanted to yell at her. He wanted to tell her she was a fool then throw her out and never speak to anyone about this ever again, but he was a creature of logic and he knew that she was right about one thing. Deep down, below the calming fuzz of the tranquilizers, he was hurt and angry, and that anger had been taken out on those he loved because he had no other outlets for it. He hated himself for that, but he didn't understand what else to do with the rage boiling inside him. It was like a volcano, bubbling up from the core of his being, threatening to erupt.

"Tell me what you can see. Exactly what?" he asked, breathless and lightheaded from the pressure rising inside him. "And… I need to know. Will there be other people out there that can see the same thing?"

"When people talk about auras, most often they describe them as halos of light and color. I can't tell you whether other people that claim to see them are speaking the truth because I can't see through their eyes. I can tell you I don't see the things that they seem to. To me, when I look at a person in a certain way, I see an image of them over the top of their physical body. Almost like a camera trick, the way a ghost looks in a movie, only very close to them, like a pale shadow. The expression your aura wears looks like anguish, pain, anger. Instead of the coloring of your own physical body, it looks gray — in places black — where you are holding the most pain."

She stopped speaking for a moment and this time it was Solana that wouldn't meet his eye. He thought again of Ed, who had told him that when people truly wished to end their pain, their auras turned black. Suddenly he found it hard to breathe.

"I don't wish to traumatize you more, but I think if I don't tell you all of what I see, you won't believe me. I know that you were handled with violence…sexual violence. There are dark-red handprints on your aura, some formed into claws, that move in a perverse way. I've always thought that when survivors of such attacks talk about how they can sometimes still feel or smell their attacker, this is what they are experiencing."

Mari shuddered again because he understood exactly what she was describing. Some nights he jerked awake with such a violent start that he imagined, just for a moment, he had dreamed everything that had happened since he had been steered down the corridor into Tomas Arregui's bedroom. He'd woken from dreams so real that he'd actually believed for a short while that he was still a prisoner in his own body on that bed. And he could not separate the present from the past. Sometimes in his nightmares he was no more than a child, neither a boy nor a girl — torn between the two, not knowing which truth to cling to. And Tomas loomed large in those dreams, always laughing or sneering, reminding him that he was never enough.

Then, in his most private moments, he'd buried his face deep in the pillow and cried in breathless silence until he had put sufficient distance between himself and his memories.

Solana was right. He was hurting. His body still ached and protested from the abduction, the nightmare of burial and whatever had preceded it — memories that he had blocked and buried with such determination. But the pain ran deeper than the stresses of his physical body.

"It's true. I can still smell him. I still feel his hands on me," he said, almost inaudible, lost in the memory. "I wash and wash until I'm raw but I still feel it. It won't let go. I had blood tests and I'm not infected, I'm not sick, but he still left me with something that I can't get rid of. I can't get clean of him." His voice shook and he turned away, refusing to shed tears in front of her.

"I'm so sorry this happened to you," Solana said in a soft, low voice that was almost a whisper. "I can help you, if you let me. I can help more than the pills you are taking. I won't touch you. I won't crowd you, I promise, but only if you allow it."

"What can you do? Can you make it go away? Because I'm trying. I try so hard to wish it away but it won't let go of me." This time he broke and fled, but he halted by the French doors, where he pressed his hands and his forehead to the sunlit glass. His tears, when they came, fell in silence and he did not turn to face her until he had them in check, though he still rubbed at his eyes with both hands. "Damn it! I'm not a woman and I can't be a man. What am I supposed to be?"

"If by that you mean you can't force yourself into typical male stereotypes like not crying when you are in pain, I'd say that's a good thing. Gender doesn't have to be black and white, Mari. Yes, male and female have their obvious differences, but not so much as some people would like to believe. We are certainly more similar than different." Solana looked at him with curious eyes. "And no, I can't change the past for you or make it all go away like magic. I can ease the pain, though, and allow your heart and head to clear enough that you can start to heal yourself. That's what I can do for you, if and when you choose it."

Mari leaned there for a moment against the doors. He was exhausted, tired of running and trying to hide from his mistakes.

"I need that to happen," he said at last. "I have to move forward. There is no other feasible alternative. I just don't know how. Promise me that you will not talk about this to my mother. I don't ever want her to find out."

"I won't discuss anything that is said between us with anyone, unless you give permission. You have my absolute word of honor on that. I will ask you once more, though, before we begin. Did you tell Jake what happened?"

Mari chewed on his lower lip but inclined his head in affirmation. "Not the details," he said, "but he understands that I was drugged and what happened after. We haven't talked about it. But yes, he is aware."

"Good, that will make things marginally easier for you. You won't have to get over the hurdle of telling him, at least. Do you still want Jake to be a part of your life?"

Tears welled up in him again at the thought of a life that didn't include Jake. He guessed that was his answer. Mute, he nodded. It took several long breaths to get his voice under control. "If he still wants me to be a part of his."

"Well, I don't know him well enough to speak for him, but he didn't strike me as a monster. He seemed to care deeply for you, so my guess would be that he still very much wants you and is probably wondering how he can make you understand that without you feeling worse. But that's just a guess." Solana bestowed a kind smile on him. "Would you like to start our first session today?"

Mari looked at the clock. It was still only few minutes after twelve and his mother would not be home for ages yet.

"How much is this going to cost me?" he asked, taking refuge in the practicalities.

Solana folded her hands on the worktop, seeming to think for a moment. "One recommendation," she said at last.

He blinked, perplexed. "One... I'm sorry? I don't understand. What?"

"Once we've finished our sessions together, if — and only if — you feel that I've helped you, I'd like you to recommend my services to someone of your choosing, should the opportunity ever present itself."

Mari was still waiting for the catch, and when it didn't come, he was left bemused. "That's all? You want me to big you up to someone else? You don't want money?" he asked with some skepticism.

Solana uttered a soft ripple of laughter. "I don't want you to 'big me up' to anyone. If you ever come across a person whom you genuinely believe could be helped by my services, I want you to give them my name and number. That's all."

"That's it?" he asked again, wondering if this was not another nightmare after all. He waited for her to peel off a mask, revealing that she had been Tomas all along, then laughing as he crumpled to the ground.

She just smiled at him. Her expression was very warm and sincere. He wondered that he he'd never noticed that before, then figured out he'd always been searching her for an ulterior motive in the past. Maybe Jake was right. He did let his overactive imagination cloud his judgement at times.

"That's it. Yes," she said at last. "Do we have a deal?"

"Um… Okay. I guess." Mari nodded acceptance, oddly humbled by the offer.

"All right. Let's start. First, please make yourself as comfortable as you are able. Sit wherever you feel best and tell me where you would like me to sit as well. We'll go from there."

Mari took a deep breath and sat down on the sofa. If this worked, there was nothing lost. If it didn't… Well, he would need to take each day at a time. After a few moments, Tonka came and sat at his feet, resting his muzzle on Mari's knee, the first time he had done so since before the attack. Mari fondled his ears and gave him a genuine smile.

Chapter Twenty-Six

Six months later

The Vault was a popular watering hole and was never totally dead, but a Tuesday night was about as quiet as it got. Jake and Cordiline sat in relative peace at the end of the bar, enjoying a beer. How Cordiline had managed to talk his coworkers into coming here for the celebration of his promotion Jake didn't know and didn't ask. They all seemed to be having a good time anyway, and Manny didn't mind playing host for the boys in blue, some of whom were 'really hot', according to him, even if they were straight.

Jake wasn't in much of a celebratory mood but he'd gone anyway, because John had asked him to. The way he'd worded it implied that he believed his work with Jake on the Cemetery Rapist case was at least in part responsible for his promotion. Manny hovered over the two of them like a big Fairy Godmother with a hairy chest and leather pants.

"It's a bit full-on down here, innit?" Cordiline said into Jake's ear during a lull in Manny's ongoing tale of Jake's voyage from greenhorn-newbie-guy upstairs to much loved bar regular. "He's definitely got the hots for you. He lit right up when he figured you didn't have the boyfriend in tow tonight. Speaking of which... How's things with you and the doctor? He's still refusing to press charges against Arregui, I hear."

"You know how it is, John, and so does Mari. He understands what he'd have to go through, and he decided it wasn't worth it. He said to tell you congratulations, by the way. He wasn't quite up to a night out." Jake took a swallow of beer.

Cordiline's expression mellowed, his gaze never quite leaving Jake's face. "You two are all right, though? You seem a bit down tonight. And I'm not fishing, before you throw that back in my face. I don't like to see you unhappy. You deserve... Well, I've already told you what I think you deserve." The freshly appointed DCI of the brand new North London Extraordinary Crimes Division took a swig from his glass and tipped it toward Manny with a nod of gratitude. "Nice pint, mate. Thanks for the tip."

"Any time, sir. I've got lots of tips if you want 'em." Manny shot him a hopeful look and wiped the same immaculate spot he'd been polishing for a half hour. He wandered down the bar when someone called and Jake noted the extra swing in his step.

"I don't think it's me Manny's got the hots for."

John's eyes widened for an instant. He covered a short bark of uncomfortable laughter with another slurp of his beer.

"Not my type, Chivis. Decent bloke, though. And you didn't answer the question." He pointed a finger at Jake.

"He's working through some stuff and that takes some time." Jake shrugged. "And how can you be sure Manny's not your type? You're basing that on looks alone. Maybe he's exactly what you need."

John glanced across at their ever-optimistic bartender and found the fellow looking their way again. He raised his glass in acknowledgment and Manny beamed.

"Too needy," he murmured, leaning in to Jake to be heard above the general chatter and music in the bar. "I don't do 'needy'."

"He's just trying to catch your eye. You're a hard man," Jake chided. "He's a good, down-to-earth guy, when you chill out and talk to him."

"I'm sure," John sighed. "I see what you're doing, Jake. Cut it out. I'm not on the pull. Do you realize how bloody long it is since I even went to a gay bar?"

"Maybe that's half the problem," Jake suggested.

"I stopped going for a reason. I got sick of being hit on by the kind of guys that went to gay bars," his companion responded with a forced laugh. "I'm sure your friend there is a good bloke, but he's gonna have to smarten up his act. I'm not dating a muppet, not that I've got time for dating."

Jake was still amused. "It's one night, not a commitment." He held up his hands when John scowled at him. "All right, all right, I'll lay off."

"Good," Cordiline responded in his best hardened-copper growl. "Sapphire got enough DNA off the previous victims to nail St. Andrews. Once the prosecution brings it all out how after he raped his victims, he buried them just shallow enough so they could dig their way out, just so he could draw the scene for his dumb comic, he'll be put away for a long time.

"The case against Arregui could still go either way. That smug bastard is denying all knowledge of his nephew's criminal activity."

Jake picked at one corner of the label on his bottle of beer and didn't respond to that.

"Will they go for the premeditated charge against St. Andrews?" Jake asked instead.

"The last girl was an aberration. He got interrupted and scarpered before she managed to get to the surface. He's sticking to that claim, that the murder was an accident. He didn't mean to kill her. They could send him down for manslaughter but his solicitor will probably push for unlawful killing, if they don't go down the diminished responsibility route. He'll be out in ten-to-fifteen years if that happens."

"And meanwhile, his victims get a life sentence of nightmares and therapy. Doesn't seem fair." Jake took a sip of his beer. It was the same lament of good cops everywhere. They got to see up close the very worst of humanity and had to still, somehow, stay human themselves. These days Jake was finding it harder to do.

"Listen, Chivis. I was going to wait to bring this up, but... I have a couple of contacts that keep me informed on certain maneuverings. Aled Mustatti was extradited today."

"Extradited? He hasn't served anywhere close to his sentence. To where? For what?"

"I would like the answers to those questions as well, believe me. However, my discreet inquiry was met with a cold shoulder and open hostility. I was told in no uncertain terms that the matter was far above my shiny new paygrade. A few less ethical inquiries led to a dead end. Literally."

"He's dead?"

"It looks that way—on paper at least. Accident in transport." John drank his beer. Jake took a drink as well.

Short of terrorist activity, Jake couldn't think of any reason to allow an extradition of a convicted murderer. Slim as that likelihood was, it was even less likely they'd somehow fuck up enough to let a prisoner like that die in transport. Unless someone wanted a ghost who could talk to ghosts. The idea that the government, here or somewhere else, had gone to all the trouble of extracting Mustatti from prison and making him disappear on paper to have their own private medium was way more crazy conspiracy theorist territory than Jake normally indulged in. But was it possible?

Jake drank more than usual but he still made his excuses well before closing time. He left Cordiline with his coworkers and friends and gave him his best and sincerest wishes for success in his new job. Out on the pavement, he took a few steps toward the apartment stairs out of sheer habit before he caught himself and remembered he didn't live there anymore. The walk across Regent's Park would probably be just enough to clear his head.

* * * *

Jake slipped in and closed the front door quietly behind him, but Tonka heard him and greeted him in the hall by bouncing all over him like his doggy birthdays and Christmases had all come at once. He found Mari in the day room, sprawled on the sofa, reading.

"Hi. You're early. I thought you'd be out with the boys all night," he said.

"I missed you." Jake gave him a kiss hello—just a brief, tender brush of their lips that still warmed him more than all the heat and chatter in the bar had. "You look comfortable. Relaxed."

"Do I?" Mari glanced down at his casual jersey yoga pants and soft, cream-colored hoodie. "Just vegging. I do feel…less anxious after this afternoon's session. We talked about moving forward and where I wanted to go from here. Solana approves of the PI business. She thinks it will be good for me to focus my energies into something constructive."

"Good." Jake was still supportive of Mari seeing Solana. He didn't have the same animosity toward her that Mari had once had, but he did occasionally wonder if Mari would be better off seeking help from a professional therapist, not that he was about to suggest that to Mari. "It will. I agree. Is Ashcroft okay with you moving to part-time hours?"

"Surprisingly, yes. I should be able to cut back next month, once we've got the current workload under control. Crime never sleeps, you know."

"Really? I hadn't realized." Jake sat down beside him and slid one arm around him and Mari leaned into his side, resting his head on his shoulder. "Is Anni asleep?"

"No. Still out." Mari ran one hand through his hair, which he had let grow again. Jake had noticed that he played with it more when he was agitated. "She got an email this morning from that children's charity in France that she's been consulting for. They've offered her a job. She's not shut up about it all day. Thankfully, she went out with an old school friend to the theater this evening and said not to wait up."

"Did she see Mr. Barnard?" Jake asked.

"She did. He says the results are consistent with her last tests," Mari told him, looking up at him with slightly misty eyes. "He is convinced she's in remission. He's never seen anything quite like it before, so he is cautiously optimistic."

"If she'd gotten this news before she met Solana, you'd be doing cartwheels. Is she rubbing it in?" Jake asked.

"What do you think?" Mari rolled his eyes and uttered a theatrical sigh. "They are both making the most of their opportunity to say 'I told you so'."

Jake laughed. "Don't pout. This is good news, Mari. The best news, actually. Right?"

"You're right, as usual." Mari sounded…not sad, exactly, but rather wistful, he thought.

Jake lifted his hand to the back of Mari's neck and stroked very lightly. Mari didn't tense up or pull away, but he stilled and Jake moved his hand to the back of the couch.

"You're going to miss her if she goes to Paris." Jake guessed at the most likely cause of his long face.

"Nah," Mari clearly lied. His shoulder blades twitched beneath his light sweater, giving him away. "It'll be good to have the place to ourselves for a bit."

Jake let him get away with the fib and Mari snuggled in closer again and looked up at him with a little smile. "Solana thinks we should be doing more than just private investigations together. She reckons that it wouldn't hurt to maybe try some personal investigating. At least I think that was the jist of what she said today. I believe my reluctance frustrates her sometimes."

"Solana thinks so but what do you think?" Jake asked. Because, while he was in no way opposed to any sort of investigating Mari wanted to do, he had to know that it was actually Mari's idea.

"I think… I miss so much about what we had." Mari heaved a small sigh. "You know that I still love you. At least I hope you do."

"Of course. And I love you, too, Mari. We don't need to rush this."

"It's been over six months, Jake Chivis. I hardly think we're rushing anything," Mari huffed, though he managed a short, bitter laugh. "I'm physically well. My body probably works just as well as it ever did. But you know how my brain has its own ideas."

Jake did know, very well, exactly how Mari's brain could override what his body wanted. When he thought about how they'd gotten through so many barriers at the start of their relationship, how happy Mari had been…and how very sexy he looked when he was getting what he wanted — Jake cut off that line of thought. The first few times, after he'd come home from the hospital, when Mari had tensed and pulled away if Jake had touched him, he had been more worried about Mari than anything else. Then he'd gotten angry. Not at Mari, of course, but at the bastard that hurt him so badly he flinched at a touch.

He'd worked on quashing his temper while Mari worked separately on moving past the hurt and anger inside him. Although they'd never specifically discussed it, Jake had decided the best way to be supportive was to let Mari initiate any touching.

Unfortunately Mari's lack of proper boundaries often meant that they took one step forward then two — or even thirteen — steps back. The only time they had really argued was over Mari's insistence that they try playing out a scene, which back before the assault, would have led to a spanking. Jake had refused and they'd fought over it. He had spent three nights at Manny's place afterward. When Mari had finally come to fetch him home, he'd let the matter drop, and Mari hadn't asked for anything like that since.

The painkillers and anti-anxiety meds Mari had been put on after he'd been released from St. Mary's hadn't helped much, in Jake's opinion. His doc had then added an antidepressant to the mix, which seemed to mellow him out but also killed what little remained of his libido. The chemical cocktail also interfered with his ability to interface and he'd started struggling to do even the minimum at his job. After only a couple of months, Mari had declared that he wasn't going to take them anymore. Since then his ability to interface had steadily picked up but his sex drive was still at zero.

"You're quiet," Mari said to him. "If you don't want to, I'd understand. I haven't been easy to live with lately. I'm sorry."

Jake had to shake his head at how far off the mark Mari was on that score. "I want you. More than anything."

Was he imagining it, or did Mari's eyes darken at his words, the pupils dilating as he gazed up at him? Mari moved to his knees beside him on the sofa and, cautiously, climbed across his thighs to sit astride them, in his lap, facing Jake with a very determined expression on his face.

"I want to kiss you," he said. "That's one thing he never did to me. One thing he can't ruin for me."

Jake had to force himself not to clench his jaw or let his hands tighten reflexively into fists. This was not about him and it wasn't about that piece of shit Arregui. The only thing that mattered here was Mari.

"You can kiss me anytime you want to."

Mari lifted his hands and let his fingers gently explore Jake's face, like a blind man refamiliarizing himself with a long-forgotten landscape. His touch set loose butterflies in Jake's chest and he turned his head, rubbing his cheek against the warmth of those caressing digits. Mari leaned in closer to him, stroking his thumb over Jake's lower lip, pressing down and opening his mouth just a little, even as his own lips parted.

They had snatched pecks of affection, here and there, brief, tight-lipped kisses hello and goodbye, but this was a different. Jake was almost overwhelmed by the tension in his whole frame as Mari bent his head closer, closer, until the soft fall of his ashen hair almost brushed his face. Then those wayward locks were trickling over his skin like silk, and Mari was cupping his chin, lifting his head as Mari lowered his. His breath was quick and warm, flowing over Jake and into him. Mari's soft, dry lips touched his, and Jake's resolve to let Mari dictate every move lasted all of ten seconds.

The soft press and nudge of lips became a more intense, searching, and Jake slid his hands up the outsides of Mari's thighs. He kept them there, although it took just about every ounce of will he had not to tug Mari onto his crotch or wander his hands more intimately over Mari's ass.

Mari tilted his head, leaning into him harder, pressing his mouth down with more intent onto his. He kissed then sucked Jake's lower lip between his, catching it with his teeth, not roughly, but enough to set off sparks inside him. When he let go, Mari's mouth covered his again and Mari's tongue darted between his lips, touching his own tongue and his teeth before retreating like a shy minnow into its own domain.

Mari drew back, but not far. His lips were still brushing Jake's mouth as he whispered, "Well, this is nice."

"This *is* nice," Jake agreed, his voice a little hoarse.

Mari sat back in his lap for a moment, studying him. He stroked one finger of his left hand gently down into the neckline of Jake's shirt and teased at the button that offered first resistance for a moment.

"Can we try something?" he asked.

"Yes." Jake ran his hands over Mari's lean thighs, a slow, gentle motion like he would have soothed a skittish horse with. "Whatever you want."

"We should go upstairs," Mari told him, his expression very earnest.

"Oh?" Jake raised his eyebrows.

"What I had in mind involves you being a bit less...dressed," Mari said, biting his lip. "I wouldn't want Mama to walk in unexpectedly."

The thought of ending their dry spell had Jake half-hard, but the butterflies still fluttered in his chest. He did not want to screw this up. He dislodged Mari from his lap and stood, taking his hand. "Let's go upstairs then."

Since moving in, they had replaced Mari's cozy bed with a larger double and now his little den was a much more intimate hideaway, with his desk and IT equipment tucked into the spare room along the landing so that he didn't disturb Jake if he was working into the night. It also gave them an office of sorts, which was useful as Jake had begun to get quite a few clients in the wake of the Cemetery Rapist case. Work was the last thing on his mind tonight, though.

Mari cupped his face and touched another kiss to his lips as they closed the door behind them and shut out the rest of the world. For a little while after their lips parted, Mari stood with the tip of his nose touching Jake's, his eyes half-shuttered by long golden lashes. Then he stroked his fingers lightly down over Jake's shoulders and chest, and began to unfasten his shirt.

Jake held still and let Mari undress him, without helping. The way Mari moved, the set expression on his face, like he was determined to prove something, reminded Jake of how he had been in the first few weeks of their relationship. He thought it best to let Mari work through whatever was spinning around in his head. When he got the last button undone, he tugged Jake's shirt down his arms almost violently. Jake let it fall and Mari attacked his fly with nimble fingers.

Jake toed his shoes off but otherwise let Mari do things his way. Mari took his time, once Jake's jeans were around his ankles, touching him gently through his boxer briefs, running one hand across the outline of his cock and balls, his quiet gaze roaming over him like he would never be tired of the view. He was careful easing Jake's underwear down his thighs, then sank to his knees and helped him to step out of them, and his socks, until he was naked. The cool air on his skin did nothing to alleviate the involuntary rush of blood to his groin that left him semi-hard. Mari still knelt before him, a little flush on his cheeks and his breath coming faster as he caressed Jake's thigh with exquisite tenderness. Those big blue eyes traveled back up from his crotch to Jake's face and he took a slower, deeper breath.

"I'd forgotten how beautiful you are," he said in a quiet voice.

Jake brought his hand to Mari's face and traced the edge of his brow, the curve of his cheek, his lower lip. "Whatever you want to do, or not, I'm completely yours. You decide everything tonight, okay?"

Mari leaned into him and brushed his lips against his thigh, planting soft, careful kisses all the way up to his hip. Then he rose and nodded toward the bed with a grateful quirk of his mouth.

"Go lay down. I'll be right with you."

Crossing his arms, Mari caught the hem of his hooded sweater, and the T-shirt under it, in both hands and drew it up, over his head. Jake sat down on the edge of the bed then leaned back among the pillows, watching as Mari dropped both garments to the floor. Mari was far too thin, he worried. His lean frame was still supple and beautiful, though, the skin soft and healthy, though paler than it had been six months previously.

Mari was gazing at him, expression quizzical, his loose jersey pants riding low on those slim hips of his. The lamplight caught on the trail of gold from his navel down into his waistband. Then he took a deep breath and pushed them down, stepping free of the pooled garment and leaving it on the floor as he came over to the bed. Jake caught his breath. It had been too long since he'd seen Mari completely naked and the sight roused him, making him anxious that his obvious interest would frighten Mari away.

He needn't have worried. Moving as light as a cat, Mari knelt on the edge of the mattress then prowled on his hands and knees toward Jake until he was able to climb astride him and sit down, straddling his lower thighs.

"Well," he said with a little shrug. "That went okay, I think."

Jake hesitated with his hands hovering just shy of touching Mari's thighs. Even though it had been Mari's idea to come up here and get naked together, Jake wasn't blind to the little twitches and shrugs and reluctance he was fighting through. It was effectively pouring cold water on his initial arousal, even though he knew it had nothing to do with him. How to fix it, how to get Mari past his discomfort and into what he was doing, was an answer Jake would have given just about anything to possess.

Just as he was about to suggest that 'maybe this was actually too soon after all', an idea popped into his head. Everything in him rebelled at the thought, but he took a breath and spoke fast, "Do you want to tie my hands to the headboard?"

For a long moment, so long that Jake worried he'd overstepped some invisible line, Mari was quiet. He didn't look away but Jake could almost see the cogs turning in that lovely head.

"No," Mari said at last, with a small, half-smile. "Not that it wouldn't look amazing but I want to feel your hands on me. I want to feel your body touching mine. I don't know if I'm ready to go further, but tonight, I want to sleep with you like this — naked — touching. Can we do that?"

"I don't know if that's a good idea — the sleeping part, I mean." Mari frowned and Jake explained, "I can hold you until you fall asleep, then I'll move over, how about that?"

"Why?"

"Mari...the last thing I want is for you to wake up in the middle of the night with me poking you in the back and feeling uncomfortable in your own bed. I don't want to be the cause of your nightmares."

"Oh." Mari was quiet again for a time. Jake could see that he hadn't thought that far ahead. He wanted to hug him and was afraid to. "Oh... I see. Yes. Still, I've woken up a few times when we had clothes on and you were—" He broke off and cleared his throat. "But it's your bed, too, and you shouldn't feel...unwelcome. Okay, we'll try that then. You can hold me and I'll hold you for a while and we can see what happens."

He walked his hands across Jake's chest then leaned forward almost too quickly, like he was afraid he might change his mind. He coiled his arms around Jake's neck and he settled down in slow, cautious increments, letting their bodies come together inch by inch until he was lying on top of Jake with his head on Jake's chest and his arms around his neck. Jake felt the rapid huff of Mari's breath whisper through the dark curls on his torso. Mari's belly was soft and warm against his crotch and upper thighs.

Jake brought his arms up around him, one hand coming to rest between his shoulders, the other on the back of his thigh. That was all they did. Still, it was more intimacy than they'd shared in months and Jake was gratified with the way every muscle in Mari's body slowly relaxed as he stroked a small circle on his back. Despite his worries and his best intentions, Jake closed his eyes. Maybe it was the beer he'd drunk earlier or the warm spot in his heart at being able to hold Mari like this again, but it wasn't long before he drifted into sleep.

Ironic that his fear had been giving Mari nightmares. He seldom remembered his dreams and even more rarely was bothered enough by them to be woken out of a sound sleep. Sometime in the early-morning hours before dawn, Jake startled awake from a nightmare of smoke and flame. He had investigated enough building fires that it took him a few moments to realize that the smell of char and melted plastics in his nostrils was only memory.

Mari lay asleep beside him, peaceful and beautiful. He was about to close his eyes again but a faint blue flash caught his attention from the floor where he had left his jeans. Jake slid out of bed and retrieved his phone. He had just missed a call, from Michigan, which was alarming because it was about midnight there. Absolutely nothing good could be on the other end of that call, but he pulled on his jeans and silently stepped out of the room.

Downstairs in the kitchen, he called the unfamiliar number back. A weary voice on the other end answered, "Jake? Is that you?"

"Yes. Who is this?"

"It's Nikan Niizh-Ziibi. I know it's late there—or early, actually. I'm sorry. I wouldn't call if it weren't an emergency. There have been four fires around town the last few months. Sheds and barns. Tonight a house burnt to the foundations before the fire department arrived. The ookomisan think it is one of our own. Jake, we need you to come home."

Want to see more from this author?
Here's a taster for you to enjoy!

Wanted: Demon Familiar
Bellora Quinn &
Sadie Rose Bermingham

Excerpt

Neil set the bushel of summer squash into the panel van with the rest of the produce ready to go to market tomorrow morning and jumped down. Mr. Yaetz patted him on the back. "That's the last one. Good job, Neil. You best head home now. Don't want to get caught outside the wards after nightfall, 'specially not in that fancy car."

Neil stifled a wince and forced himself not to look around to see who might have overheard the mention of his 'fancy car'. Mr. Yaetz didn't mean anything by it, but the car was a sore point with his co-workers at the small greenhouse and urban farm lot. None of them had their own vehicle, much less a sleek convertible sports car. Explaining that it was his mother's, not his, hadn't stopped the digs about his 'slumming with the common folk' or brought him any closer to the camaraderie the rest of them shared.

"Thanks, Mr. Yaetz. I'll see you tomorrow," Neil told him and turned toward the front lot. He glanced at the horizon automatically, judging how much time he had. About forty-five minutes, maybe an hour. More than enough for the short drive home. He wasn't likely to come across any shadow beasts here on the outskirts of the city but a pack hunting farther afield was always a possibility. Of course, if he did run across shadow beasts, they would have to catch him first and the Maserati was both fast and agile.

Neil slid behind the wheel and the powerful engine purred to life. With the sun slowly sinking behind him, he swung the car out onto the road and headed for home.

As expected, Neil pulled into the driveway with plenty of daylight left and no encounters with any creatures that came out after dark. Climbing the front steps, his thoughts preoccupied with a shower and dinner, he almost missed the broken seal on his front door. He stopped cold. The warding glyph, usually a subtle shimmering gold, was inert, dull gray and cracked with lines of black. A sick knot cramped in his belly and Neil pressed his thumb down on the latch and pushed the door open but hesitated on the threshold.

"Mom?"

He listened. No answer.

Neil stepped into the foyer and slowly moved into the hall. A picture had been knocked off the wall and the broken glass from the frame glittered in the fading sunlight streaming in behind him.

"Mom?" he called again, louder.

Something crashed in the kitchen, the metallic clatter of pans hitting the tile floor. Neil ran in that direction.

His mother screamed, "Neil, get out! Get out!"

Heart hammering, he skidded into the kitchen. A black-clad, hooded man held on to his struggling mother. Another man stood next to them with a curved knife in his hand — his eyes were flat black and icy cold as they slid over him. Neil rushed them, yelling, "Get away from her!" The man with the knife lifted his free arm and flung the outstretched fingers of his empty hand at him. Neil hit the stop spell so hard it jarred him from teeth to toes, knocking him on his ass.

"Neil!" his mother shrieked.

He lifted his head in time to see the man who had floored him lift the knife and draw it down the side of her throat and across her shoulder in two professional, vicious slashes. The other man let her go as her eyes went wide and her hands flew up to clutch at the wounds. The blood didn't spray everywhere like it did in the movies. It welled up in a gush of red that soaked the front of her shirt as she choked and gasped then fell down on her knees.

"Mom! No!" Neil scrambled to his feet. The two men moved toward him in unison as his mother crumpled, face down on the floor. Her body sounded like a wet rag hitting the tiles and a shocking pool of red spread under her.

"Take him," the one holding the bloody knife said. His voice was low, emotionless and without accent, like an automaton in one of the old films they occasionally streamed when the comms satellite was functioning.

On autopilot, Neil grabbed the pendant that hung on the chain around his neck and ripped it off, throwing it on the floor. The man reached to stop him, but it was too late. The glass pendant shattered and a wall of noxious smoke rose between him and the killers. It wouldn't hold them long, a minute if he was lucky. Probably less. He turned and ran back down the hall, fleeing the house.

He stumbled down the steps and fumbled the keys from his pocket, hitting the lock button. He yanked the door open and was shaking so badly he dropped the keys on the floor.

"Fuck! Fuck!" He reached down and his fingers just touched the ring as the killers came running out of the front door. Neil grabbed the keyring and jammed the right key in the ignition. For one horrible second, he was sure it wouldn't start even though he'd just driven the car home. The engine turned over as smooth as a kitten's purr and he slammed the shifter in reverse just as the man with the blade grabbed the driver's door handle. Neil put his foot down on the pedal. The tires squealed and the car shot backward down the driveway and into the street.

Blood pounded in his ears, almost drowning out the engine sounds as he threw the car into drive and floored the gas, clutching the steering wheel hard enough to turn his knuckles white. He looked in the rear-view mirror as he sped away. They would come after him. He turned at the next intersection. Then turned again. And again. He tried to focus on what to do next but all he could see was the shock and anguish on his mother's face before she fell, and that bright pool of red spreading out under her. He looked in the mirror again but saw no sign of the men that had killed her. That didn't mean anything. They could come, he knew it. He was heading out of the city following pure instinct, but now he slowed the car for just a moment. At the next turn, he doubled back the way he'd come.

Out of the city might seem safer, but it wasn't. He had little money and the car would take him only so far. He needed resources.

He forced his fingers to relax on the steering wheel but his hands still shook. When he took a breath, it was shaky too. The red had been so stark against her blonde hair. Her eyes…had they been blank before she fell or after she hit the floor? No. No he couldn't think of that now. He raised and hand and swiped at his wet cheeks.

Bone Men. Their name whispered across Neil's mind in his father's voice, from one of his many lessons. Assassins. Twisted by the sorcery that enhanced them, marked by the lives they took. Had she been their target? Was her death retribution for something his father had done? Or...or were they there for him?

His mind raced as fast as his pulse and the car he was driving. He took another deep breath and eased his foot back off the pedal a few degrees. He needed a clear head. He needed a plan. But first he needed somewhere to hide. Instinct told him to find someone he trusted, but his training overrode that idea. He could hear his father's voice in his ear again. *Trust no one, Nielob. If they come for you, go to ground. Speak to no one you know. Hide and wait. I will find you.*

Not if he could help it. If he had his way, he'd lose both the Bone Men and his father, for good. The car would get him a good distance but he couldn't keep it. It was traceable. He'd drive into the city, find someone he could sell the car to for scrap and use the money to get a ticket to as far away as it would take him.

He couldn't take the car directly to a salvage yard without a title, too risky. He needed a fence. Months ago, while he'd been watering seedlings at work, he'd overheard Carl bragging about how his uncle was going to get a real car, one with a combustion engine. No one had believed him and Carl had gotten mad. Insisted his uncle knew a guy that dealt in contraband autos in the city. Hammersfell Road, next to the old Ackard Motors factory. There was a warehouse where they had raves. The fence organized them. Neil had no way of knowing if the bragging was just lies, but he had filed the information away anyway. His chin gave an odd quiver and the tightness in his throat squeezed hard enough to choke him. No. He couldn't give in to tears now. He couldn't afford to let out the sobs that threatened him. A safe place first. The grief tasted of bitter acid and wanted to strangle him, but he swallowed it down and kept going.

About the Authors

Bellora Quinn

Originally hailing from Detroit Michigan, Bellora now resides on the sunny Gulf Coast of Florida where a herd of Dachshunds keeps her entertained. She got her start in writing at the dawn of the internet when she discovered PbEMs (Play by email) and found a passion for collaborative writing and steamy hot erotica. Soap Opera like blogs soon followed and eventually full novels.

The majority of her stories are in the M/M genre with urban fantasy or paranormal settings and many with a strong BDSM flavour.

Sadie Rose Bermingham

A storyteller since before she started school, Sadie also enjoys reading, photography, live music and long walks on the beach.

Sadie has worked as a bookseller, a pedigree editor for the racing industry and a local and family history researcher. Originally from the north of England, she has been working her way across the UK ever since. She currently resides on the south east coast with her long term partner, where she hopes to buy a mobile home and establish a whippet farm.

Bellora and Sadie love to hear from readers. You can find their contact information, website details and author profile pages at http://www.pride-publishing.com.